Lies, Love, & *Loyalty*

A Novel By

Jan' Nine Parker

This is a work of fiction. Any references or similarities to actual events, real people, living, or dead, or to real locales are intended to give the novel a sense of reality. Any resemblance in other names, characters, places and incidents is entirely coincidental.

Author JanNine Parker
janninelparker@gmail.com
Facebook/Jannine Parker

Typeset by Rukyyah
Cover designed by Brand Concepts Creative Media
Editing team: Rukyyah and Leila Jefferson

Printed in United States of America
10 9 8 7 6 5 4 3 2 1

Dedications

I dedicate this book to LA thanks for the inspiration.... To the inspiring beautiful women Janee Bass, LaQuita Burden, Vernica Burton, NeNe Johnson, Queta King, Kisha Lindsay, Keisha Parker, Pauline Phillips, Chartan Smith, Dana Thornton.... Rather I know you personally or not I see you, and you inspire me, Thank you.

And to the Women that are down for their men without limitations; know your worth, a Real man would never allow you to do something he wouldn't do.

Acknowledgements

First and foremost, I want to thank God for all of his many blessings. All the praise goes to him. I have been through so much, some good things some bad but no matter what the experience it has taught me a lot. I wouldn't change a thing because of it I am the person I am today. I thank him for giving me a talent that I can share with the world. Thank you for never giving up on me and also for never allowing me to give up on myself.

To my kids, who, I love more than my own life. Thank you for believing in me. This was a journey for me and through it all you all were right there pushing me toward my dream. I love you with all my heart. Andre Bonds you're like a son to me I'm glad you are in our lives, love you. To my sister, Cheryl thank you for always believing in me and always giving me positive words of encouragement, I love you. To my father, thank you for all that you have done for me, you always said to me "never give up and to follow my dreams" over and over again. I was listening even when you thought I wasn't I love you and you will forever be my father. To my second Mother, Evelyn I love you so much. You being in my life means the world to me, thank you for all the talks, support and shoulder to cry on when I needed you most. I did it just like you said I would. To my cousin Jasmin, we have been through a lot together. Regardless of our differences you never stopped believing in me thank you for taking the time out to sit and listen to me share ideals about the book. When I was frustrated and wanted to give up, you wouldn't let me. Our bond will always be a strong one no matter what's thrown our way, I love you Jazz.

To the one that was there from the start, Lanickia aka Poohbear thank you from the bottom of my heart for reading my manuscript over and over again. You never complained or anything you were very supportive then as you are now this has been a two year project and you've been there every step of the way and for that I thank you and love you. To my closest friend, Monique Spencer thank you for being there when I needed you, although you had your own issues going on you still took the time out to read my book and give me feedback. I questioned myself and this book many times and you were always there asking me why. Thank you for believing in me you will never know how much I appreciate that and you. I love you friend. To my partner, Cassandra aka Case thank you for all the information you gathered for me, all the input and most of all for your honesty. You know me and there isn't too many who really do, thanks for always being there when needed. We gon' need cameras in the back lol... I love you Case. To my friend, Melissa you are everything from a friend to a counselor, if you can help you will no matter what it is, if you can't do it then and there you will make a way to get it done. You pushed me in more ways than one, instead of always giving me the answer or resource you would make me look for it on my own. I thank you for that. I still remember us coming up with the character names you were there from the start and I just want to say thanks and I love ya. To Myisha, I couldn't ask for a better friend than you. God brought us together at the right time in our lives. I love you like a sister. You and only you know how much I value our friendship. With you I can just be myself, if I'm wrong you will tell me I'm wrong. Thank you for always encouraging me to keep moving forward, and for staying on me about everything. You believing in me pushed me because I knew that you were sincere. Like we always say to one another," if you up I'm up; so when I shine you shine," no jealousy-just real shit between two real women. You always said my dream should be like my baby and that no one would love my baby like I would therefore I have to be the one on top of everything. Yes people are willing to help you but no one is going to care like you do because it's your dream. You were right, I didn't give up and thank you for not allowing me to only you know my real struggles. Love ya …

To my editor, Rukyyah it was a pleasure working with you. Thank you for doing an excellent job. My proofreader, Leila Jefferson it was great working with you. Thank you for all the feedback you did a good job. Special thanks to, Anngela Berger you've helped me from day one. You will never know how grateful I am that you took time out to help me pursue my dream. You will forever be my friend love you.

To Calinda aka Lynn Lynn my friend who I can call on at any time doesn't matter if we talk every day or once every six months the friendship remains the same and is one of a kind. Thanks for the help along the way, love ya. To Tiffany Smith, you always, lift me up when I'm down you don't know how many times you're kind words helped me. I love you. To my trainer, my brother, my friend Antoine Smith aye you know me better than people I've known for years, we clicked from the start. Thank you for always pushing me to never give up on anything and for always telling me to know my own worth. You helped me in so many ways and for that I thank you. I love you and Tiffany. Special thanks to my girl Tick we were hanging tight when I started writing this book you listen to my ideals and all of that thank you for that but more importantly thanks for being there for me when I needed you, love you. To my NBH family, Thank you for always inquiring about the book, asking if it's finished or when will it be out thanks for just caring and showing support remember Team work makes the dream work.

To the ONLY man I have ever been in love with one of my best friend's RC thank you for allowing me to let go. You helped me in more ways than you could imagine. You are one of my best stories, I'll love you always. To Cool Breeze you know who you are, thanks for pushing me when I was bull shittin and not taking care of business. You came along at the right time and yep you were a distraction but a good one. I'm happy to have you around, clean slate remember, Luv ya.

Special thanks to all my family and friends that believed in me I love you all.

Last but not least I want to thank my number one fan, my mother Judy Jordan. I couldn't ask for a better mother, friend, confidant. Because of you I am the woman I am today you believe in me no matter what and you never gave up on me. Our bond is unbreakable we don't always agree but at the end of the day I know that you will always have my back. You're the Best, I love you Mama……..

Prologue

Coco was, on a date, having a good time with King. They finished dinner and had planned to go bowling afterwards. While waiting on the check, her phone rang.

"Why is Rel calling me? Shit, I'm going to have to hit him back later," Coco said. She glanced at her cell phone for the third time.

"Why does he keep calling me?" she asked herself. Coco apologized to her date. "I'm sorry, but I have to take this," she said to King. He shook his head as he finished his drink.

The moment Coco heard Rel's voice, she knew something was wrong. His words were hard to make out. She suddenly felt fear creep up her body. All Coco heard was "children's hospital" her mind went blank. An eerie scream escaped her lips and she started shaking uncontrollably. She felt light headed and, faint.

"Where is my baby?" she screamed repeatedly. The sheer terror in her eyes caused King to grab the phone.

"Who is this? What the fuck is going on?" he asked.

"Ay, just get her to Kosair Children's Hospital now," Rel said and hung up.

King didn't say anything else. He grabbed Coco's purse, her hand, and they hurried out the door. He was damn near dragging her. She couldn't catch her breath. She was in such a panic. He made it to his car and got Coco inside.

"King, what did Rel say to you? Is my baby ok? Please, tell me my daughter is okay." Coco was nervous.

You could tell by the look on her face, and, not to mention, she shook like a leaf in the wind.

The hospital was not that far from where she and King were.

"King, get me to my baby! Lord, please, let my baby be alright, and let her know Mommy is coming!"

"Fuck this!" King said while turning on his distinguished, bright flashing lights. He saw an alley and cut off a truck in his Bentley coupe, which demanded respect and space. King ripped through the alley, hitting pot holes and all. He whipped his car around the corner and the hospital was only two blocks away.

"I need to call ZO," Coco said. ZO was Coco's ex and Brandy's father. Coco called, but got his voicemail. She tried again and got the same thing. She left a voice message saying that he needed to meet her at the hospital. King made it to the hospital and parked in the ER entrance. Coco damn near jumped out of the car before he could even stop. Coco ran inside and spotted Rel. The look on his face confirmed that something was very wrong.

"Where is Brandy?" Coco screamed as she ran over to him with King right behind her. When she got within reach of Rel, she could tell he had been crying because his eyes were blood shot red.

"Rel, what is going on? Where is Brandy? Damn it. Where is my daughter?"

Tears streamed down Coco's face. Before Rel could say anything, Coco lost it. She punched and hit Rel uncontrollably.

"Tell me damn it!" was all she screamed. King tried to take hold of Coco, but she was unable to tame.

"Cori Matthews," Coco heard the doctor say. "Are you the mother of Brandy Carter?"

"Yes, where's Brandy?" As the doctor explained to her what happened to Brandy, she stood there in shock.

Her legs gave out from underneath her. She shook so much it was visible from across the emergency room. She was on the floor sobbing. Suddenly, there was no other noise in the ER except for Coco's voice.

"No, not my, baby!" The sound of her voice screaming through the ER was deafening. No one could control her. She was hysterical and began to hyperventilate.

Coco felt claustrophobic as if she were trapped. Her heart raced. The doctor called the nurses over to help calm her. The doctor gave her a shot of Ativan. It immediately began to work because Coco was no longer aggressive. She sat there expressionless, in shock and talking to herself.

"God, please, this can't be real," was what she kept repeating. "This year was supposed to be my year. What did I do to deserve this?" Coco glimpsed back to the beginning of the year.

Damn, how things have changed, she thought before she passed out.

Chapter 1
The Past

"Coco bitch, we are bringing in New Year 2013," Asia yelled from down stairs.

Why am I going out? Coco thought. She hadn't been out in months, but it was New Year's Eve and she planned to bring in her New Year right.

"Damn, Asia, I'm going to get faded tonight," Coco said.

I'm in a better place, she thought as a tear slid down her face. Coco was beautiful and that night, she looked like a beauty queen. Her makeup was flawless. Her dark coco chocolate skin had a natural glow to it. Coco had perfectly French manicured hands and pedicured feet. They looked great.

She wore a short Dolce & Gabbana sequined dress that was silver with the back out. Coco had the perfect shoes; Dolce & Gabbana Alexa Crystall embellished pumps.

The shit was on point with her hand clutch to match. She wore costumed, three karat platinum and diamond mesh chandelier earrings, and beautiful diamond watch along with a tennis bracelet to match. Coco looked like a million bucks. She always turned heads. Men and women, it didn't matter, she required attention and always got it.

Coco was mixed, her mother black and her father Cuban. Standing, five feet nine, one hundred and sixty five pounds. She had a small waist, flat stomach, wide hips, and small breasts. Coco's shape was nice, she wasn't thick, but she wasn't skinny; she was just right. Not to mention, she had pretty light brown eyes the shape of almonds, and eyelashes that most women would swear weren't hers. She paid Asia good money to keep that illusion.

"Damn it, Coco, you not done yet!" Asia yelled.

"Hold up a minute. I'm putting on my smell good, plus what's the hurry? Mina isn't even here yet." Coco continued to get ready looking at herself and touching up her hair. She loved the new short coal black pixie haircut. Coco always had worn her hair long and decided for the New Year she wanted a new look. The hair style fit her perfectly.

Coco sprayed on her D&G *"The One"* perfume and walked down the steps to find Asia there looking gorgeous. Asia and Coco had been friends for years; truly they were more like family. Asia was Coco's sister Samone's, best friend from college. Over the years they got tight and were always there for one another.

"Well, hello, Diva, you look like money, Asia. That old money, that shit they keep hidden and stored like a nice bottle of Chateau Lafitte. One glass of that and you won't want or need shit else all night. Plus, you're wearing that pant suit." She smiled as Coco complimented her.

"Coco, you know how I do. I decided to give these motherfuckers something to talk about! Yea, I'm on one tonight!"

Asia was feeling herself. She was a bad bitch and she knew it. She moved her hips to the music that came from the speakers in the other room.

"Coco, turn that up." Coco turned the music up. Rick Ross *Bag of Money* banged through the speakers. Both the women loved that song. Coco sung along with Rick Ross, she always stepped out looking like a bag of money, no matter if it was in some high fashion or just something plain. She wasn't into the labels, she stepped out as a fashion diva when necessary, but other than that, she felt she could rock an outfit from Target and look just as good.

The music had Asia in a zone. She got on the pole that was in the middle of the family room and put on a show for Coco, something she always did as long as she had an audience.

"Okay, you better work it," Coco yelled.

"Told you, I'm on one tonight .I'm feeling myself tonight. Yea, I'm about to make it well- known that I'm that bitch." Asia said with confidence.

"Call Mina and see how long she will be. I'm about to freshen back up," Asia said as she headed toward her bedroom.

Coco didn't bother calling Mina, she knew that she would be there so she just chilled and listened to the music.

"Damn, Asia, it took you long enough. You look amazing, China Doll, you went and changed your outfit. I love it, though."

Asia had on a sequined dress by St. John with the V shaped back. In vibrant, colors of violet, aqua, navy, and pink. She wore matching Gucci sling backs and a clutch handbag. She accessorized her look with simple, yet stunning Tiffany earrings and bracelet. Asia always adorned herself with that special set given to her by her true love.

No matter how much or how often Coco complimented Asia, she could never accept her beauty for what it was. Asia Nadia Coleman was a jaw dropper yet she didn't think so. She was five feet eight and one hundred and seventy pounds. She was what you would call "*thick*". Most southern men loved Asia. Her bra size was a 36D, waist was an average twelve, and her hips; were curvaceous. Her sun-kissed, honey complexion, dark chink eyes, thin eyebrows, and pouty lips gave way to why Coco nick named her friend China Doll.

Was China of Asian descent? Was she even bi-racial? Hell no! Both of Asia's parents were from the North and full-blooded African-Americans. Her parents were a nice-looking couple in their younger years and had grown to be a well-groomed couple, reminding you somewhat of the First Family, the Obama's.

Her mother had always been a stay at home mother and wife, and her father a businessman. No one actually knew what business Asia's father dealt in, but they knew it was lucrative, a business her grandfather passed down.

Asia seemed to have it made; she was beautiful inside and out, however she had serious esteem issues. Asia's breast size and definitely her "not- runway" waist size made her feel like she was fat. She always looked for the newest gimmick for weight loss or to make her physical appearance what she thought it should have been.

"China Doll, why did you change outfits?"

"Well, I just thought this look would complement my frame a little better." Coco placed her hands on her hips and shook her head.

"Okay, Asia, you agreed in the New Year you would get off that hang up about your weight. I hate when you start that shit."

"Everyone can't be small like you. I'm good Coco, you do you and I'm gon' continue to do me."

"If you, say so" Coco she stated as she rolled her eyes.

"What's going on in here?" Mina said as she walked in the room.

Asia rolled her eyes. "Not a damn thing. What's up, Mina? You are looking beautiful this evening."

"What the hell were you two arguing about and don't say nothing because I heard you all when I walked in. Tonight is not the night for this shit, so whatever it is, brush it off. Take this blunt and fire it up. I'm trying to be high and you two bitches will not spoil this shit for me tonight."

Asia took the blunt and Coco stood there looking upset.

"Stop looking all mad, Coco, you looking too pretty to be all frowned up, plus I love the new haircut I can't believe you cut your hair." Mina said.

Coco rolled her eyes and smiled. "Thank you Mina."

It was always Mina who came in and changed everyone's mood. Mina didn't bite her tongue for anyone. How she called it was how it was. She was real and that was why Coco loved her. She knew that Mina would always keep it real with her even if it hurt. Like Coco always said, 'Hurt me with the truth, but never comfort me with a lie.'

Coco and Asia were a lot alike. They always seemed to have words. They both thought that they were right and the other was wrong.

"I'm sorry, China Doll, do you forgive me? I love you and I only want you to see what we see. Which is a beautiful woman inside and out." Asia smiled and turned to Coco.

"We're good, Coco, let's just enjoy the night."

With that said they turned back up the music and started their smoking session.

"Mina, I love your look," Asia said.

Mina had on all black Giorgio Armani jersey jacket and pencil skirt, the neckline rounded perfectly as her breasts sat up in the one button jacket. She wore beautiful accessories by David Yurman. Graphite Ice tassel earrings with the Cable Coil necklace to match. All black accessories with diamonds beaming off of it. She wore a pair of Jimmy Choo Teazer Satin feather sandals with a Jimmy Choo Sweetie Plexiglas clutch, her shit was on point.

Mina was five feet seven and one hundred and forty five pounds with a small frame, resembling that of Jada Pinkett-Smith. She had a slender nose and lips, and hazel eyes, with long, black pretty hair. Mina's olive complexion was flawless. Her body was banging. Mina had 38C breasts and a small waist line. Her ass was round and firm. It didn't look like it belonged on her small, petite frame, but she was fit and in shape. She loved the gym just as much as she loved weed.

One could never tell that she smoked. Mina didn't play when it came to weed. Like a nigga, if she didn't have it, she had a fucked up attitude until she got it.

"Asia, whose ideal was it to get a driver for tonight?"

"The only bitch that hates driving, Coco's ass, she set this shit up last month."

"You know I hate not driving myself, but because Coco hasn't been out in months, I'm going with the flow," Mina said.

"Aw, I love you, Mina. Thank you all for getting me out, shit I'm back! Watch out, ladies, keep your men close because Coco is back on the scene." Coco smiled from ear to ear.

"That's what I'm trying to hear you say, Coco. I love it when you are on your shit" Asia said.

"Right, China Doll, tonight, I must reclaim myself. Can you believe it's been six months since I stepped out?"

I'm shocked myself, what was I thinking? Love is a powerful thing, Coco thought.

"Thanks for staying on my ass, you two."

Coco stood there in a daze, she thought about her best friend, Toni, who lived in Detroit. *Shit isn't the same without my bestie here.*

Coco was still thankful for those two women. They had been there when she needed them most. If not, who knew how long she would have stayed cooped up in her house thinking that she would never get over a man that walked out on her months ago, leaving her feeling insecure.

Coco made up her mind that she would never let another man get her down. Her motto was, 'these niggas better come correct or not come at all.'

"Let's go, ladies, our driver is here," Asia said.

The women did a last look over and out the door they went. They pulled up in a Rolls Royce Phantom Black-Taringa. All eyes were on the luxury car that sat directly in front of The Gillespie. The driver opened the door and Asia stepped out first, being the diva that she was. She got love from those standing in the long line to get in. Coco stepped out with a smile on her face. Mina stepped out last to be greeted by her man, Ty.

"Damn, baby, you're looking beautiful," Ty said to Mina as he gave her a passionate kiss.

"Ladies, are you ready to party?" Ty said as he gave Asia and Coco a hug.

"You three look like you should be on the cover of a magazine, damn!"

"Ty, you know how we do," Coco said.

"Come on, let's get a picture before we step in," Ty said.

They took the picture and headed in. Once inside, heads turned as always. Ty escorted the women to the VIP section and had a bottle waiting for them.

"Alright, baby, I'm about to go do my thing. You want to come with me or chill with the ladies?"

"I'm good, baby, we got about an hour before the New Year. I'll see you then." Ty kissed Mina, and then he headed off.

"Mina, your man is looking good in his Armani suit, damn, and he smells good, too. That man knows he stays on point, better yet, you keep him on point," Asia said.

"Yes, my baby looks handsome," Mina said with a smile on her face.

Ty, towering at six feet two and two hundred pounds all muscle, broad shoulders and chest. He had a walk that demanded respect. Ty was a tall, dark chocolate, and a grown ass man. His smile was sexy as hell with a dimple on the right side. With soft looking lips. Keeping his low even fade lined up and fresh always. His swag screamed approach with caution and approach only if you have your shit together! With an intoxicating smell, Ty was definitely a man that made you wanna be caught up in his world.

Mina smiled as she thought, *Ty is my baby and yes his ass is looking good. I love that man.*

Chapter 2
Coco

Coco was ready to get the party started. That night was her night to get back out and enjoy herself. She rocked her hips to the music. It was as if she was in her own zone.

"Shit, let's pop this bottle we got here and get it in," she stated.

"Okay, let's get turnt up, but before we do that, bitch did you eat something today?" Asia asked.

"Yes, I ate today." Coco laughed, she knew why Asia asked. Coco was the one who always went out and wanted to drink all damn night, but never had shit on her stomach.

"Tonight isn't the night for that sick shit, Coco. What all did you have today?" Mina asked.

"What are you two, my fucking dietitian or what? I said I ate, I'm good let's take some shots!"

The women agreed and they headed to the bar. They wanted to move around and see what was going on. They were too dolled up to just sit. They made their way to the bar where they ordered a triple shot of Peach Ciroc.

"Let's toast to new beginnings," Coco said as they held up their glass and tossed back their shot. She had a smile on her face.

"Damn, that felt good going down, let's get another one?" she said. The two women looked at her crazy.

"Here you go. Damn, we just took a triple shot and you talking about you want to take another one," Mina said.

Coco looked at Mina, then at the bartender, and asked for another shot. That time, she only ordered a double shot.

I don't know what Mina is thinking, I'm trying to enjoy myself tonight. I plan on drinking all night long, Coco thought as she took the shot.

Coco could feel the liquor tingle through her body, she was feeling just right. The confidence that she lacked a few months ago was back. The liquor gave her a little extra boost to her already over the top attitude.

Mina looked at Coco, she was happy that her friend was out having a good time. If a shot was what Coco wanted, then that was fine with her.

"Coco, you deserve to have as many shots as you want tonight, sweetheart, just don't get sick," Mina said.

They laughed. They knew Coco was the drinker of the three and as long as she ate, she could hold her liquor. Mina and Asia were the smokers, although, they did drink, just not as much. Coco, on the other hand, didn't smoke.

The ladies mingled around the party, they talked and socialized with many. They made their way to the third level and it was a half hour before the countdown.

Everyone had a ball. The third level was wall to wall with fine ass men.

"Damn, it's some fine men in here tonight," Coco said.

Asia smiled a sexy grin. "That's one thing I can say about Louisville, they have some good looking brothers."

As they made their way to the table, Coco paused dead in her tracks. She had a look of surprise on her face.

"Am I seeing correctly? Is that... naw, couldn't be. I'll be damned it's him," Coco said.

Asia and Mina looked in the same direction as Coco and saw Rel on the other side of the room with an unfamiliar woman. Rel was Coco's ex. He was the reason why she hadn't been out in months. She hadn't heard from him since July and he was there. The look on Coco's face was a confused one.

"Aw shit," Mina said under her breath, but loud enough for the other two women to hear. Mina knew that Coco seeing Rel was about to be the a start of a long night.

"You okay, Coco?" Mina asked. Coco smiled at her friend before she answered her. She may have had a smile on her face, but you could tell by the look in her eyes that she was hurt.

"Yes, Mina, I'm okay. As a matter of fact, I'm going to say hello." Coco walked in the direction where Rel was. Asia grabbed Coco's hand and Coco gave her a look as to say let go.

"Coco, you sure you want to do this?" Asia asked. Coco stared at Asia and Mina as if they had both lost their damned minds.

"What you mean do I want to do this? Why wouldn't I? Damn, I'm okay." Coco continued to walk over as the ladies followed behind her.

Rel looked good as hell. His tall, muscular frame was eye catching. He was six feet five and about two hundred and thirty pounds. He was one of the most handsome men that Coco had ever laid her eyes on. Coco admired his red toned skin color. He always looked like he was glowing. She loved everything about him, his sexy eyes, slender nose, and full lips. As Coco headed toward him, she smiled at the man she saw before her.

Damn, look at his fine ass. Rel is always at his best. Coco thought to herself.

His goatee was lined up perfectly and his hair was cut in a low, even fade all around. He had nice, wavy hair.

He looked like he was Puerto Rican. He was fine and he loved to dress. He wore an all-white Gucci Suit with shoes to match. He had on the Latin Grammy special edition watch by Gucci and he wore all white Gucci sunglasses; the man was just that, *the man.*

The first time Coco laid eyes on Rel, she was smitten by the way he carried himself. He was so smooth, one would have thought he was an arrogant man, but he wasn't. He was just confident and he had every reason to be.

Coco had second thoughts as she made her way over to him. I can't believe I told them I was going over here.

"Here goes nothing," Coco said as she got closer. Out of nowhere, Big R appeared. He was Rel's friend. They were more like brothers, you never seen one without the other.

"Hello, Big R," Coco said with a smile.

"How are you doing, Coco? Damn, I haven't seen you in a while. You stay looking good, ma."

"Thanks, Big R, you're looking handsome as always."

Big R resembled Rick Ross' weight, height, and carried it well. He stayed dressed and his shoe game was always tight. He was tall, dark, and handsome with pearly white teeth. He was a big teddy bear that you just wanted to hug up on.

Coco didn't have time for small talk, so she continued to make her way across the room. Rel spotted her instantly.

"Damn, she's beautiful," Rel said under his breath.

Coco's presence was so strong. She was beaming off of the strobe lights. There wasn't a man in the place that wasn't looking at her, which she didn't notice because she had her eyes focused on one man and one man only.

As she approached Rel, she smiled, she couldn't help it. Being in his presence always made her feel good. Her stomach had butterflies. The man did something to her that she just couldn't shake.

"Well, hello stranger," Coco said with a smile spread across her face.

Coco was in a zone. She paid no attention to the woman that stood right next to Rel. She was a bold bitch when she wanted to be.

"Coco, how you been?" Rel asked as he pulled her closer to him for a hug. The two looked good together.

It feels so good being in Rel's arms. Damn, I missed his touch, Coco thought as he embraced her tighter.

He whispered in Coco ear, "It's so good seeing you."

At that moment, Coco pulled away as Mina and Asia walked up. The look on Rel's face was a happy one.

"How are you doing, Rel?" Mina asked.

"I'm good. Mina, you look good."

"Thank you, Rel, you look nice as well."

Asia kind of stood off to the side as if she tried to avoid Rel.

"Asia, come give me a hug. Where have you been hiding?" Rel asked.

Asia walked over and gave him a hug. Coco noticed the strange look they gave one another.

What the Fuck are those looks for? What does he mean where has she been? I'm going to make sure I ask her about this shit later, Coco thought.

"Hello," Coco looked at the woman standing next to Rel.

"My name is Ciara."

Everyone was quiet as the female introduced herself. Ciara was gorgeous; she had long black hair with golden highlights throughout the front. She had beautiful dark, chocolate skin. Ciara had large breasts, a small waist-line, and a big ass. Her ass would be considered ridiculous by most men.

The three ladies looked at Ciara as to say, 'who are you?' To them, she was just a bitch that was there standing next to Rel.

"Excuse him, my fiancée, Rel, is rude." Ciara stated.

Coco's eyes grew wider when she heard the word *fiancée*. At that moment, Mina giggled.

"Rel, you're engaged? Hell, naw congratulations," Mina said as she shook her head and introduced herself to Ciara. Mina wasn't for any shit, she knew she had to get the fuck away from there before she said something she had no business saying.

"Coco, I'm about to head over to Ty. It's about ten minutes 'til the countdown. You gon' be ok?"

Coco fought to control her emotions and tears. She knew at any given moment a tear would escape her eyes. Coco was hurt and pissed all at the same time. She heard Mina's voice, but really had no idea what that she was saying.

"Mina, I'm good," Coco said.

Mina knew better. She could tell that her friend was hurting. Coco let Mina know that she would meet her back at the table and told Mina to have a drink waiting for her. She desperately needed another drink after hearing that Rel was engaged and, not to mention, Coco had no idea Rel was still in Louisville. He never once bothered to contact her and there he was, standing before her. Coco wished she had never gone out, but she wasn't going to let it show that she was hurt.

"Congratulations Rel." Coco extended her hand to shake Ciara's hand as she introduced herself.

"My name is Coco, nice to meet you. Rel, why are you so quiet? You have a pretty fiancée. I'm so happy for you, truly," Coco lied. She was far from happy, but she couldn't let Rel know that he broke her heart once again.

"It was nice meeting you, Ciara. Rel, I wish you nothing, but the best, you take care."

Coco walked away with her head held high as she made her way to Mina's and Ty's table. Mina had her drink waiting. She knew that Coco was not really over Rel.

"Coco, are you sure you're ok?" Coco looked at Mina and smiled.

"Yes, I'm good, trust me. Bitch, enjoy your night. Don't worry about me."

Coco gave Mina a half of a smile as she stood there and sipped on her drink. Out of nowhere, Asia walked up.

"Damn, you just left me over there. Mina, where is my drink?"

Mina handed Asia her drink without saying a word.

"I mean, come on, Asia, did you really think I would continue to stand over there and hold a conversation?"

Asia cut her eyes at Coco, but Coco paid Asia no attention. You could see that there was tension between the two women.

"Can I toast with you for the New Year?" Big R asked Asia as he walked up on her.

"You sure can," Asia said in a sexy tone.

Big R grabbed Asia and gave her a hug. Coco had a look on her face as to say, 'how this happen?' Coco assumed that Asia hadn't seen Big R in a few months, yet, they were all hugged up.

I'll be damned. I guess I'm toasting solo, Coco thought.

The countdown began. "Happy New Year!" everyone screamed. Couples kissed and hugged. Coco looked over at Rel as he hugged Ciara. He spotted Coco looking at him and their eyes locked. He saw the hurt in Coco's eyes, but there was nothing he could say to her. He felt bad.

"Coco, baby," she heard. It was Xavier. He was Coco's best friend and her ex man from back in the day. They were together for a couple of years, but they decided they would be better off as friends. Xavier was a ladies' man. He always kept a woman or two.

Coco knew before they decided to be exclusive that he was a male whore, yet, she loved him. She thought she could change his cheating ways. She was wrong.

Xavier stood there looking handsome as ever, his tall frame and masculine body could turn on any woman. Not to mention his pretty brown skin and baby face. His smile was what did it for most women. He had a grill and whenever he smiled his gold fronts always shined.

Coco loved his thuggish look. He sported a low fade that stayed waved up. On top of that, Xavier could dress. His swag was one of a kind. He mainly rocked jeans, tee, etc., but when it was time to get clean he showed up and showed out.

He wore True Religion dark, denim jeans with brown stitching, a matching button down shirt, and a pair of Rockport shoes. His gold cross lay on his chest, and he sported a Raphael Leon Swiss made diamond watch. He loved jewelry. Not to mention his tattoos from his neck down. The man was eye candy. His appearance was always smooth and sexy.

"Coco, Happy New Year, baby," Xavier said.

Coco hugged him. He wore one of Coco's favorite colognes by Paco Rabanne, One Million.

Damn, he smells good; Coco thought. She was happy that he was there at that moment.

"Xavier, why didn't you tell me you were going to be here? I was alone during the countdown."

"I'm here now, baby, shit, let's start our own countdown." Xavier had a devilish smile on his face.

The two counted down together. Coco loved Xavier. He could always put a smile on her face no matter what mood she was in. Ten, nine, eight, seven, six, five, four, three, two, one, Xavier pulled Coco closer as he gave her a kiss. Xavier and Coco had chemistry. When the two were a couple they did everything under the sun. They both loved attention, actually, Xavier craved it.

"Who are you here with, Xavier?"

"Shit, me and the FAM, you know how we do. I dipped out on them. You know I got to move around." Coco looked at him and shook her head.

Xavier laughed because Coco knew him all too well. He couldn't get shit past her, even if he tried.

"You know how I am, Coco. I got to see what's happening in here. I'm glad I did because I spotted your fine ass."

Xavier stood there rubbing his hands together as he licked his lips and stared at Coco.

"Damn, you are looking good in that dress. Turn around for me."

Coco turned around as she modeled her dress. When she looked across the room, she noticed Rel staring. At that moment, Coco decided she would give Rel something to see. She turned back around and kissed Xavier.

Rel knew she did that shit on purpose. She was mad, so he tried not to feed into her bullshit. But, seeing how close the two looked from across the room had him heated.

Coco and Xavier headed to the bar. As they were walking off, Rel was walking toward them. Coco looked surprised to see Rel headed in her direction.

"Coco, can we talk?" Rel asked.

"What's up, Rel?" Xavier asked. He looked over at Xavier.

"Shit, I'm good."

Xavier knew all about Rel and Coco's relationship.

"Coco, I'll go grab our drinks and meet back up with you." Coco stood there looking at Rel.

"What's up, Rel?" Coco said, trying to be smart. She wasn't really trying to give Rel the time of day. She felt like he had humiliated her once again.

"Shit, you tell me, Coco, so you back with your ex I see."

"Well, not that it should matter to you, but no I'm not. We're just kicking it for tonight. Unlike you, I didn't go out and get engaged."

"About that, Coco, can we talk?"

"What is there to talk about, Rel? Hell, you didn't take the time to talk to me six months ago when you cut me off without any explanation. I didn't even know you were back in the city!" Coco was livid.

"I never left the city, Coco," Rel said with shame in his eyes.

Caught off guard by what Rel said, she asked him to repeat it and when he did, she couldn't believe what came out of his mouth. Coco's eyes watered. She was hurt. To hear him say he never left cut her deep.

"Coco let me explain, please damn..." Rel tried to explain to Coco, but she cut him off.

"Explain what? You have the nerve to stand here before me and expect me to hear you out? Not to mention you are engaged and you been here this entire time? You didn't even bother to pick up the damn phone and tell me why you just stopped fucking with me. FUCK you Rel!" Coco lost it.

"Do you have any idea what I been through emotionally? I sat around wondering what I did for you to just up and leave me like you did."

Rel pulled Coco closer to him. He couldn't stand to see her upset. He knew that Coco would be hurt, but he didn't think it would affect her like that. Coco always came off so tough, like she didn't have feelings, but Rel saw just the opposite. She wasn't insecure, she was just hurt, and she had given him her heart and in return got nothing.

"Rel, like I told you earlier, congrats I wish you nothing but the best, I truly do." Coco hugged Rel, and said, "Happy New Year."

"I never stopped caring for you and I'm sorry," Rel whispered to her.

A tear escaped Coco's left eye and he wiped it away. Coco looked into his eyes and smiled.

"I'm sorry as well," she said before walking away.

A part of Coco didn't want to leave him, but she knew she had to. Rel was no longer her man, plus, he was with Ciara and one thing Coco wouldn't do was compete with another woman. If Ciara was who Rel wanted then Coco was happy for him. Xavier watched Coco from across the room. He hated seeing her upset.

"Coco, you okay, baby?" She gave Xavier a smile.

"I am now," she said as the two walked off, sipping on their drinks.

As they headed down the steps, Coco saw Ciara walk toward her looking like she was lost.

"Hello Coco, have you seen Rel? We keep getting separated. This place is a nice size." Xavier looked Ciara up and down as he admired her body.

"Here comes your fiancée now. Take care, Ciara." Coco grabbed Xavier's hand and walked off before Ciara could say another word.

"Damn, you could have introduced me." Coco kept walking as if she didn't hear what Xavier said.

They made their way around the club and enjoyed themselves. Coco worked on another drink that she ordered when she saw Asia on the dance floor. She watched her friend do her thing until the song went off.

"Where the hell have you been, Coco?" Asia asked her.

"I should be asking you the same thing but I got my answer, you been on the dance floor."

"You know I love to party. The DJ is killing this shit tonight. So, are you ok, Coco?" Asia had a look of concern in her eyes.

"I'm good. You see I got Xavier with me, he been keeping me company. His ass is over there dancing with that big booty chick. That negro knows he needs to stop."

They stood there talking and laughing when Big R and Sean walked up. Sean was another one of Rel's partners.

"Coco, long time no see, baby. You look good as always," Sean said.

"Thank you, Sean, you looking rather good yourself."

Sean looked gorgeous with his coal black skin and hazel eyes. Sean stood there licking his lips while looking Coco up and down.

Damn, Sean is looking good, his smile is sexy with his deep dimples and don't let me forget his gold fangs.

Lies, Love, & *Loyalty*

Plus, I love his dreads. They aren't for everyone, but for this man, they fit him perfectly, Coco thought.

"So, Sean, you think I can get a dance?" Coco was ready to party. The Ciroc had her feeling good once again.

"I'll dance with you all night if you want me to," Sean said with his deep, manly voice.

Coco knew what she was doing. She knew that Sean was feeling her from day one.

Coco is a beast, Sean thought. Coco grabbed Sean's hand and led him to the middle of the dance floor as Rick Ross came on.

"*You the Boss*" was bumping through the speakers. Coco must have forgotten she was in the damn club and that she was dancing with one of Rel's friends because she danced all up on Sean. He loved it. He had his hands around her small waist while she swayed her hips from side to side. Coco and Sean danced so close on one another there was no space in between the two.

Coco smiled at Sean when Kelly Rowland's "*Motivation*" played. Coco took Sean by the hand as she sang the lyrics along with Kelly. Coco danced like she was performing. She loved that song and she knew how to work her body and she did just that. Once the song went off, she and Sean hugged.

Rel stood from a distance. His eyes were glued to Coco. He couldn't believe she was out there with Sean like that, but there wasn't shit he could say or do about it.

"Sean, we need to dance more often. Looks like our audience loved it," she said with a smile on her face. They both laughed as they walked off the dance floor. Mina walked up to Coco shaking her head.

"What were you doing out there? You back, bitch. Just like you said you would be." Mina was happy to see her friend with a smile on her face.

"Here I was worried about you and I walk up to see what everyone was staring at and it's your ass out here freaking Rel's friend."

"Damn, Mina, was I out here like that?"

Mina looked at Coco in surprise.

"Yea, you were. You were looking good, though. You had men and women staring. Men wished they could have been that nigga out there with you and women wished they could either be you or move like you. Either way, you held everyone's attention for the last two damn songs, including the one and only Rel. He wasn't happy at all. He watched for a while before walking off, leaving his fiancée yet again. He dipped out on her ass all night. I almost feel sorry for her ass." Coco and Mina laughed

For the rest of the night, they all enjoyed themselves by, taking plenty of pictures and having plenty of drinks.

"Coco and Mina, come with me for a second before we head out," Asia said.

"Tonight was fun. This was a good start to a New Year. I'm about to leave with Big R. I just want to tell you two to be safe tonight and that I love you very much. I'm happy to have you both in my life."

"Aw, China Doll, I love you, too. Tonight was fabulous. I miss times like these. I'm glad we're all friends, may nothing ever come between us," Coco said.

"You two are too much, but I love you all as well and nothing or no one can come between us if we don't allow them to," Mina said, meaning every word.

"Mina, are you about to head out as well?" Coco asked.

"Yes, my baby and I are about to leave shortly." Mina looked at Asia.

"So, Asia did you know that Rel was still here in town?"

Mina stood there waiting for Asia's response, but before she could answer, Ty walked up and asked if Mina was ready to go. Mina looked at Asia and rolled her eyes.

Bitch you lucky Ty walked up, Mina thought.

Why the fuck would Mina ask me that shit? I'm glad Coco didn't hear her, Asia thought.

"Yeah, I'm ready, Ty, we were just saying our goodbyes. So, Coco, what are you going to do?"

"Shit, get in the Phantom and go grab something to eat. I'm not tired yet." Coco looked around for Xavier, who had obviously forgotten about her. Coco laughed to herself.

"Coco, where are you going?" Xavier shouted.

"Damn, what you screaming for?" Coco asked, irritated.

"Now, you aren't fucking with me, Coco, damn, it's like that?" Xavier was drunk and, slurring his words.

"Quit playing, Xavier. What are you about to get into or, better yet, who are you ready to go up in?" Xavier smiled.

"What you talking about, Coco? I'm headed home by myself."

"Yea, your ass is trying to fool me!" Coco said, laughing as she pushed him.

"I'm dipping out with a friend. I just wanted to tell you bye and let you know I enjoyed bringing in 2013 with you." Coco looked in the direction of the woman Xavier planned on leaving with and shook her head.

"Coco, so I'm still your date for the New Year's dinner over Mina and Ty's crib, right?"

Coco ignored Xavier, she signaled for the female to come over. The chick introduced herself. Her name was Paula. Coco skipped the greeting and let her know that Xavier was not to get behind the wheel to drive.

"I'm Coco. Xavier is my best friend, and could you please drive his ass home?"

Coco was protective of Xavier. She held her hand
out and told Xavier to give her the key. He was being
stubborn and said no. Coco was mad.

"Look, hand me the keys."

"Coco, I can drive!" Coco tried to snatch the keys
out of Xavier's hand, but he pulled back before she could
grab a hold to them.

"Give me the damn keys or I'll drive you home
my damn self." Xavier pulled out his keys and handed
them to Coco.

"Here, take the keys. You still think you can run a
nigga."

Coco smiled.

"I see you gave up the keys. Here you go, Paula,
be safe and Happy New Year."

Coco made it home and took a long shower. She
was relaxed in bed, thinking about the events from the
night. She reminisced about the first time she met Rel. It
was at one of Ty's parties. It was an all-black affair.
Coco stepped out with Asia and a few of her friends.
Coco had run into Rel on her way to the bathroom. When
she saw him, she couldn't take her eyes off of him and he
couldn't take his eyes off her. She figured he was from
out of town because she had never seen him out until that
night. Not to mention, his entire look was different. He
approached Coco, asked her name and offered to buy her
a drink. Coco introduced herself and for the rest of the
night the two were inseparable.

Rel was a true gentleman. He wined and dined
Coco doing all the things she loved. He was attentive to
her every need and on top of that, he treated her daughter
like a princess.

Coco got teary eyed as she thought about the past.
You couldn't have told her six months ago that Rel would
dip out on her, but he did.

Coco wanted to be mad at Rel, but she couldn't. She cared for him and always would. She cared about his well-being and his happiness. Although, he didn't reciprocate the same feelings for her, Coco still wished him nothing but the best and if Ciara made Rel happy, then what could she do? 'I'm happy for you, is the hardest lie to tell when your old love has found someone new.' Coco fell asleep that night with nothing but Rel on her mind.

"This Iz It Boutique," "yes, we are open today 'til five p.m.," Coco said to the customer on the other end of the phone. Coco was the owner of her own boutique and had been for three years. She didn't mind working on holidays. Coco was all about her money.

Damn, time has flown by. I can't believe how busy it was up in here today. Shit, let me close up and head home I can't be late to Mina's.

"Home sweet home," Coco said as she walked into her house. She sat down on her bed as she went through the mail that had been sitting there for two days.

"Aw, she didn't forget about me," she said as she looked at the pictures that she had received from Toni. They were family pictures of Toni, Toni's husband, and their son. Coco truly missed them.

Toni stays looking good. That bitch knows she's the shit. Coco picked up another envelope. It was from ZO. She opened up the envelope and it was a card that had a letter and picture inside. She looked at the picture and smiled at the photo.

ZO had been her first love. Coco opened the letter and began reading it.

Hey, how are you doing? I hope you're doing fine. Last time we talked, you were going through some shit with that nigga, Rel. You know you don't need to be out there sweating no man, right? You too beautiful for that, remember that. I know a nigga like me did you bad, I was wrong, and regret that shit every day. I miss you and Brandy. When I get back out, I want to make it up to you and our daughter and start over. Just think about it. You know I don't give a damn about any so called "man" you got, so just know that I'm not going to stop coming to you about this until you mine again. We got too much history and we've invested too much time. I know Brandy is with my sister and her husband for Christmas break, so give her a hug and kiss for me. I love you and miss you. Take care and send me some pictures, please. PS I don't have forever, so don't count me out too soon!

Coco shook her head as she read. She refused to move backwards. She would forever love ZO, but what she wouldn't do was be with him. Coco put the letter in her nightstand and the picture on her dresser. She was running behind.

Damn, let me get in this shower. Time is flying. The dinner is at eight o'clock. Mina made the dinner late because she knew I had to work, so I damn sure can't be late, Mina would kill me.

Chapter 3
Mina

"Baby, where are you about to go? You know we have company coming in less than an hour, right?" Mina asked as she watched Ty walk to the front door.

"Yea, baby, I know. I'll be right back. I have to go take care of something down at the club. I'll be back before anyone arrives. Do you need me to pick up anything while I'm out?" Ty asked, pausing at the doorway.

"No, I'm good. If I think of anything, I'll call. Love you, be careful, and hurry your ass back," Mina yelled from the kitchen.

"Love you, too, baby," Ty said as he closed the door.

Mina took a look around her surroundings and sighed. Not knowing where to start, she focused on the kitchen sink and washed dishes. Staring into the sink as it filled with suds and water, she thought of how blessed she was to have a life full of happiness. Being thankful for all that she had despite her trial and tribulation, she was truly happy. As she rinsed the glass, she watched the crystal clear water as it ran down it, with the realization that she was not the woman she used to be.

Wiping off the marble island, she set the dinner table for her guests. Mina had a two story, European French Country home and it was lovely. The house was four thousand, twelve square feet, four bedrooms and four baths.

Mina and Ty purchased the house two years ago and one would think they had just moved in. Everything was perfect and that was the way Mina loved it. In her eyes, she had the perfect man, home, job, and life. Things could not be better for her.

Mina had known Ty for four years. They started out as friends and their relationship grew into more over the two years. At the time, Mina was involved with Michael, her first true love, he was her everything. Mina and Michael went to high school together. Michael was a senior and Mina was a sophomore. She had a crush on him, but Michael never really paid Mina much attention. She was younger. Once he graduated, he went to college and once Mina graduated, she headed off to college as well. One day Michael ran into her, and from there they became friends and awhile after they were a couple.

Michael got drafted his junior year in college to play in the NBA for the Lakers. They always knew he would be successful, even if he didn't play basketball. Michael was a smart man. But, like most men the money and power went to his head. Michael's ego was over the top.

Michael favored Carmelo Anthony with mocha chocolate skin. He wore his hair in a curly DC fade. He was drop dead gorgeous.

Michael made a name for himself. Every woman wanted him, but Mina didn't care. In her mind, she had that man. He wasn't going anywhere, but things eventually changed. You know how the saying goes; 'more money, more problems.' In the beginning it was okay because he adored and treated Mina like his wife, but that was the thing, she wasn't *his wife*.

Mina hoped that Michael would propose, which he never did. One minute, he sent for her for every game, and the next he pushed her off to the side. He still took care of her financially, anything Mina wanted, she got. Regardless of all the different women Michael messed around with, Mina was his trophy. He would always love her no matter what.

After the third year of being a LA Laker, things changed for the worse. Mina was no longer happy with the arrangements they had. She wanted more, seeing him here and there wasn't working for her. She could have easily picked up and moved with him, but at the time Mina's father was very ill and she wouldn't leave her family when they needed her most. On top of that, her younger brother, Taye was reckless as hell in the streets. Moving was not an option.

Mina felt as though Michael could have been there more when he wasn't playing ball. He showered her with gifts, but money couldn't buy her happiness. One may think it could, but Mina knew first hand that it couldn't. They stayed on the go. Mina had traveled around the world, seen a lot of amazing places, but she was tired of it all.

She was lonely and needed companionship from a man. One night Mina, Asia, and Coco went out, and that's where she met Ty. She stood at the bar ordering her drink when he eased up beside her. He signaled for the bartender. "I got her drinks for the night." Mina looked up at the man that stood beside her with flattery.

She had seen Ty plenty of times, but they never exchanged even a hello. Leaning against the bar with confidence, Ty introduced himself.

"How are you doing? My name is Tyrese, but everyone calls me Ty, and your name is?"

"Mina, and thanks for taking care of my drinks."

Mina thought Ty was attractive and couldn't stop staring at him. Ty let her know that whatever she and her girlfriends wanted was on him. He parted by telling her to have a good time before he walked away.

Mina stood at the bar in a daze, wondering, *what the hell just happened*? She couldn't believe she let him walk off like that. Just as Mina was about to turn to leave, Ty asked, "Would you and your girlfriends like to chill with me in VIP?"

Smiling, Mina said, "Yes! Of course, let me find my friends first."

"That won't be a problem. I'll have them paged," he said as he slightly bit his lip.

Mina laughed when he told her that. Ty couldn't understand what was so funny. He looked at Mina with a sexy smile on his face and let her know that he would take care of it. He asked Mina what her friends names were and the next thing Mina heard was the music paused and a female voice paged her friends. When Ty came back over to Mina, he grabbed her hand.

"You ready to go, beautiful? Your girlfriends now know where to meet you, so let's make our way there." Mina smiled and proceeded to walk with Ty.

Well damn, shit, I like his ass already. Taking charge is what I love in a man.

As Mina and Ty made their way through the club, all eyes were on them. There wasn't a woman in the place that didn't want him. Mina and Ty made it to VIP where they sat and chatted while waiting on her friends to get there. Asia and Coco walked through the doors and smiled when they saw Mina sitting with Ty.

"Bitch, did you have us paged?" Coco said. Mina looked and laughed and before she could say shit, Ty responded.

"I see you two made it. I'm Tyrese, but call me Ty."

Mina stood up and introduced her girlfriends to Ty. Everyone hit it off well. Ty had told the ladies if they need anything to let the bartender know. Ty pulled Mina to the side and let her know that he had to take care of some things and that he would be back. As soon as Ty left the room, Coco and Asia started with the questions.

"Ok, bitch, how did this happen? Do you know who the fuck that is, Mina?" Asia asked. Mina looked confused.

"No, who is he? I mean of course I seen him out. I saw him at events out of town when I was with Michael. Other than that, I have no idea who he is. What I do know is that he is fine as hell."

"Well, he owns this spot and I believe a few other spots. I'm not sure if they're all clubs. I just know his money's long," Asia said.

Mina listened, but the statement about Ty's money being long didn't impress her. Shit, she was with one of the highest paid NBA basketball players around, she already had money. What she wanted was companionship.

"What about you, Coco? Do you know anything about Ty?" Mina asked.

"I know that he is single and that he was with some female for some years. She has a son from a previous relationship, but Ty takes care of him as if he was his own. I also know he deals with ZO, not sure what type of dealings they have with one another, but you know what ZO is into. Other than that, he seems to be what every woman in the city wants."

Mina knew that she wasn't going to do shit, despite the fact that Michael was playing her. She still loved him and when she was in a relationship she was loyal until the end.

The women partied all night. Ty stayed under Mina the entire time. He showcased her as though she was his woman and she loved every moment of it. She got all kinds of looks that night from different women, most of them wondering who the pretty bitch was he had on his arm. Mina didn't care, she loved the attention and so did Ty. In his mind he was single, fuck whoever didn't like it or him. He had the prettiest woman on his arm and he wasn't letting her out of his sight. The night had come to an end and the ladies were headed out to Mina's car when they heard Ty.

"Mina, damn, baby, you just gon' leave me without saying good- bye?" Ty had a smile on his face as he walked beside her.

"I'm sorry, I seen you were busy, but since you're not now you can walk me to my car."

That night, Mina drove her Mercedes Benz E-Class Coupe Carlsson. The car was all black with the darkest tint, you couldn't tell who was in the car and that was how she liked it. '*Keep them guessing'* was her thing. As they reached the car, she unlocked the doors for Coco to get in. Asia had driven her own car.

"So, Mina you think I can get your number?" Ty finally asked.

Mina was feeling Ty and she did want to get to know him, so she asked him to give her his number. Ty gave Mina his number and told her to make sure that she called him. He let her know that he would love to see her again.

"So, Mina how does tomorrow sound?"

Mina didn't have shit else going on, so she agreed to meet up with him. She thought about him the entire drive home. She was torn. She felt guilty and kept telling herself, *'It's not like I'm cheating on Michael.'* Mina knew she needed to let Michael go. She just wasn't ready.

The next day Mina met Ty at Stony River Restaurant at five p.m. They sat, talked, and had drinks. Mina was so relaxed around him, like she had known him for years. She was up front about her relationship with Michael. Mina didn't want there to be any surprises between them.

He knew a lot about Mina. He had been interested in her for some time. He knew Michael was in the NBA and he also knew what came with his success. Ty knew that at any moment Michael would fuck up and when he did, Ty planned to be right there to mend Mina's broken heart.

Men stepped to Mina on a regular. She was beautiful. Ty had to have her. He loved how she looked and she was perfect in his eyes.

Ty went on to tell her about his past relationship and explained to her that he and his ex-just grew apart. He took care of her son as if he was his own. He was actually happy being single. He was just waiting for the right woman to come along. Mina asked him about the club business and what else he did. Ty ignored the question, so she didn't stress it. She knew she was being nosey, but wanted to ask, anyway. He did, however, share his dreams with her as well as his goals. He was a man with a plan. But, in his plan was a woman to share the spotlight with.

Although Ty was very private, he opened up to Mina with no problem. Mina was intrigued by Ty, he said all the right things and she knew he meant what he said. What Ty wanted to give his woman was love, honesty, and trust & that was all Mina longed for.

From that day on, the two became close friends. They were together as often as they could be. Mina went to business school, she one day planned to run a night club just like Ty. She loved the glam life, she loved music, and she stayed in Ty's spots helping any way she could. Shit, he needed her. She was the icing on the cake.

Things flowed smoothly between them.

They hadn't had sex. It had been a year and a half and Mina was still with Michael. Michael had no clue that his woman was slowly but surely falling out of love with him. His ego was so blown up that he barely recognized he was fucking over the one woman who loved him more than her own life.

Things were good in Mina's life until the day she got a phone call from an unfamiliar female. Mina picked up the phone, not recognizing the number.

"Hello, may I speak to Mina?"

Mina had no idea who the female was, but she answered,

"This is Mina."

"My name is Michelle. You don't know me. I was calling to let you know that I have been seeing Michael for over a year now and that I am pregnant with his son."

Mina sat on the phone in dead silence, taking in all that she heard. She felt like she had been shocked with a stun gun. Unable to speak, she finally gathered her thoughts, but they all came out at once and she laid into the woman on the phone.

"Bitch, what the fuck you mean you're pregnant? Who in the fuck are you?" Mina was livid. She couldn't believe that bitch called her.

"I'm not calling to start shit. I just thought you should know for the last six months Michael has said that you two were no longer together."

When Mina heard that it just added fuel to the fire. She was pissed off. She could feel the heat come off her skin like boiling water. She had never been so mad in her entire life. Both women sat silent on the phone. Mina was deep in thought. She couldn't believe that Michael had gotten some female pregnant and she was hurt that he said that they were not together.

"Look, Michelle, I don't know you and don't care to know you. What I do know is that you can lose my number and don't call me anymore. I will handle this situation and Michael."

Mina hung the phone up and called the airport. She was catching the first flight to Atlanta. That was where Michael was for the weekend.

Fuck calling this nigga, Mina thought. She felt that it didn't need to be discussed over the phone. It required a face to face conversation. Mina couldn't think straight. She was upset and hurt. She gave her heart to Michael and he had broken it.

I gave him all of me and then some. He has the nerve to go out and get someone pregnant, so fuck protecting me!

Mina was a mess, she couldn't stop crying and she kept asking herself how Michael could be so careless. Mina knew Michael cheated. She would be a fool not to think, so, but she thought he would be smart enough to protect himself. He had ruined their entire relationship for some pussy.

Mina didn't know who to call. She was ashamed and hurt. After she found out what time the next plane was heading out, she called Coco to ask her to take her to the airport. Of course, Coco said yes. She had no clue that her friend had just got the worst news of her life. Coco arrived at Mina's and let herself in with her key.

When Coco walked in, she found Mina on the couch crying her eyes out. Coco rushed to Mina's side and asked her what was wrong. Mina couldn't even speak, she was crying so hard. At that point Coco didn't know what to think because she had rarely seen Mina cry, so she knew that something was wrong.

"Mina! What is wrong? You're scaring me. What happened?"

Coco was frantic. Mina sat up and tried to calm herself, and Coco got her a warm wash towel to wipe her face. She gently wiped off her friend's face. Seeing Mina cry made her cry. Although she didn't know what was wrong, if Mina was hurting so was she. Mina didn't speak a word and Coco didn't continue asking her what was wrong. She knew that Mina would tell her when she was ready.

"Mina, honey, your flight leaves in an hour let me get you to the airport. Are you sure you want to be alone? I can drive you to Atlanta, that way we can talk. How's that sound?"

Mina finally spoke and said yes. She told Coco she didn't want to be alone. Coco gathered Mina's overnight Chanel bag, then she grabbed some clothes that she kept in the guest room. Coco called ZO and let him know that she was driving with Mina to Atlanta and that he would need to pick up Brandy. Coco loaded the overnight bags into her silver 2010 Escalade and within minutes, they were headed to Atlanta.

The ride was silent for the first two hours. Coco put in Monica's *Making of Me* CD and once the fourth track start playing "Why her" that was when Mina let it all out. Coco offered to turn the music off, but Mina told her not to. Coco listened with disbelief as she told her the events of the day. She tried to keep a calm expression as she listened closely as her friend revealed that Michael got some bitch pregnant.

Once they arrived in Atlanta, Mina had Coco take her to Michael's condo. Mina let Coco know that she would call her when she was ready to be picked up.

Mina let herself into the condo. To her surprise Michael was not there, so she decided to go into detective mode. First thing she found were condoms.

Isn't this a bitch, what the fuck he got these for? He obviously wasn't using them with a baby on the way.

Mina was furious, all she saw was red. At that moment, she could have exploded into flames. She couldn't continue to sit there and wait. Just as she was about to dial Michael's number, he walked through the door with shopping bags. When Michael saw Mina, he was puzzled and looked very confused.

"Mina, babe, you came to surprise me?"

Yea, motherfucker I got your surprise, Mina thought.

Michael could tell Mina had been crying. He went to the closest and put the bags away. Mina thought that was strange, but wasn't concerned with that at the moment.

"Come here, Mina, baby, give me a hug."

He walked to Mina and what he got was a fist to the face. She punched his ass so hard, his damn head jerked to the side.

"What the fuck is wrong with you, Mina!"

That pissed her off even more. She started stealing on him, didn't matter where her blows landed.

"You son of a bitch, so you out here cheating on me and saying we not together anymore? Is that what I mean to you, Michael?"

Mina looked crazed. She was at her breaking point and seeing Michael had taken her over the edge.

"Hold up, Mina, what the fuck you talking about?" Michael had a look of confusion on his face.

"Damn It don't you dare attempt to lie to my face. At least admit the shit, if you have an ounce of respect for me left, please, just keep it real. I gave you my all and what the fuck I get but a phone call from your bitch, Michelle, telling me that you two have been fucking around for a year now and that she is having your baby."

At that moment, Michael tried to comfort Mina. He didn't deny it. What he did was apologized from the depth of his soul, but his words fell on deaf ears. Mina was no longer sad, she was a woman scorned. She realized in a blink of the eye she lost everything she ever loved. In her eyes, Michael was her everything. True, she turned her head on a lot of things that he did, but she wasn't dumb. She knew what came with his career. She just thought Michael would be smarter than the rest, but he was a man and they all think with their dicks instead of their brain.

Mina grabbed her phone and texted Coco, letting her know she was ready and would be out front. Mina walked over to the closet that Michael had put the shopping bags in, and when she did you could tell by the look on Michael's face that something was about to go down.

"What's this you went shopping for today?" Once Mina saw the items and clothes in the different shopping bags, she went off.

"You're an inconsiderate motherfucker. Seriously you out shopping for baby shit and maternity clothes for your bitch? You done lost you're fucking mind, right? You must have, that is the only explanation," Mina said with flared nostrils.

Mina went to the laundry room. She grabbed bleach, lighter fluid, and ammonia. She poured it all over the shit he purchased, then took a match and set that shit on fire.

"Fuck you, that bitch, and your unborn baby. I hope you rot in hell, you low life son of a bitch."

Before she walked out of the condo, she spit in his face just to let him know he wasn't shit.

"Do not contact me and stay the fuck out of my life!" Mina walked away, meaning every word she said.

The fire she set burned in the background. Michael wiped the spit from his face as he stood there speechless. All he could do was shake his head.

How the fuck did I get myself into this, damn? Michael thought as the fire department arrived.

Coco sat out front confused as she watched residents exiting the building.

"Mina, what is with all the fire trucks?" Mina looked at Coco with hate in her eyes as she got in the truck and slammed the door.

"I just pulled a Left Eye move! Let's get the fuck away from here," Mina said with attitude.

Coco drove off not saying shit. She knew her friend was no longer sad. She was a mad and if you knew Mina, then you knew not to fuck with her when she was angry.

"Coco, I don't want to go sit up in that damn room. Let's go to the mall." Coco had a puzzled look on her face and just smiled.

"What you got that look on your face for? I want to shop. You say all the time how it relieves your stress. Well, I want it to relieve mine. Let's go run up this nigga's cards. Shit, he owes me and I'm gon' make him pay for my pain and suffering."

Coco headed to Lenox Mall. She put in Young Jezzy's *Thug Motivation* 101 and played that shit loud. Coco had a blunt ready she lit it, and passed it to Mina. A smile spread across Mina's face.

I love Coco. She drove me all the way here never pressuring me to tell her what was wrong. Then look, she got the weed on deck for me. I love her for just letting me go through this.

Once in the mall, the ladies shopped. Mina was no longer crying or upset. She was high and felt good, although, the two knew once they got back to the room and settled down that Mina would be sad again. That was okay, she just enjoyed the moment.

After shopping, the ladies decided they would go eat. They ended up going to Longhorn. They had drinks and dinner, talked and laughed. They worked on their second bottle of wine when Mina got a text.

Hey, beautiful, I haven't heard from you today. I have tried calling you a few times, baby, let me know you ok. At least reply back to this. I'm missing you, thinking of you, Ty.

"Aw, just what I needed to make me smile."

"Let me guess, that was Ty. He's the only one that can put that kind of smile on your face. So, you're feeling him?" Mina smiled as she answered the question.

"You know what, Coco. I am. It's been damn near two years since he's been in my life. He's good to me. I love our friendship. I'm glad it happened like this because it gave us a chance to build something strong and stable. Our friendship is unbreakable."

Mina had opened up and let Ty into her life. He was there for her when she felt alone. All the times Michael didn't reply to her messages or return her calls, it was Ty's shoulder that she cried on and not one time did he ever make her feel ashamed about crying over Michael's cheating ass.

"Coco, you know the one thing I love and respect about Ty is that he never once hated on Michael. He knew despite what Michael put me through, I loved him no matter what. Ty respected my feelings and he never once pressured me about giving him some pussy."

"Yeah, bitch, I'm still tripping on that. You two are together like every other day. How the hell didn't you fuck?"

"Trust me, it was hard, but I wanted to remain loyal to Michael. Yea, he was a cheating bastard, but that didn't have to make me one. Coco, I would have never thought Michael and I would be over had someone said that shit to me years ago. I would have cussed them out. Damn, he was my baby. I love that man and look how he treats me in return. I guess the saying is true, 'A woman's loyalty is tested when her man has nothing and a man's loyalty is tested when he has everything.' Michael is going to miss me."

They made it back to the hotel tipsy and tired. Mina had decided she would call Ty.

"Hey, baby, you ok?" Ty asked as soon as he picked up the phone.

Mina let Ty know that she was ok and that she'd be home the next day. She told him that she didn't want to discuss anything over the phone, but rather face to face. He agreed and they made plans to hook up once she was back in town.

"Before I let you go, I just want you to know that" he cleared his throat. "I love you."

Mina responded without hesitation, "I love you, too."

She hung up the phone, tears streamed down her face. Not because she was sad, but because she was happy. Despite all that took place, she felt as though that was in God's plans. For the first time, she wouldn't put a question mark where God had put a period.

The next morning, the ladies drove back to Louisville. The ride was relaxing. Coco played her CD while Mina drove.

"Coco, I just want to thank you for picking up like you did. Just to be by my side, you will never know how much this means to me to have a friend like you that truly cares. Just know that I love you and value your friendship."

"No problem. I love you, too Mina. I know you would do the same for me."

Once back in the city, Mina drove to her house. Coco helped her get her things in the house and they hugged one another goodbye. Mina unpacked her bag, ran a hot bath, and poured a glass of wine.

"This water feels good. I just want to relax right here at least for an hour."

Mina laid her head back, closed her eyes, and thought about Michael. She couldn't figure out how things between them went so wrong. She wondered how she allowed herself to overlook Michael's cheating ways.

Mina knew about the other women, she just didn't care. She figured in her mind they were just jump-offs and that she was, *"The One,"* but only thing she knew was that she was just one of the *"ones."* Mina felt that she was just as much to blame as Michael was.

She knew that Michael was wrong and that he fucked up, but Mina fucked up as well. No one made her stay. She chose to; therefore, she placed herself in the position to get played and hurt. Mina didn't hate Michael she was just disappointed that he turned into everything he said he'd never be.

Lord, I bring to You my burdens and you know my situations. You know I can't make it without You. Comfort my heart, give me strength, and help me to carry on. Amen. She stepped out of the tub.

She felt relieved and refreshed. Mina got dressed she wore dark blue with white stitching True Religion, Becky jeans with a blue and white graphic tank to match. As always, she looked stunning.

When she pulled up to Ty's house, he stood in his driveway. He opened the car door and held out his hand. As soon as she was out the car, he hugged her tight and gave her a kiss on the forehead. When they got inside his home, Mina grabbed him and hugged him again. She thanked him for being so concerned about her. Just knowing that Ty was there for her made everything better.

Ty didn't know what had taken place the day before in Atlanta. He figured Mina would tell him when she was ready. He just wanted her to know that she was not alone.

Ty's intentions were to gain Mina's trust and her heart. He wasn't trying to rush into anything. He let her know that if something was meant to be, it would happen.

"So, you know I got you right, Mina?" Mina looked up at Ty.

"Yes, I know this."

He asked her if she understood what he meant by that. He explained to Mina there was a difference. He wanted her to understand that every man wasn't the same and that he would wait for however long until she was ready. He knew she was worth the wait. She just got out of a long term relationship with a man that she loved damn near more than she loved herself. That shit wasn't going to be easy to move on from. Ty wanted Mina's heart, her trust, and her loyalty.

Mina stood there as she tried to fight back her tears. She loved Ty, didn't matter that she just broke it off with Michael. She loved him and how could she not? For two years, he had played the role of her man. He was the one there when her father fell sick again, and it was Ty that was there when she cried at all hours of the night because of all the shit she knew Michael did. Even then, she felt the love for Ty growing and she tried to ignore the feelings because she felt as though she was being disloyal to Michael.

Mina thought, *damn if I wanted so badly to be with the wrong person just think how amazing it will be when the right one comes along.*

Two years later, and Mina and Ty are still going strong.

Chapter 4
Ty

Ty was handling some business across town.

"Damn, where this nigga at? Mina is going to kill me."

He sat in his truck waiting for his connect to give him the okay to come in and he did. Once inside the house Ty opened the bag that held one hundred G's, and the man looked inside the bag. He didn't need to count it because Ty always came correct with the money. Ty was in a rush and you could tell.

"You got that for me? I'm in a hurry," Ty said as he rubbed his hands together.

"Hold up, Ty, damn, what's the rush?" He looked at Ty all serious like he couldn't understand why he was rushing, that wasn't like Ty.

"Man, Mina planned that New Year's dinner and you know she wants me there on time. I'm fucking around with you and I'm late as hell."

Ty's connect laughed because he knew Mina didn't play. Although, he talked a good game, he knew that she ran shit. He dealt with his connect for more than a few years, so the two knew one another well, business and personal.

Ty let him know that he'd be hitting him up in the next couple of weeks. The shit he was supplying always went fast. He headed out the door with the large duffle bag. He had one more stop to make before heading home.

Ty had a house on the south side that he owned. Once inside the house, Ty went into the basement, lifted up the floor boards, and took the bricks out of the bag and sat them down neatly. Ty rushed out the house not really paying attention to his surroundings because if he had, he would have noticed the black Monte Carlo car that was parked on the corner.

Ty hopped in his Range Rover and headed home as fast as he could. On the way home his phone rang, he saw the caller ID and sent the call to voicemail. He didn't feel like dealing with any bullshit. He was relieved once he finally made it back to the crib. He hoped that Mina wasn't pissed off. He had a special surprise for her that evening.

"Mina, baby, where you at?" Mina rolled her eyes at Ty.

"Don't come in here, babying me. Where the hell have you been at, Tyrese?"

Mina was upset. She never called him by his name unless she was mad at him. Ty pulled Mina up on the kitchen counter and whispered in her ear,

"I'm hungry can I get a taste of you?" Mina smiled and placed her legs over his shoulders so Ty could get the meal he craved.

Chapter 5
Asia

"Asia, damn your pussy is wet, baby, ride this dick!"

Twan repeated over and over how good Asia's pussy was.

"That's right, baby, you love my pussy, don't you?"

Asia knew she had Twan gone off of her. It hadn't always been like that, but Asia played her hand correct and she had that nigga open. That was how she liked it.

Asia eased down real slow as straddled his dick, rocking her hips in a clockwise direction. Twan held on to her hips, she played with her pussy, and placed her fingers in his mouth, so he could taste her juice box.

"Taste good, doesn't it, baby? You want some more of this candy to taste?"

Twan sucked Asia nipples he knew what time it was. He laid her back and gave her head. She loved the way Twan ate her pussy. The man had skills. He had a nice, thick tongue that could do just as good as his dick. Asia threw her pussy all in his face. Twan didn't mind, he loved the taste of her. He flickered, his tongue on her clit real gentle. Asia always told him how she loved it when he did that.

"Turn over for me, baby. Let me hit it from the back."

Twan smacked Asia's ass. He slid his dick right into her wet pussy. He loved watching it go in and out. He stroked her long and hard.

"Damn, handle your pussy, baby."

Asia bucked her ass back on the dick. She trembled uncontrollably. After she came, she told Twan to lye back, as she got in-between his legs. Asia took his nine inch dick into her mouth. He tasted so good. No thanks to her. She loved the taste of her own pussy. Twan knew Asia's head game was fire. She did shit to him that no other woman did.

Asia stroked his dick up and down at the same time, making slurping noises as she sucked faster. Twan had a hold to her hair. He fucked her mouth and Asia loved it. She couldn't wait to taste his cum. Asia worked on the head of his dick. She knew that was his sensitive spot. She sucked on the head like it was a blow pop and just as she expected, he busted right in her mouth. She sucked every drop out of him.

Asia got up with a smile on her face. Twan tried to catch his breath. He couldn't say shit. All he could do was smile and shake his head.

"Alright, baby, let's get a move on it. You know we got to be at Mina's for dinner and you know how she gets when folks run late," Asia said.

"Damn, Asia, can a nigga catch his breath?" Twan wiped the sweat from his forehead.

"I'm just looking out for you, Twan. You're the one who has to go pick up wifey, or did you forget?" Asia said with a smirk.

Twan looked at Asia. He did forget that he told his wife about the dinner. Twan's wife blew up his phone all afternoon. He was so busy with Asia that he didn't bother to return her calls. Asia went to her closest and picked out her outfit.

Damn, that man does something to me, too bad he's married.

Asia has been creepin around with Twan for a year and no one knew, that's the way they both wanted it. Twan was Ty's best friend. Asia met him at a barbeque held by Ty and Mina. Twan had just moved in town from Indianapolis. As soon as Asia laid eyes on him, she knew she knew he could get it.

Twan was tall and his skin was chocolate like a Hershey bar. Asia loved dark skinned men. He was bald head, had a goatee and a grill in his mouth. Even if he didn't have a grill, he still had a killer smile, plus, his body was built like Allen Iverson and had tattoos all over.

Asia knew that she shouldn't be fucking with Twan since he was married, but she couldn't help herself. She developed feelings for him that she couldn't shake off.

Twan was in the shower and, called out for Asia to bring him a towel. As she handed him the towel, he yanked her naked ass in the shower with him. She was upset and he knew it, but he didn't care. He wanted to taste her sweet pussy again. He lifted her leg on his shoulder while he was down on one knee, and he sucked on her pussy as she moaned. Her moans alone turned him on. He turned her around and continued to eat her pussy from behind. He grabbed her fat ass and sucked the shit out of her pussy. She could no longer take it. She wanted to feel him inside of her.

"Baby, put it inside me." Asia played with her clit.

"What you say, baby? I can't hear you. What you want Twan to do?"

"Twan, please, put it inside me."

Asia was frustrated. She wanted some dick and she wanted it at that moment. He had her exactly where he wanted her. She talked big shit like she wasn't feeling him and he had to set her straight. Let her know that he was calling the shots and running the show. Twan stopped, turned off the water, stepped out the shower, and dried off. Asia stood there speechless.

"Hold on, Twan. I know you playing, right?"

"Shit Asia you stressing about the time and shit. I just thought I'd give you a little something to hold you over for later."

He continued to get himself together as Asia finished showering. Once she was done, she slammed the door, exiting the bathroom.

"This nigga play too many games, but that's cool. I got something for his ass later on tonight. When he sees me, we gon' see who has the last laugh."

"Alright, Asia, I'm ready to head out."

She walked into the room with a royal blue panties and bra set on. She looked good, baby oiled up.

"Aw, damn I see you got on my favorite color. Come let me kiss those lips."

Twan tongue kissed Asia and slapped her on the ass. He let her know he would see her later.

He left out of Asia's and didn't notice that his wife, Keisha, was parked across the street watching his every move.

"Damn, I've already started off my year wrong," Asia said out loud as she locked the door.

Lately, she felt down. She had the life any woman wanted. The only thing that was missing was love. She was tired of fucking around with Twan and the rest of them niggas. She didn't want to be someone's spare time. Yea, she was getting a wet ass, but that was all she got.

Asia was single with no kids and she owned her own hair salons. She had three that she managed and she still did hair on a regular, although, she didn't have to. She was paid and the men she dealt with had to be as well. She was accustomed to the life style of having and getting what she wanted. She had always been spoiled.

She got dressed as fast as she could. She wore her Miss Me jeans with a white miss me top and five inch Jessica Simpson heels that were all black with a silver heel. She grabbed the clutch purse to match the shoe and her accessories were diamond hoop earrings and a silver diamond cross. She looked casual, yet, sexy as hell. She placed her hair in a neat bun, considering she got that shit all wet in the shower. She wore light makeup and lip gloss. She truly looked like a china doll with her hair off her face. She grabbed the pineapple upside down cake for the party and headed out the door.

Chapter 6
Rel

Rel pulled up to his crib when he saw Big R getting out of his Ivory 2012 Cadillac truck. They showed one another love as they always did. They grew up together in Atlanta. They had been through a lot together. They started their own construction company. Their business took off from the start. Rel's father had a lot of connections, so it all worked out. He was a take charge kind of man, so once the business went how he wanted it to, he sat back, chilled, and stacked his money.

Rel's family moved to Louisville shortly after he was born. His family made him return to Atlanta when he was five years old. He visited his parents often, but it wasn't until he was grown when he decided that he wanted to relocate to be closer to his family.

"Big R, so what did you think about that whole situation last night with Coco?" Big R rubbed his bald head.

"Damn was all I said when I saw Coco walking toward you. I was like some shit's about to hit the fan, but Coco always plays it cool. She's always a lady first. If she was hurt, she wasn't gon' allow us to see it."

Rel nodded his head in agreement, and thought *where'd we go wrong?*

"Yea, nigga, you fucked that up right there, and then to top it all off, Ciara ass talking about you two are engaged. What was all that about?" Rel looked at Big R as to say, 'How in the fuck I should know.'

"I'm not sure why Ciara said that shit. I wanted to smack fire out of her ass. I didn't say anything. I let her run with it and she wonders why I don't want to fuck with her on that level. I'm about to hurry up and get her ass back to L.A."

Rel couldn't understand why Ciara said they were engaged. He knew Ciara heard Coco's name before. He hadn't kept it a secret that he had met someone new. Ciara used to be Rel's woman. They were together for four years and had been apart two years, but, of course, he still fucked around with Ciara. Shit, he loved her and always would. But, at the same time he couldn't stand her. Ciara fucked around on Rel and got pregnant a year or so after they got together. She tried to say it was his baby. Once she had the baby girl, he had a paternity test and it came back that he was not the father. He was hurt, of course, but being the man that he was he took care of the baby as his own. Ciara apologized to him numerous times, but things between them were never the same.

"So, you headed to Mina and Ty's crib with Asia?" Big R smiled, showing his pretty white teeth.

"Yea, she's actually on her way here to pick me up."

"So, what's up with you and Asia?"

"Shit, same ole shit. She cool as hell and beautiful, but she be on her bullshit. She wants to fuck with a nigga on her time and her time only. You know that isn't working out for me too well, but for right now, I'm gon' let her think she got a nigga. Asia better start playing her position."

Big R stood there in deep thought after he made that statement. He was feeling Asia, but he didn't have time for her games.

"Ay, so what's up with Coco and Sean?" Big R said. You could tell by Rel's body language that he wasn't trying to have that conversation.

"I'm not worried about that shit."

Rel stood there silent. He wasn't trying to think about Coco and Sean. He knew that Coco would never do know shit like holler at his partner. He knew that she still loved him.

As the two stood there loose rappin' Asia pulled up. The men showed one another love. Rel went in his crib and kicked back. He wanted to meet up with Coco to explain things to her. He decided that he would text her and let her know that she was on his mind.

Coco, seeing you last night had me thinking of all the good times we shared and I would love if you would just give me the opportunity to explain to you why I did what I did. All I'm asking for is just the chance to explain and if after you hear me out, you don't want to fuck with me anymore, then so be it. I'll walk away. I know you got feelings for me because I still have them for you. Hopefully, we can work shit out. Get at me, Rel.

Rel sent the message feeling confident that Coco would text him back and agree to meet him. He sat there with a smirk on his face until he saw Ciara walk into the room. She asked him if he was hungry. He told her he was good and let her know he was about to step out.

"So, when you heading back to L.A., Ciara? Don't you think it's about time you get back to Carman?"

Without waiting for a response, Rel said, "Yea I'm gone get you a ticket out of here on Friday." He walked out the door.

Rel got into his red 2012 Chrysler 300. He sat there for a while, and then he noticed his phone lighting up. It was Ciara.

"Damn, what the fuck does she want?"

Just as he said that shit, Ciara walked in his direction with a look of disgust on her face.

"Rel, what, you don't see that I'm calling you!" Rel jumped out the car.

"Lower your fucking voice, C. That's that shit I be telling you about all that's played, babe." Ciara rolled her eyes at him.

"What the fuck you mean that's played? What you trying to say, Rel, that I'm played?"

Rel laughed. "You said it, not me."

"You know what, fuck you, Rel. Since last night you have been acting brand new. What's this about, that bitch Coco?" Ciara was pissing Rel off.

"Again, watch your tone and watch who you calling a bitch!"

Ciara mugged Rel in the head. "I know you just didn't defend that bitch!"

Rel snatched Ciara up. "Look, I told you to watch your motherfucking mouth and I'll give you a pass on putting your hands on me. After that shit you pulled last night, you're lucky your ass isn't back on a plane as we speak. Ciara, don't act like you been down here and we just this happy couple, get that shit out your head because it's not happening."

Rel got back in the car and drove off, leaving Ciara standing there with a confused look on her face. She knew how to get under his skin and she knew that he would never hurt her physically, that wasn't in his character. What she did know was that she had over stepped her boundaries and he wouldn't put up with that shit too much longer.

Chapter 7
Coco

"Where in the hell is he at!" Coco said out loud.

Coco was waiting on Xavier. He was supposed to be going with her to Mina's for New Year's dinner. She called him, but got no answer. That really pissed her off. She left Xavier a voicemail message.

"Since you aren't picking up the phone, I take it you're not coming. Get at me when you can. You're fucked up for this shit, and if you still with Paula tell her I said she's on my shit list as well."

Coco hung up the phone.

I can't believe his ass. Hell, I may as well drive Mina's car to her house since she left it here last night. But, then who will bring my ass home? Coco thought.

Coco grabbed Mina's keys. Ty got her the new GS 350 F Sport Lexus. The car was bad as hell and all black, of course.

Before pulling off, Coco's phone went off. She figured it would be Xavier texting her on some 'I'm sorry' shit. But, when she looked down, it was a message from Rel. Coco read the message and a tear fell from her eye. She had a lot of unanswered questions that desperately needed answering. She needed closure so she could move on.

After sitting there another minute or so, Coco texted Rel back and she felt better as she pulled away from her home to head to Mina's. During the ride, she thought about Asia and how Rel acted when he saw her. She wondered if Asia knew the entire time that he was still in town. The thought of that upset her only because Asia watched what she went through those months. For her to know something like that and not tell her could ruin their friendship.

Coco had a lot on her mind, but that night was not the night for all that. She planned to relax and enjoy herself. Something she hadn't done in a while.

This is my fresh start from here on out. I'm going to leave the past in the past. No more feeling down and sitting around crying. I have a lot to look forward to this year. I am truly blessed. I have a beautiful daughter, she is my reason for living, and family and friends that love me know matter what.

Chapter 8
Mina

"Happy New Year," Mina said as she opened the door to let Asia and Big R in.

Big R looked handsome as always. When he walked in the door, he hugged Mina. Asia and Mina hugged as well. Mina told Big R to make himself at home and she offered to make him a drink. Asia looked at Mina as if to say 'Bitch, what about me'. As Mina walked away to make the drink, the doorbell rang.

"Asia, since you can't fix your man a drink do you mind answering the door for me, please?"

Asia rolled her eyes at Mina as she headed toward the door. When she opened it, to her surprise, it was Twan and his wife, Keisha.

Asia was caught off guard, but she played the shit off.

"Hello, you two." Asia extended her hand and introduced herself.

She was a little jealous. Although, she had seen pictures of Keisha, it wasn't anything compared to seeing her face to face. Keisha was a jaw dropper. For the first time Asia wondered why the hell Twan was cheating.

Mina walked up and thanked Asia for answering the door. Asia was more than happy to get the fuck away from Twan and his wife. She headed to the bar to fix a drink because she knew she would need a buzz to make it through the night.

While Mina introduced herself to Keisha and showed her around, Twan was busy texting Asia. He told her to meet him upstairs in the hallway bathroom. She got the message from him and laughed.

Wish I would meet his ass anywhere in this house tonight. I guess he must have forgotten about that little stunt he pulled earlier in the shower. I haven't forgotten. Fuck Twan.

Twan's phone vibrated, he was all smiles until he read Asia's text message *Meet your wife in the bathroom.*

Twan smiled. *Okay, this how she wants to play this shit? Cool, I'll play her game for right now.*

The guests arrived one right after another. *Where the hell is Coco?* Mina wondered. The doorbell rang, and Mina opened it and shook her head. She couldn't understand why Rel was standing in her doorway.

"Rel, what are you doing here?" Mina said with a slight attitude.

He knew then that Coco hadn't told Mina she had invited him. He stood there in the doorway feeling awkward. Coco sat in Mina's car watching and laughing. She knew Mina would give him a hard time.

Rel looked good. He rocked all-white Rock Rival jeans with a button up to match. He left the shirt unbuttoned with a long sleeve white tee underneath. He had on a pair of all white Air Force and sported an all-white L.A. hat. White definitely was his color.

Mina was just about to say something when she saw Coco walking up. Rel looked relieved. *I bet her ass was parked somewhere watching,* Rel thought.

"Mina, Happy New Year," Coco said before hugging her friend.

"Before you come up in here, did you invite Rel? Because you know his ass isn't stepping foot in here unless it's okay with you."

Coco couldn't stop laughing. She advised Mina that she did invite him.

"Alright, Rel, come in and show me some love as long as my girl isn't mad at you I'm not, either."

"So, Rel, can I get a hug?" Coco asked.

"Get your ass over here. You did that shit on purpose, didn't you?" Coco smiled as Rel took her into his arms. Rel smelled good, he wore Armani Code by Giorgio Armani.

"You look good tonight, Rel."

"Thank you, Coco, you look beautiful as always."

Coco was all smiles. Her night was already off to a good start. She wasn't concerned with why she hadn't heard from Rel in months. She was just happy being in his presence and it made her face light up.

The night was good and everyone enjoyed themselves. There were all kinds of shit to do, play pool, spades, XBOX, dominos.

Mina, Coco, and Asia made their way into the kitchen to talk. "Coco how is it that you and Rel are here together?" Asia asked.

Coco stared at Asia and said nothing at all. Truth was she wasn't feeling Asia. She watched during the night how Big R and Asia interacted. It bothered her because for Asia not to have seen Big R in months, they seemed rather close. Asia was puzzled, but she didn't have time for the bullshit. She was already pissed about Twan and his wife. Then, on top of that, Coco was being a bitch. Mina could tell that something was about to go down so, as always, she stepped in before anything was said.

"So, what do you all think about Keisha?" Mina asked, trying to redirect the conversation.

Coco smiled and said that Keisha was cool and how pretty she thought she was. Mina asked Asia what she thought, but, of course, Asia didn't have much to say. She walked out of the kitchen and made a drink. Mina and Coco continued to talk. Coco didn't mention how she felt about Asia. It wasn't the time or the place, but you could best believe that she wasn't gon' let that shit slide.

Chapter 9
Ty

Dinner was finally over and everyone was relaxing. The majority had left except Rel, Coco, Asia, Big R, Twan, and Keisha.

"Mina, come on out this kitchen. Damn the shit is as clean as its gon' get. Relax and enjoy yourself."

Ty knew she was a neat freak. She couldn't stand for her home to be a mess. As soon as she got finished, she walked out to the family room. Ty went to the bar and poured Mina a double shot of coconut Ciroc.

"Sip on this, baby, and fire this blunt up. Enjoy your friends, ok?" he told her as he kissed the back of her neck.

Mina headed out onto the patio and Asia joined her. She needed to get some air because it felt strange with her and Coco being in the same place and not speaking. Mina lit the blunt and hit it a few times, and then handed it to Asia. She knew Asia wanted to talk about what Coco's problem was, but Asia didn't because she knew Mina didn't like a lot of drama. She tried to avoid it and that was why she didn't fuck with a lot of females. They made small talk, finished the blunt, and went back inside the house.

Ty told everyone to join him in the family room. Mina didn't know what he was about to do. When she walked up he took her hand, got down on his right knee, and pulled out a box from his pocket. Mina's eyes watered before he even gotten a word out.

"Baby, you're my friend, my lover, my world. I'm truly blessed to have a woman like you in my life. I would be honored if you would be my wife. Mina Olivia Smith, will you marry me?"

Ty opened the box and the ring was beautiful. Mina looked down at the ring, and then looked at Ty. She could hardly get the words out. "Yes, I will marry you!"

Ty put the ring on her finger and kissed her passionately. The ring Ty had picked for Mina was a stunning, glittering Tiffany diamond paved-set on a platinum band that showcased the bezel-set center diamond. The ring was breath taking and Mina felt so special. Everyone clapped and congratulated them.

The women, of course, had their moment; although, they didn't know Keisha, she was there crying along with them. She could feel the love Ty and Mina had for one another. Everyone could. It was the kind of love that many women would long for and some never found.

Mina took a moment and went outside by herself.

"God, I just want to thank You for finally letting me experience true love. Had I not went through what I went through with Michael, I may have never got the chance to know what real love feels like. I am here and now engaged to my soul mate. Bless us as we become one." When Mina opened her eyes, Ty was standing in front of her.

"You okay, baby?" He asked as he kissed her cheek.

"Of course, I am. You have made me the happiest woman in the world tonight. I love you, Ty, and I promise to always love you."

The party continued. Rel and Coco were caught up in the moment happy to be around the other.

Big R and Asia were all hugged up. Asia couldn't front, she liked Big R and after witnessing Ty and Mina, she wanted to have that one day. She knew she couldn't have it with Twan, so why continue to fuck around? She wanted something more and, to be honest, Keisha, she was cool. She felt a bit guilty for fucking her husband.

Keisha and Twan, on the other hand, seemed as though they were distant. It may have something to do with the fact that he was mad and jealous that Asia was all over Big R. Every time he turned around they were hugged up kissing. At first he thought she did it on purpose, but then he realized she really wasn't paying his ass any attention, and that pissed him off. He knew at that moment that Big R had her attention, her full attention. He could not take it any longer. He told Ty that they were heading out. Keisha said goodbye to the women and they all agreed to have lunch later that week. They each took Keisha's number as they hugged her goodbye. Twan said good bye to everyone except Asia and no one noticed, but Coco.

Asia thinks she's so slick, that bitch keep playing with fire she just may get burned, Coco thought.

Coco knew that Asia was fucking Twan. Hell, everyone knew that was Asia's problem. She always thought she was on the low. She wasn't, she was so busy juggling all the men that she was becoming sloppy with her shit.

Ty's cell phone went off as he fixed a drink. He looked down at his phone and shook his head as he read the message.

I heard you just proposed to Mina. I'm hurt that you didn't bother to tell me you were gon' pop the big question to her. Why would you let me find out like this? We tell each other everything! I know I can't stop you because I'm married, but you could have prepared me for this. I can't stop crying. I can't talk to anyone about this; no one because no one knows. We have been secretly seeing one another for years. You mean to tell me you didn't have enough respect to let me hear the news from you first! I had to find out on Twitter and Face book. I guess this is where our story ends. You will forever hold a place in my heart. Love your #1.

Ty couldn't believe what he read. "Damn, she found out quick." He stood there as he read the message once more before deleting it. He knew he was wrong, but that night was all about Mina. "I'll contact her later," Ty said before he turned his cell phone off.

Alright, time for their asses to get out. They ain't got to go home, but they got to get the hell up out of here, Ty thought as he looked at Mina and knew he made the best choice possible. He loved that woman.

Chapter 10
Asia

Asia was still hurt behind the shit with Coco, but she let it go. She drove in daze, thinking if she should say anything to Big R about the two of them being exclusive. It was almost two years since they had been messing around. Asia knew deep down inside that she wasn't feeling Big R like that, but she was tired of being alone. Being with all the different men had her feeling even more alone than she actually was.

Twan was married and had no intentions on leaving his wife. Asia didn't want him, anyway. She knew if he could cheat on his wife he would cheat on her as well. He was just a fuck. She saw the potential in Big R. He was a keeper, she felt like maybe he could grow on her. Asia didn't want to be alone while her friends were all in relationships.

"Big R, can I talk to you about something?" Asia didn't know what his response would be.

"Come on, Asia, baby, you know you can talk to me about anything you want. What's on your mind?" Asia was nervous. It was written all over her face.

"Well, what is it that you want to gain from us kicking it together?" Asia looked away as she asked the question.

"Huh, baby, what you mean?" Big R pushed her for an answer.

Damn, I'm nervous as hell. What if he rejects me? I can't handle that, she thought.

Asia sat there silent for about two minutes before Big R spoke.

"Are you trying to ask me where you and I stand?"

"That's exactly what I'm asking you," she said, feeling slightly relieved.

"Where do you want us to stand, Asia?"

Asia thought Big R would make it easy for her, but he didn't. He wanted Asia to tell him that she wanted him. She was so used to niggas sweating her and letting her have her way.

"It's like this, Big R, I'm feeling you."

"What do you mean you're feeling me?"

Huh, is he trying to fool me? He's fucking with me now. He got to be. Asia rolled her eyes as she turned and looked him in his eyes.

"What I'm saying is we have been kicking it for almost two years now and I want something more with you."

Big R sat back with a smirk on his face. "Damn, finally we get somewhere."

Asia drove straight ahead, never looking at Big R.

Why isn't he saying shit? Out the blue, he said, "Pull ova." Asia turned on her signal and pulled to the side of the dim road.

"Step out the car, Asia." She looked at him like, 'nigga, please.' "Man, you heard me step out the car."

She got out the car and he walked around to him. "That's all a nigga been waiting on you to say. Now, was that so hard, baby?" He pulled her close to him as he kissed her.

Asia smiled. She was happy at that moment. She didn't give a damn that she was pulled over on a dark ass rode in the freezing cold. She was glad that they were on the same page. Her night was almost complete. She couldn't wait to get back to the house to fuck his brains out but for right now, she had something better for him. She was a pleaser and there was nothing she wouldn't do to make her man happy. She knew that giving him some head on the way home would blow his mind.

Asia told Big R to drive and, of course, he did. Once inside the car, they got warmed up. He moved his seat all the way back. He was a big guy and needed room. Plus, he was certain that she was gon' get him together.

He was a freak and loved watching Asia suck his dick. She sat back in her seat, reached over, and unbuttoned his pants. She stroked his manhood and had it brick hard in no time. She grabbed some pop rocks from her purse and kissed the head of his dick. Big R moaned and the more he moaned the deeper she took him in her mouth. After she made it all way down to his shaft, she came back up real slow, placed the pop rocks in her mouth, and sucked the shit out of his dick.

"Fuck, baby, keep doing whatever it is you're doing to my dick. That shit feels good."

That was all Asia needed to hear, she performed her ass off. She looked up at Big R and he had his eyes closed.

"Bae, if it feels that good that you need to shut your eyes, then I need to stop."

Big R didn't even say shit. He took his hand and placed it on the back of Asia's neck as to let her know to keep going and she did just that. She wasn't gon' stop until she sucked that nigga dry.

The music played as Asia did her thing. "*Representin*" by Ludacris and Kelly Rowland came on, and Asia reached with one hand and turned it up. She sucked his dick to the beat. Just before the song went off, he busted in her mouth and she slurped up every drop of his cum.

"Asia, you know you got a nigga gone off that fire head." Asia smiled. She was a pro at giving head. She would challenge Super Head any day.

Chapter 11
Ty

"Baby, I'll be up in just a minute," Mina yelled to Ty. She couldn't stop looking at her engagement ring. He had done well, she loved her ring. She had no idea that he would ask her to marry him.

She made her way to the master bedroom. Ty was already in the shower, which gave Mina some time to get the room together like she wanted. She lit candles throughout the entire room, and ran into the guest bathroom and took a shower. She was out before him. She oiled down her body and waited for him to come out.

Ty walked out the bathroom with his towel wrapped around his waist. When he saw the bedroom, he smiled. He loved what she had done. Mina hit the control button and Maxwell began to play.

"Damn, baby, when you have time to do this?" Ty asked with a big ass grin on his face.

"You know I can get some shit together in a heartbeat. Come over here so I can take care of you," Mina said with a smirk of innocence.

She reached out her hand as he walked to her. She took the towel from around his waist and sat him down on the bed. She then sat on his lap and stroked his dick as she kissed his lips. Ty's hands were all over Mina's body. He placed small kisses all over her breasts. He placed his hand between her legs. Then, put his fingers inside her warm pussy. He played with her clit while sucking on her breast. She was so turned on as she threw her head back in pleasure and let out a small moan.

"Ty baby lay back." Ty laid back on the king sized bed as Mina got in between his legs. She took him into her mouth. She devoured his dick. She loved giving him head and he loved receiving it. He had a hold of her hair as he watched her greedily take in his nine inches.

"Damn, baby, shit feels too damn good. I'm about to cum if you don't stop." Mina stopped just before Ty was about to nut. She stroked his dick before she climbed up on top of it. She sat down on his dick and rode it like a cow girl. She squirted everywhere and he loved that shit. He had her by the waist as she popped her pussy up and down his long dick.

Ty could never understand why that nigga Michael cheated. Hell, Mina was a freak in the bed, she believed in pleasing her mate, and that she did.

After Mina rode the shit out of Ty, she wanted to taste him again. She took him in her mouth as she sucked the shit out of him. The taste of her own juices on his dick was appetizing to her. It tasted like sweet nectar. He could no longer hold back, he came in her mouth and she sucked every drop of cum out of him. She kissed his lips.

"I love you, Mina, you ready for round two?" Ty smacked her ass.

Mina smiled. "I was born ready."

He made her tap out after round three. She couldn't take it anymore, she threw in her towel. Ty, on the other hand, couldn't sleep. He was up thinking about the text message he received. He grabbed his phone to turn it back on. To his surprise, he had several different messages from family and friends telling him congrats. He listened to messages from his voicemail. "Damn, how many messages did she leave me? Fuck, I knew I should have told her about me proposing to Mina."

Ty had a woman on the side he had been messing around with for years, way before Mina was even thought of. Once he got with Mina, he told himself he would end things between the two. He knew things could get complicated if he ever got caught. Ty didn't want to admit it, but he was in love with his secret lover. For some reason, he couldn't let her go, he slowly pulled away from her, but he could never stay away. They had a connection, but the thing was she was already married, that was the reason Ty didn't understand why it bothered her so much that he proposed to Mina. He knew he should have called her and let her know about the engagement, but he never made the time. Ty knew she would find out. She knew too many people in Mina's circle. He played it too close to home. He couldn't take the chance of Mina ever finding out. If she did, it would destroy their relationship and her friendships she had with others. Before he headed back to bed, he sent her a text saying he would call her soon he got in bed, and put his arms around Mina's waist *I'm right where I want to be,* he thought as he kissed the back of Mina's neck.

Chapter 12
Coco

Coco was up early. She had a long day ahead of her. First, she needed to get Brandy's things together for school because the holiday break was over. She grabbed her phone and called Asia. She wanted to hook up and have breakfast.

"China Doll, wake up. What you doing still in the bed?" Asia rubbed her eyes.

"Bitch, what time is it?"

"It's fifteen minutes after nine, what difference does it make, damn it."

"It makes a big difference if I don't have to be anywhere this early."

"Well, you do have clients today. I thought you started at eleven because Brandy has appointment at noon or, did you forget, Asia?"

"Damn, I'm getting up. Where you want to eat, Coco? I know that's the main reason for the call. Your ass stays hungry."

"I was thinking Wild Eggs. How long will it take you before you leave out? We got two hours, China Doll, hurry up!"

Coco thought about the night before as she got ready. She was so excited for Mina and Ty.

"That's what true love looks like. She so deserves to have a man like him who loves her unconditionally."

Coco was happy for her friend, and she thought eventually she would find the love of her life as well. She thought about Rel and smiled. They had good times together. Rel apologized to Coco the night he took her home from Mina's. Coco didn't want the night to end, so she invited him in and they talked things over. She told him that they could be friends and if it became something more, they would take it from there. He agreed. He knew that he would have to earn Coco's trust back and even if they didn't get back together, they both agreed that they would always be friends.

Coco got dressed and was applying her makeup when she got a phone call from Toni.

"You must have read my mind," Coco said. She was happy that her friend called. She filled her in on all that took place.

"Yeah, I saw all over Facebook, Twitter, and IG that Mina and Ty were engaged. So, do you think he really is in love with her?"

Coco sat on the other end of the phone wondering, why Toni would ask her some shit like that.

"Bitch, please, Ty is crazy in love with her."

"Coco, what makes you so sure?"

"That big ass rock he just put on her finger. Did you see that shit? The ring is stunning."

"Yea, I saw the ring along with a thousand other pictures the bitch posted."

"Damn, is that why you called me this morning to bitch and complain about some shit that has nothing to do with you? Hell, I thought you would be happy for Mina."

"That's your friend, Coco. Her happiness ain't got shit to do with me. I see that you back talking to Rel. How in the fuck did that happen? I know you ain't thinking about fucking with him again, not after that nigga just up and disappeared."

Coco got madder by the second. She didn't know what Toni's issue was, but she wasn't in the mood to hear her negative shit.

"Actually, we are talking again and if you would give me a chance to talk and stop being so negative this morning, I could fill you in on what has been going on."

"Who's being negative? Just because I'm not team Mina like you are, I'm being negative, or is it that you know I'm right about that nigga, Rel? Don't let him make an ass out of you a second time. Damn is you that thirsty for a man or what? Coco, everybody has been stupid for somebody before, but damn, give that shit an expiration date."

Coco couldn't believe her ears. She didn't know what to say. Of all the people in the world to down talk her, she never thought it would be her best friend.

"Okay, Toni. I see that you clearly have some shit going on that has put you in a foul mood and you decided that you were gon' call me and lash out. No sweetheart, not today. And, let me make this clear, I'm far from being a thirsty bitch. It's all good for you to give your husband multiple chances when he fucks up, but let me try to work shit out with Rel, now that's a problem. Call me back when you ain't on the bull shit."

Coco hung up with tears in her eyes. She continued to get ready. She wouldn't let anything or anyone ruin her day.

Damn, not even a week into the New Year and my best friend is on some bullshit.

Chapter 13
Rel

"Nigga, wake up!" Rel heard at nine a.m.

What the fuck could Ciara have to argue about this damn early in the morning? Rel laid there as if he were sleep.

"Rel" Ciara yelled again.

"What the fuck is wrong with you, C?" Rel was pissed.

"So, where were you last night? You were with that bitch, weren't you? Don't deny the shit because I smell the bitch's perfume."

Rel got up and walked into the bathroom. Ciara quickly followed behind him.

"Damn, what, I can't piss in peace? What is it that you want to know? Shit, you got your answer. You said you smelled her perfume. Haven't I made it clear where you and I stand? I guess not, so now, how about I show you."

Ciara stood there with her hands on her hips looking confused.

"Go get your shit packed. You're going home today." Ciara had tears in her eyes; she couldn't believe what she heard.

"What? Are you deaf all of a sudden? Go pack your things or should I pack it? Better yet, I'll give you some money so you can just get some new shit and you can be on your way. Yea, that sounds better. Get your purse, we can just roll to the airport and get you a flight out."

Rel stood there with a blank expression on his face.

Man let me hurry up and get her ass up out of here. She trying to do too much she must have forgotten who she's fucking with. So, now I got to show her.

Ciara was in the master bedroom getting her things together. "Fuck I should have just left the issue alone about Coco," Ciara said quietly, knowing she fucked up.

Ciara knew he didn't like that shit, yet, she did it, anyway. He let her slip with that fiancée shit, but the jumping off talking crazy and questioning him. Anyone that knew Rel knew doing all that was a deal breaker. He didn't and wouldn't allow anyone to question him.

"Ay, you ready to go?" Rel yelled.

Ciara walked into the living room with her suitcase and bag. Rel carried the bags to the car. She walked out the door with tears streaming down her face. He never asked if she was ok, he just put the shit in the trunk and headed toward the airport. She cried the entire ride.

Once at the airport, he parked the car and grabbed the bags. She followed behind him.

At the clerk desk, Rel spoke to the attendant. "Yea, I need a one-way ticket to Los Angeles, California for your next flight out," Rel said. Ciara found a seat. She was tired and had a headache. After all the arguing, she knew it was just time to let Rel be. He wouldn't change his mind.

He walked over with her ticket in hand. "Your flight leaves in an hour, here's ten stacks for right now. I'll send you some more cash later this week." Ciara took the money and placed it in her purse.

"Rel," Ciara said before he cut her off.

"You take care of Carman and call me once you touch down." He turned and walked away.

Ciara stood there in shock. She was hurt by the fact that Rel didn't even hug her goodbye or act as if he cared. It really bothered her. She knew in her heart that it was over and their relationship would never be the same. She took out her phone and texted him to say her final goodbye. He was on the expressway when he received the text. He shook his head as he read the message.

Rel, if I could go back and change things, I would. I am sorry about how I acted. You have been by my side from day one and I owe you so much for that. For me to question you and act a fool was not right. I now know that you have not loved me for some time now, yea you got love for me, but that's as far as it goes. I pray one day we will be back together all I can do is hold on to that little hope. I'll always love you, Darrel Andrew Vincent. I will only contact you about your daughter. Thank you for loving her like she was your own. Love you forever, Ciara.

Chapter 14
ZO

"Brandon Lorenzo Carter, number 169419, Kentucky Inmate, please, step forward. Brandon Carter, you have served thirteen months and one day of your five year sentence in the Marion County Correctional Center. Do you feel as though you are ready to join society again?"

"Yes, I do!" ZO said with excitement.

"Please, give us your reason for why you think you should be given a second chance."

ZO looked at the Parole Board Panel. So many inappropriate choice words rushed to his mouth, but he knew he had to tell them what they wanted to hear. He would say anything. He was ready to get the fuck up out of there. He was on some get back shit as soon as they opened the gates to let him out. He had some niggas to be dealt with on the street. First, he'd start with the nigga that crossed him. Being released so early would catch everyone off guard and that was how he wanted it, for niggas to not see him coming. He wanted them to be surprised. Catch them when they least expected it.

The parole board made their decision rather fast.

"Brandon Carter, we grant you your parole and we hope to not see you again. This is your chance. Make it count."

ZO smiled from the inside out. He made his way back to his cell. He lay back on his cot and talked out loud to himself, something he always did.

"Hell yea, I'm free. Thing is, I don't want anyone to know I'm out. I have to set my plan in motion."

He wondered if he should at least tell Coco or not. ZO hated not being honest to her, but he had to do what he had to do in order for his plan to work. He missed Coco and Brandy. He sat back and thought about where he went wrong with her. He loved her and he knew she loved him, but he took her for granted. She was his one true love. She stuck it out with him through whatever. Back in the day, he wasn't trying to see her like that. She was pretty, but he had too many women to be tied down to one. He explained that to her and she respected that. It actually made her like him even more.

ZO saw that Coco wasn't backing down, so he gave in a little, he was feeling her. It started off good. They had an understanding that they were just friends with benefits. She never got mad or jealous of any of the other chicks because she knew that he wasn't feeling any of them. Once they graduated high school, they sort of drifted apart. He was on some get money shit. He didn't have time to kick it with Coco.

She kept a nigga by her side, even though she was gone off his ass, but she still kept it moving. ZO wasn't trying to be in a relationship with anyone. Coco had it bad. It didn't make a difference if she was in a relationship with someone else. If he called, she would drop whoever and whatever. He did the same for her.

Shit went bad when ZO got locked up his first time. Coco was there for his entire bid. She visited him and did whatever he needed her to do. She stayed loyal and never changed up on him, not once, and she wasn't even his woman. He knew that she was his and no one could tell him differently. He had her heart, so he figured why commit? He still got what he wanted, Coco and other women on the side.

After ZO got out of jail he was back to his old ways and Coco was fed up. She started tripping about little shit like why he didn't call her back and where he was. ZO wasn't trying to be on anyone's time schedule, so he was like fuck Coco and she was like fuck him, too.

Coco started fucking with Xavier. Word on the street was that Coco was gone off him. ZO would call her, but she stopped picking up his calls. The shit was fucking with him, for the first time Coco didn't put him first.

One day, ZO ran into Coco. She looked beautiful as ever. When she saw him, she smiled and the two hugged. They talked for about thirty minutes just catching up. She explained to him that she was happy with Xavier and she hoped that ZO would be happy for her as well. He snapped on her, letting her know he didn't give a damn about her and some other nigga. He made it clear that he wasn't trying to hear that shit. You could see the hurt in her eyes. He knew he hurt her feelings. He couldn't believe that Coco honestly thought he could ever be happy for her with another man. The two had so much history together, he didn't have to question her love it was genuine. He didn't want to commit to her, but he damn sure didn't want to see her with another man.

Two years later, Coco and Xavier's relationship ended. Shortly after, Coco and ZO got together and shit was good.

Although, he had finally made Coco his woman, it didn't stop him from fucking around. He slowed up once she got pregnant, but hell, even then he still cheated. After years of cheating, she was finally fed up with him. She knew she deserved better, so she ended it for good. She was tired of his broken promises and looking stupid, but the main thing she was worried about was her daughter. She didn't want her growing up thinking that was how a woman was to be treated.

ZO adored his daughter. He wouldn't even raise his voice at her. Coco and Brandy was ZO's reason for living. Two years later and there he was still thinking about Coco and how he could get her back.

"Carter," the officer said which broke his train of thought.

"Yea, Wassup?" ZO said to the officer.

"Do you have arrangements for pickup from here or will you need transportation? Because if you do that won't be until the end of the week if you need to be taken wherever it is you're going," the officer said.

"Yea, man, I got arrangements. My ride will be here tomorrow morning at eight a.m.," he said before he turned and walked away.

"This nigga got to pay. He lucky I don't make him pay with his life, but that would be too easy. That nigga ain't gon' see me coming. I took the fall for this shit and this bitch nigga don't answer my calls. Nigga think I forgot about my money. Thinking a nigga got forever, well wrong. I'm about to show up and show out. Because of this bull shit, I lost my woman and my daughter. I can't really blame that nigga for what took place with me and Coco, but had I still been out there, I know we would have made shit work. I remember that shit like it was yesterday," ZO said as he had a flash back of what landed him in jail.

"*Damn, ZO, you trying to get pulled over with all this dope in the car or what?*" ZO was on his shit, he was high and he felt like he was on top of the world. He gunned his Charger.

"*Mitch, I'm good, my nigga, calm down, I got this shit.*" Just as he said it, a police officer came from out of nowhere and flashed his lights.

"*Fuck, I can't pull ova.*" ZO lead the officer on a chase. He got off the expressway and went in and out of sides streets.

"Nigga, when I come to this turn, jump the fuck out take the drugs, the money, and get ghost!"

Mitch did just that and the shit worked. ZO still lead the officers on a high speed chase. There were five cop cars in pursuit. He knew the shit was gon' end in disaster, but he didn't give a fuck.

"Isn't shit they can charge me on but fleeing, the nigga got the drugs and money, I'm good."

ZO went so fast that he lost control of his Charger and found himself wrapped around a pole. He was arrested. The cops found a pound of weed in the car along with two guns, that he forgot to pass along to his partner. He was so worried about him getting out with the drugs and money that he forgot about the two guns under his seat. Shit wasn't looking good for ZO. He carried concealed weapons, and that hurt him. He got sentenced to three years for the charges. When they gave him parole after a year and a month, he was not complaining.

"Yea, let me get myself all groomed up. A nigga came in looking handsome as ever. I'm leaving out the same way."

ZO was arrogant. He knew he was handsome. He stood six feet three, two hundred and thirty pounds, and all muscle. He was cut up with tattoos everywhere. He had light mocha caramel skin, nice, thick eyebrows with light brown eyes, and long eyelashes. He had nice, soft lips with a grill on his top teeth. The grill, plus his luscious lips, full beard, and bald head had women in love.

After he got himself together, he lay down for the night and he thanked God for his early release. "Tomorrow is a new day," he said before he drifted off.

Chapter 15
Rel

Bang! Bang! Bang! Rel opened one eye with confusion. He wasn't happy because someone was basically tearing down his door.

Who the fuck is that? He thought as he jumped out the bed.

"Whoever the fuck is at my door better have a good reason for banging on my shit at six in the motherfucking morning," he hollered as he approached the door.

He looked to see who it was; it was his sister, India.

"What the fuck is wrong, Indy?"

"I'm sorry. I came busting down your door, but I need to borrow some money, please."

"Man where's your key at? And you mean to tell me you came over here at six a.m. to ask for some money? Man, bye, Indy!" Rel was disgusted.

"Rel, please, I called you all last night. You didn't pick up, so I had to just show up. I'm sorry, but I need to borrow this money."

He turned and walked back to his room.

"You always say you need to borrow some money. Why don't you just say give me some money 'cause you never pay my ass back. How much you need?"

India stared at Rel. She was gorgeous, she was five feet eight and one hundred and sixty pounds, and she was thick as mud. Men loved her hour glass shape and along with the perfect body was a beautiful face. India had flawless honey complexion skin, chinky eyes, and small, perfect lips. She had long, pretty chocolate hair, with red highlights. She could pass for being Asian but she wasn't. She just had strong features. India had a small birthmark behind her right ear it was shaped like a half of a heart.

"I said how much do you need, Indy?"

"I need like ten stacks. Rel, please, don't question me on what I need it for. I just need it. I couldn't ask daddy because he tries to be in my business too much and I can't stand that shit."

Rel stepped closer to India. "What the fuck you mean you can't stand that shit? You asking for a lot of loot out the blue and can't let me know what it's for? You are tripping. Shit, your ass need to get a job. You running round here shopping and shit, going out of town on other people's money. Then, you have the nerve to get mad if someone questions what you need it for. Hold on, I'll get it for you. This is the last time for this shit. You hear what I'm saying, Indy?"

India rolled her eyes. "Yeah, I hear what you saying, Rel." India knew he would be pissed, but she could care less. All she was worried about was getting the money.

"Here you go, put this shit in your purse and be careful. Give your big brother a hug. I love you, Indy."

"I love you, too, Rel, and again thank you."

Once India left, Rel kept thinking about what she could have needed the money for. He had no clue and he felt like calling his father, but changed his mind. He didn't want to upset him and didn't want India to be mad at him. She looked up to Rel.

"Yea, I'm gon' keep my eye on my sis. She is doing too much." Rel couldn't go back to sleep, so he decided to watch TV. He checked his cell phone and he had three messages.

Damn, what the fuck am I, an *ATM?* Rel said to himself. Ciara sent a message saying she needed some money.

"Ciara got me fucked up. I'm not taking care of her, only my daughter. She has gotten too accustomed to this lifestyle." Rel deleted the message as he got back in bed and fell asleep.

Chapter 16
ZO

"Brandon Lorenzo Carter, your ride has arrived," the correctional officer said.

"Hell yea, I'm free. I'm about to get my piece of the pie, plus, some extra slices. These niggas about to get caught slipping," ZO said out loud.

Damn, look at her fine ass. She's thick as a motherfucker. I'm gon' fuck the shit out of that pussy all day and night, ZO thought as he made his way out the gates.

"Hey, baby, I'm so glad you're out. I've missed you, daddy." India gave ZO a kiss, his dick jump inside his boxers.

Damn, I can't wait to ride that dick, I'm gone eat this nigga up.

"Damn, ma, you got me over here brick hard with that kiss. You gon' show daddy how much you missed him on the drive home?"

"You know I got you." India got in on the passenger side and ZO got in the driver's side.

"Ma, did you get that paper for me like I asked you too?"

"Yes, of course I did, baby. I got the money at home waiting for you. I told you your baby was gon' come through, didn't I?"

Hell yeah, she had come through. She just didn't know she was going to work perfectly for my little plan.

ZO met India a few years back. She stepped to him on some real shit. India was a beast with her shit. She was beautiful and she was sexy as hell. ZO had to have her. He had no intentions in really getting caught up with her, but he did. She was cool, never nagged him, none of that shit, and she always wanted to please him. No matter what, she played her position. She never tripped about him having a woman. She knew Coco was ZO's one and only true love. His intentions was just to get some ass from India from time to time, but slowly but surely he let her in his world, and they had been kicking it ever since.

Coco knew nothing about India. She didn't know he had been fucking with her for two years. Once India and ZO started kicking it that was when he found out that Rel was her older brother. When he found out, he didn't trip. He felt as though he could keep up with Coco that way. There was no need for India to ever think she would be ZO's woman. She was just something to do at the time.

Before they had even pulled off, India had ZO's dick out front and center.

Look at this pretty motherfucker. I'm about to hit this nigga off with some of the best head he ever had.

India stroked his dick. His manhood throbbed in excitement as India took him into her warm mouth. He tried to watch her as he drove.

"Damn, baby, I need to pull over. Shit feels too damn good." ZO had been locked up a little over a year. He wanted to enjoy the moment.

"No, baby, keep driving. Don't stop."

ZO kept driving as India slurped up and down on his dick, never once coming up for air. She circled the head of his dick with her tongue she began to suck faster, and the faster she went the more his dick throbbed.

ZO came in her mouth and she continued to suck his dick, which sent chills up his spine.

"Damn, I missed your sexy ass, ma."

"I missed you too, daddy," India sat up and kissed ZO on his neck. She truly did love him. She didn't realize he was only using her to get what he wanted and that was revenge.

Chapter 17
Big R

"Where the hell is India? She needs to answer her damn phone," Big R said with disgust. He knew that India did it again. She ran game on him every chance she got. He was a trick that didn't mind throwing her money and there was no limit. Whatever she asked for, she got. She had him gone off her.

India just came and borrowed fifteen racks from me but wouldn't say what for. Now, I call her a day or two later and she don't want to take a nigga's call. She's been acting strange as hell. She ain't been trying to give me any pussy. I asked her if she fucking someone else she says no. She's a fucking lie. A nigga ain't stupid. I shouldn't be fucking with her no way. Shit, Rel is my best friend, my brother. If this nigga knew I was fucking his sister, then shit wouldn't be the same. That nigga told me day one his sister was off limits, but I tested the waters, anyway, going against what my brother said. Now, I'm two years in and fucked up about India. She is on some bullshit. I don't understand, her one minute shits good and the next it's not.

That's why I started fucking with Asia like I did. She wasn't on the games, plus, the two look alike. They were both super thick. Asia is more of a lady and a freak in the sheets. India, is a freak in the streets and between the sheets, only thing was she didn't leave anything to the imagination. She let it all show. Damn, you got to keep a nigga guessing. I love her ass, I can't deny that.

Fuck India when she calls, I'll let her ass see you can't play a real nigga like me. It ain't that type of party. I can have any bitch.

Chapter 18
Ty

Damn, the year is moving along alright. Shit is going good. It's damn near March. This nigga keeps me supplied with that good shit. Let me hit him up real quick. Hopefully, he can meet me today. My shit went faster than I thought.

Ty called his connect. "What it do, Ty? What you trying to do my man?"

"Shit, you know what it is. When can I come through?"

"Give me thirty minutes, and then be on your way," his connect told him.

Ty stopped by the club to kill sometime. When he arrived there Mina's brother, Taye, was there.

"Taye, what brings you by?"

Ty really didn't fuck with him. He was a wild, young nigga, just out of control. Taye was always in some shit. He didn't hustle, but he had a reputation of being a stick up kid. Everyone knew it, but he always tried to deny it. He always tried to make a come up off the next man. Therefore, Ty didn't truly trust him he only dealt with him because he was Mina's brother.

"How you been, Ty?" Taye said a little sluggish. He was well over six feet tall with light brown skin and light brown eyes. He was handsome and a clean cut guy.

"What's up Taye?"

"Shit, Ty, can you put a nigga on or what?"

Taye was once again trying Ty's patience. He always stepped to him on the same shit.

"What you talking about, Taye? I don't fuck around, you know that."

Taye laughed. "Nigga, come on, Ty. You think the streets don't talk? You got clout in these streets. Let a nigga get on."

"Taye, you heard wrong. Like I said, I don't fuck around, so fuck what the streets are talking about. You talking to me now and I'm telling you, but if you want, I can let you work in one of my clubs," Ty said with disgust.

"Man, fuck you! Ty, what the fuck makes you think I want to work in your motherfucking club?" Ty hit Taye in the mouth with a blow that knocked him on his ass.

"What the fuck is going on in here?" Mina said as she walked in to see her man knock out her little brother.

"Man, get this nigga up out of my face. Taye, don't ever step foot in here."

"Fuck you, Ty. I got something for your ass. Bitch nigga, fuck your club."

Ty was about to get in Taye's ass again but Mina stepped in front of him.

"Look, I can't stand here and allow you to put your hands on my brother. Taye, you need to leave. I'm not sure what just went down here. But, y'all need to stop!" Mina said with tears in her eyes.

"Yeah, ok, I'm out of here, but you got a buster for a fiancée. You think you know this nigga, but you really don't, sis. You heard what I said, Ty, don't get caught slipping, nigga." Taye walked out the door with a crazed look in his eyes.

Fuck that Taye. I will hurt that lil 'nigga if he ever comes to me again. Damn, I wish Mina had never walked in here now I got to tell her ass something and I don't want to lie to her. Everything's not for her to know. Plus, what in the fuck is Taye talking about? I don't fuck with too many niggas for anyone to know what the fuck I do. That nigga got some nerve stepping to me the way he did.

Ty's thoughts were interrupted by the sound of Mina's voice.

"What was that about, Ty? You're fighting my brother and for what? Look at me when I'm talking to you!" Mina yelled.

"Man, calm down, Mina. Your brother stepped in here on some bullshit. This is my motherfucking spot."

"So, what you saying, fuck my brother? You had to put your hands on him?"

"Hell yea! I had to and I'll do it again if he ever comes in here or approaches me like he did. I'm sorry, baby, but your brother is grown. Taye's out here robbing motherfuckers, worry about that instead of me kicking his ass. I got somewhere I need to be, Mina. I'll see you back at home."

Ty kissed her on her cheek and walked out the club. He drove to the East side to meet his connect at his house.

"Damn, he lives too far out, shit. He ain't got to worry about getting any pop up visits. I much rather met him at his condo."

Ty pulled into the gated community, the shit was peaceful out there. His connects crib was tight. It was somewhat of a mansion. Ty rung the door bell and was let in.

"Ty, you looked pissed off, you good?"

"Yea, I'm straight, just had a run in with Mina's brother, Taye. That lil' nigga got me fucked up! Coming to me talking about let him get on."

"Word, that nigga know you in the streets like that, Ty?"

"That's just it, he don't know shit. Hell, Mina doesn't even know and I want to keep it that way. I don't need him or anyone else in my business. Here go 200,000 for you. What you got for me, my nigga?" Ty tossed the duffle bag with the cash in it on the floor.

"Shit, I got what you asked for, Ty. Calm down. Don't go out here all hot headed. Here, take you a shot of this Remy. Ay, plus, I know that's your woman's brother, but watch his ass. I heard about how he gets down. That's why I don't fuck with a lot of niggas here. They ain't about business like you. I been don' put one of these niggas in a body bag."

Ty chilled a little while longer, and then he headed out. He was on his way to his spot to drop his shit off and head home afterwards. Once inside the spot, Ty went to his stash and put the drugs away. He locked the room and proceeded to head out the door. He noticed an unfamiliar car parked across the street, he could tell it was a female inside, so he didn't think anything of it.

Maybe she's waiting on someone, Ty said to himself as he hopped in his car to head home.

Chapter 19
Asia

"Hey, everyone Good morning," Asia said as she walked in the shop at eight a.m.

"Well, good morning, diva," Red said. He was Asia's assistant. He was gay and funny as fuck. Red was medium built and cut in all the right places. His ass could dress like a motherfucker and always rocked the latest styles. He was nice looking, too.

"Bitch, what you do last night, coming in here talking about good morning. Who laid that pipe to you last night?" Red said to Asia. The women in the shop laughed. Red always said some crazy shit.

"Shut the hell up, Red. Damn, can I just be thankful for waking up this morning?"

"Yea, if your ass was waking up to some dick, bitch." He was the life of the party. Asia loved him to death that was her ace.

Damn, I wonder if Coco is going to come in today. Since our little discussion we had over breakfast a few weeks back, the bitch been acting funny and shit. She asked me if I knew about Rel being here all along and I told her I did. I couldn't lie to her. I felt like I was protecting her, but in her eyes, I wasn't being a loyal friend. She felt as though I was protecting Rel, which is a fucking lie.

I had no idea why Rel stopped calling Coco. I never asked because it wasn't my business and I should have said something, but I didn't. For that, I'm sorry. She doesn't have to get all brand new and shit. She comes in here, get her hair done, and then roll out, not saying too much of anything. The tension is killing me. I miss my friend. I have so much going on that I want to share with her. We got to talk later if she comes in, which I'm sure she will because she never misses an appointment, Asia thought.

"Miss Thing, guess who I got under the dryer, bitch!" Asia looked at Red as if to say, 'who?'

"India. So you're doing her hair again?"

"Yea, I am. I saw her a few weeks ago, said she wanted to come back. Shit, you know I don't pass up any money. Plus, I don't have a problem with her. That shit is between her and Coco, feel me?"

"Um, bitch, I don't feel you and neither will Coco when she gets here. You two are already half speaking and now this? Oh, shit, it's going down in the spot today. Coco gon, whoop both you bitches." Red laughed, he knew that some shit was about to pop off.

Damn, Coco is gon' be pissed. I kind of hope she doesn't come in, Asia thought.

Asia knew she had fucked up because Coco and India didn't like one another. It was like India was jealous of Rel and Coco's relationship. India acted like he was her man that shit pissed Coco off.

"Oh, guess who just pulled up in her cream Armanda? Oh, it's about to go down!" Red said.

"Coco is about to be pissed. What the fuck am I gon' tell her? I need to hurry and get this bitch India out of here." Asia said quietly.

"Good morning, Red. Why you looking like you're up to something?" Coco said as she walked through the door.

"Coco, what are you talking about? I'm just glad to see you this morning. Aren't you glad to see Coco, Asia?"

"Red, can you please go do some work?" Asia said.

Asia couldn't be mad at Red. She knew he loved drama. Red could sense that Asia was upset, so he left it alone and went to the back.

"Coco, what are you getting done today?"

"I just need a black rinse. What you think, China Doll?"

Aw, she called me China Doll. She must not be as mad as she was because when she is pissed at me she calls me Asia.

"Yea, that's cool. Make your way over to the shampoo bowl, please. I'll get you together. On the way to the shampoo bowl, Coco spotted India.

I know that isn't India's ass sitting under the dryer, Coco thought, but didn't say anything because she really couldn't tell.

Just as Asia was about to finish molding Coco's hair, India came from under the dryer, and sat in the waiting area. *Fuck, here come this bitch, aw damn,"* Asia thought. Her stomach felt queasy. She knew Coco was gon' be upset.

"Hey, Asia, how are you doing?" India looked pretty as always.

"Hey, India, you dry girl?" Coco turned around to see India.

"Coco, how have you been?" India knew Coco couldn't stand her ass, hell, she couldn't stand her, either.

"I'm good." Coco wanted to jump out that chair and smack the shit out of India, but she played it cool.

"I'll be with you in a minute, India, as soon as I get Coco under the dryer."

"Asia, when did you start back doing that bitch's hair? You doing her hair again knowing I can't stand that bitch?" Coco smartly blurted the words out.

"Coco, this is business, I'm not into all that bullshit."

"You not in to all what shit? Bitch, it's plenty of stylists here in the city. She is one bitch you could have said no to, but you didn't. Once again, you disregarded my feelings. I would never put you in an awkward situation. Get me under the dryer so I can get the fuck done and get out of here. You fucked up."

Asia put Coco under the dryer. The fact that Coco questioned her friendship and loyalty made Asia feel a certain type of way. She was getting tired of Coco's spoiled ass. If shit didn't go her way she wanted to bitch and complain.

Yea, let me hurry up and get Coco out of here, bitch think she gone continue to talk shit. She mad at me because she don't like India.

"You okay, Asia?" Red said as he walked up and laid his head on her shoulder.

"Yep, I'm good. I'm not letting that shit Coco said ruin my day. This is my business. My money flow aint gon' stop for no one and I mean that."

"Damn, I mean Coco is like your little sister, that shit doesn't matter, huh? You know how she feels about India, although, you're right, this is a business, but damn, at least schedule those bitches on a different day." Red walked away, laughing his ass off. He thought the shit was funny.

For the rest of the day, Asia was in a zone. She knew it would be awhile before her and Coco would talk again.

Chapter 20
India

Damn, Asia can do some hair, my shit is looking good. I like Asia, although, she's fucking Big R.

India knew all about them. He made it very clear that Asia was his woman. India found the shit funny because he was still trying to get up in her pussy. She cared about him, but they could never work. India played him and he would do just about anything for her and she would do anything for ZO. That was why she continued to fuck with Big R, the money was too good.

Despite the fact that ZO had a bad temper at times, India loved that man. Only thing she couldn't stand about him was that he damn near worshiped the ground Coco walked on. India didn't care that Coco was the mother of his only child. She was jealous and that was what it all came down to. On top of that, she had Rel's ass gone off her, too, which only made India hate her more. She knew it was selfish, but she wished that ZO didn't have any kids. She wanted to be his only concern.

Fuck Coco, that bitch was pissed when she seen me at the shop. I know she said something to Asia, I could tell because as soon as that bitch was finished getting her hair done, she was out with not even so much as a goodbye. If she only knew I was fucking her daughter's father, she would be livid. Yea, in due time, that bitch gon' know just who the fuck I am, India thought.

When Rel first introduced India to Coco, they got along. After a while, India got tired of seeing the bitch. He no longer had time for her. India let Rel know that she was jealous of their relationship, but the truth was she was really just jealous of Coco. Coco was beautiful and about her business and India knew this, on top of that she hated the attention ZO gave her. He would do anything for Coco.

When India first met ZO, she had to have him. She loved his entire swag and on top of that, he was getting money. India made it a point to always be wherever he was. He thought India was beautiful, so when she stepped to him they hit it off perfectly.

He told India all about Coco and that he had no intentions on ever leaving her, so if she was cool with being his side piece, then good. But, if she had a problem with him having a woman, then she needed to keep it moving. India didn't care; she figured he couldn't be too happy at home. So, she chose to play her part and be the sideline because that was exactly what she was in his eyes. Whenever the two were together and Coco called, he would bounce on India every time. But, India never once said shit. She continued to play her role. She was down for him. India was finally happy once Coco ended it with ZO.

She finally thought she had him. She could tell he was hurt behind the break up because a few months after that, Coco met Rel and ZO wasn't pleased. The more time Coco gave Rel, the tighter India and ZO's bond got. They were always in and out of town on business runs that ZO set up. India thought the two were Bonnie and Clyde. She finally won his trust completely and he actually was really digging India. Did he love her? Naw, but he had love for her, but she could never replace Coco, ever.

Once ZO got busted, things weren't the same for India. She missed him. She visited him every weekend, sneaking weed and dope for him to sell while he was locked up. She wanted so bad to prove to him that she was down for him, that she would go as far as risking her own freedom. He had her right where he wanted her, gon' off his ass. He knew anything he asked of her, she would do. When he came to India with his plan, she was down.

India stood in the mirror as she looked herself over. She smiled because things were finally in her favor.

I finally got my man. I feel bad using my brother and Big R like that, but my baby needed me. He still needs me. His so called partner fucked him over and he's on some pay back shit and I'm all a part of his plan. I got his back and he's got mine, I'm sure to be wifey after all this goes down.

Chapter 21
Coco

Coco stepped in the shower, she was up early. She had a lot to do. It was inventory day at the boutique, so she knew she would be there all day. Brandy was at Mina's house, she stayed the weekend with her once a month. Coco two stepped to the music she played as she stepped out the shower. She wanted to be casual, so she put on a Juicy Couture jogging suit with a pair of all white Air Max.

I need to make sure I go through the mail from yesterday. I haven't heard from ZO in a while. That's not like him at all. He usually calls Brandy, but it's been damn near two months with no call. Shit, it was just New Years it seemed like, now it's March. Time is flying, Coco thought.

Coco looked through her closest to grab something to put on later. She and Rel had plans to meet up. They were cool and things were flowing between the two. She really didn't care if the two would get back together or not. That was just like her, she was all about the chase. When he wasn't checking for her and dipped out, she was heartbroken, but since he let her know he wanted them to work on things, she lost interest.

Fuck this shit. I wish I would change clothes for his ass. We're only going to grab something to eat and then to the casino.

Coco grabbed her bag and headed out the door. She planned to meet India that morning. The week before, Rel asked her what the problem was between her and his sister. He wanted the two to at least try to get along. Coco agreed to meet up with her. She would be cordial, but if India said one slick comment, Coco advised

Rel she would fuck his sister up. She cared about him because if she didn't, she wouldn't have ever considered it.

Coco pulled up to Crackle Barrel and parked. She decided she would head in and wait for India. Before she made it in the door, she heard a horn blow. She turned around to see India pull up in a blue Charger. She thought about ZO because that was what he drove before he got locked up and on top of that it was blue just like his. *I miss ZO*, Coco thought as India walked up.

"Good morning, Coco. I like that jogging suit you rocking." India was in a good mood.

"Good morning and thank you." Coco tried to be nice, but something didn't seem right, but she decided to give it a chance. 'Keep your friends close and your enemies closer.' In that case, India was the enemy.

"We have about twenty minutes before we have a table, so we can just sit in here and chat until then. So, India let's just cut to the chase. What is it about me that you don't like? I never understood the problem that you have with me. We started off cool, and then you start acting like a real bitch toward me, why?" Coco looked India dead in her eyes to let her know she wasn't bullshitting.

"Well, you're right, Coco, we did start off cool, but to be honest with you, I felt like I was losing my brother to you. I just reacted with a *fuck you* attitude and I know I shouldn't have, but hell, Rel is all I have. I don't have a lot of female friends. He's my brother and friend all in one. So, when you came along all that changed. I was used to getting attention from him and I wasn't getting that. I hope now that you know this we can put this shit behind us and move forward. I hope I didn't cause any beef between you and Asia since she started back doing my hair." Coco laughed.

"Asia and I are good. If we got a problem, it has nothing to do with you. Yea, we can put this behind us because your brother wants us to very much get along and I don't see any reason on why we shouldn't be able to."

The waitress got the ladies seated. They talked about different things, but mainly about Rel. They both tried to feel the other out. Coco was willing to try to get along, but India, on the other hand, had an agenda. She didn't really want to be Coco's friend. She was only getting close to her because ZO told her to and what ZO said, India did.

"Well, India, I got to head to the boutique. I have all kinds of inventory that I need to put out and I have to do it by myself, so I need to head out."

"Do you need some help? I don't have shit to do 'til later. I don't mind. Plus, I need some new outfits. I love the shit you be rocking. Being that you couldn't stand my ass, I decided never to come to the shop, although, I wanted to," India admitted.

"Hell yea, you can help. And, you can shop afterwards." Coco laughed.

"Coco, before we leave, just know we are cool, but if you fuck over my brother, we gon' have it out. I love him and I know he loves you 'cause if he didn't, he wouldn't give a damn if we liked one another or not."

"India, if we do fall out, it won't be for that reason." With that being said, both women headed to their vehicles and drove off to meet at the boutique.

Chapter 22
ZO

ZO sat in the car parked across the street from his ex-partner's trap house. He had been watching his moves ever since he got released from prison. If he wasn't watching him, he had India watch his ass. That night, he was done watching and had his shit set up perfectly. Once he saw Ty exit the house, ZO waited for about twenty minutes to make sure the nigga didn't forget shit and come back. The night was perfect, there was a storm coming and he knew everyone would be in.

This nigga did not one time accept any of my calls. I mean, did the nigga think I had forever? Ty thinks he could just run off with half of my money. The nigga showed no loyalty to the game. It could have been both of us going down, but instead, I let the nigga flee, taking the fall for the shit. And, this is how this bitch nigga pays me back? I never could find out who this nigga's connect is, but fuck it. I'm not worried at all. I'll find that out soon enough, ZO thought as he put on his black leather gloves.

He made his way around the back of the house and kicked in the basement window.

Stupid muthafucker, he knows he should have had an alarm and bars on his shit. Ty never bothered to get an alarm system. He never took anyone to that crib, only ZO, who he thought was still locked up. Once inside the crib, he went straight to the basement, pulled up the floor boards, and took all the dope.

"This nigga is getting money, look at all this dope. Who in the fuck is his supplier, I got to know," he said out loud. He filled up a big ass army tote with about fifteen bricks. The dope on the street was at least worth twenty five thousand dollars a brick.

I know if this nigga got all this shit here, he has to have some cash here, too.

ZO tore the house up when he finally hit the jack pot. Ty had 200 G's there. He smiled from ear to ear. He couldn't believe that Ty was getting paid like that. He was getting money while he was out, but nothing like that. Once he got all the shit put inside his car, he ran back into the house with some gasoline and set that bitch on fire. He took off in his car and didn't bother to look back.

"This is just the beginning, this nigga gon' feel my wrath."

Chapter 23
Mina

Where the fuck is Taye? My parents said they haven't seen him in a week. I have been blowing up his phone. I'm not sure if he is still pissed at me about what went down with him and Ty. The shit is crazy. Taye is my little brother and even though he does some fucked up shit, he's blood. I know he can piss a nigga off, hell he pisses me off, but still he is my family. Maybe I should have done something, but what would I have done? Hell, I wasn't gon' leave Ty because he hit my brother, but maybe I could have come to Taye's defense instead of allowing Ty to sweep the shit under the rug.

Mina really wanted to ask Taye was he the one who set fire to Ty's house. Mina had no idea that Ty had over 300,000.00 worth of dope in his house, Ty failed to mention that to her.

Since the fire, Ty had been in a foul mood. Mina would ask him what the problem was because she couldn't understand why he was so angry. The house was insured so in her mind she thought shit was okay. Thing was Ty was robbed and he didn't know who did it. Mina didn't want to think about that shit because she had too much on her mind. Club Essence's grand opening was that night and she was excited. It was her dream come true to finally open up a club. Mina sat on her bed and a tear slid down her face.

I can't believe Ty is so worried about that damn house catching fire that he left me to do all the last minute preparations, which is fine because I handles my business, but damn, it's like I'm all excited and he's acting like he could give a fuck. But, I'm not gon' worry about that. I'm going to relax the rest of the day before I get ready for tonight. My girls are coming out to support my grand opening. I'm so glad Asia and Coco got over whatever they were going through with one another and I can't believe Coco and India are friends. Shit has been happening all around me. Damn, I hear my phone. Where the hell is it? Mina grabbed her phone. To her surprise it was Taye.

"Negro, where are you?"

"Damn, sis, I miss you, too. Shit I'm here in the Ville."

"Negro, don't play with me. You've been missing for like a week and a half. Now you talking about you here in the Ville anyway are you coming to the grand opening tonight?"

"Mina, did you even have to ask that shit? Hell yea, I'll be there. I wouldn't miss it for the world. I support all that you do, although, Ty don't want me there."

"Taye, I don't want know shit started tonight. Is that understood?"

"You should tell your dude that. I'm good, sis."

"Well, first of all, he's my fiancée and I'm telling you. This is my night, so, please, I just want to enjoy it."

"I got you. I won't act a fool unless your fiancée does. Love you, Mina." Taye hung up the phone before Mina could respond.

Damn he hung up on me. Hell, I'm just glad to know he is ok.

It had always been her and Taye, he was her heart. Mina got her outfit together for later that night. She felt good about everything finally coming together.

Chapter 24
Rel

It was ten in the morning and Rel was ready to head out of town. He told Coco that he would be gone for about a week and that he had some shit he had to tend to. He was slipping on a few things and needed to get his shit back tight. He was damn near up Coco's ass trying to patch shit up, but she wouldn't give in that easy and he knew it. There was a knock at the door and it was Big R. He was expecting him.

"Wassup, Rel? You ready to go?"

"Yea, I got my shit together. Thanks for looking out and taking me to the airport. I plan on being back in a week unless some shit comes up. I'll let you know for sure when I will be back."

"Rel sounds good. I'll make sure everything straight on this end here." Rel got his things and secured the house before he walked out.

"Big R, while I'm away, look out for India for me. I got a feeling something aint right. Her ass borrowed like ten G's from me a while back, and then wouldn't tell me what it was for. Shit doesn't seem right. She's been hanging tight with Coco. I'm glad they worked out whatever issues they had with one another."

"I got you. I'll keep an eye on her, but you know she's gon' do what she wants to do." Big R walked out the front door with hurt in his heart. He felt used. He knew India was up to something. It had been awhile since she fucked with him actually he hadn't heard from her.

They arrived at the airport, showed one another love, and went their separate ways. Rel headed inside to catch his flight. While waiting, he called Coco and got the voicemail, so he left a message. *Damn, I wanted to hear her voice before I left. I'll call her when I touch down.*

Rel's phone rang. "What's up, my nigga? I'm at the airport right now. Big R handling shit while I'm gone. Meet up with him, I'll be away for a while. That shit that took place is way too close to home, nigga. You need to be careful, shit, you hear anything yet? When you do let me know, but business is the same. I just need to clear my head and from the looks of things, you should, too. I'm out, I'll hit you up."

Damn, that man is always on the grind. I ain't mad at the nigga, though. He just needs to lay low for a minute.

Rel shook his head as he hung up the phone. He boarded his flight to L.A. He let Ciara know he would be there for about a week or so and, of course, she wanted him to stay with her. He said he wasn't trying to give her any reason to trip or think that maybe it was possible they could work shit out. Lately, Ciara hadn't called and when she did, it was to let Carman talk to him. Rel finally thought that Ciara was changing. He would soon find out that he thought wrong.

Chapter 25
Coco

Where in the hell is India? She was supposed to be here thirty minutes ago. Her ass was picking up some peach Ciroc for me and she hasn't shown up yet.

Coco and India had got real tight, since their talk. India even worked at the boutique. Coco pretty much had her in charge of the store when she was away.

I bet that bitch is with her friend. She won't tell me who it is, but she is open off that nigga. I try not to be nosey, but if she wants me to know, she'll tell me. She's like that damn Asia, always secretive. The two remind me so much of one another. Shit is crazy. Damn, speaking of Asia, I need to call her ass. I know she said that Big R was coming tonight. I like Asia with him, even if it is just for the moment, Coco thought as she reached for her phone to text India to make sure she was ok.

Coco was getting her things together for later that night when she heard a knock at the door, "Come in!" Coco yelled.

"Damn, I thought you got lost," Coco shouted to India

"I had to make a few stops before I got my night started," India said with a smile on her face. They laughed. "Coco, when is Rel coming back?"

"I'm not for sure. You know how his ass is, all secretive and shit, but he's supposed to call me when he gets to L.A."

"Let me ask you something, Coco. You not the least bit worried that he may fuck Ciara while he is there?" India asked hesitantly.

Coco looked at India. She didn't need to respond, the answer was written all over her face.

"Bitch so it hasn't crossed your mind that they may fuck? You said the two of you aren't fucking, so shit, he is a man and he has needs."

"Look, Ciara is no threat to me. Not sure what gave you the impression that I gave a fuck, but honestly, I don't. If Rel and I get together we do and if we don't, then we don't. It is what it is. Real talk, if Rel wants to fuck Ciara, he can. He's not my man. We're not exclusive. Just like if I decide to fuck someone, he can't be mad, feel me?" India could tell that she struck a nerve.

"Okay, Coco, you talk a good game, bitch."

"Whatever, India, you really think I'm some square bitch, huh? Like I just let a nigga run ova me? Yea, Rel had me fucked up with how he up and left, but don't let that fool you, bitch. I ain't with the bullshit. I can have any nigga, if you really want to know, I'm good on just being Rel's friend for now. He needs to earn a place in my life. I know he isn't trying to fuck this shit up a second time around because it's not three strikes you out, its two over here. Trust me he isn't fucking Ciara or any other bitch. He'll wait on this pussy, he knows what it is."

"Ok, Coco, your shit's like that, huh?"

"Bitch, you better Google me! Anything else you want to ask me, India?" Coco was done with the conversation. She just wanted to get her drink on.

"Yea, I do. Why don't you ever talk about your daughter's father?" Coco rolled her eyes in the back of her head.

"Why would I? Don't get me wrong, I love the ZO, always will, but I'm good on him. We will never be together. He lost my trust, respect, and all of that. I loved him, yet, I hated him at the same time. The loyalty, let's say that shit took a back seat. To sum it up, I devoted my life to making him happy. He didn't appreciate that or me, so why would I give him a second thought? I'm good."

"Wow, I'm sorry. I didn't mean to piss you off," India said.

"Girl, miss me with that. I'm not pissed. I just answered your question that's all. Plus, I haven't heard from ZO. He doesn't call or write, so to me, he's like fuck his daughter, so fuck him. I'm done talking about his ass. Shit, let me make us a drink. Are you ready for one?"

Coco made the drinks, but she felt a little uneasy. She couldn't figure out why India wanted to know about ZO. She shook the thought out of her mind so she could get back to her night. The ladies enjoyed their drinks as they got ready for the opening of Mina's new spot.

"I can't wait to go out. It's been a long time since New Year's. I'm ready to mingle. I'm so happy for Mina. I hate that Ty's house burned down. That shit was fucked up, wasn't it?"

India was quiet when Coco made that comment. She didn't really give a care about Ty or his house. He had crossed her baby, so in her eyes he deserved the shit.

"India, I'm about to take a bubble bath. You know where the other bathroom is. I already got your towels out for you."

"That's cool, you smoking tonight, Coco? If so, let's blow before we step out."

"There you go, naw, I'm good with my drink. But you think you could drive tonight?"

"Yea, I'll drive. Coco, you don't ever want to do no driving." They laughed as they went to get ready for the night.

Chapter 26
ZO

Damn, I needed some rest. Let me get my ass up so I can get this new 2013 blue Dodge Charger. Hell yea, thanks to Ty, I'm back on top. Wait 'til this nigga finally see me, he gone think he saw a ghost, bitch nigga. Taking from that nigga wasn't enough because what I took was mine to be taken. Now he's going to have to pay. Let's see how he feels when his freedom is taken away. In due time, his world will come crashing down right before his eyes.

ZO was pleased that his plan was flowing in the right direction.

He, jumped in the shower, and got dressed for the evening. He wore Polo from head to toe. He always stepped out looking fresh. He drove India's Monte Carlo to the car lot off of Preston Highway. The salesman that dealt with ZO had all the paperwork ready. All he was waiting for was the cash. They made the exchange and he signed the paperwork. The dealer had everything set up with the info he needed to make the sale look legit, being that ZO was a street nigga and had no job.

"If we're done, let me get them keys." The salesman passed ZO the keys. "Nice doing business with you," ZO said as he got behind the wheel of the Charger. He popped in Rick Ross' CD *God Forgives* and played *Hold Me Back*. He was feeling that song ever since the first time he heard it. "Hell yeah, these niggas won't hold me back," ZO rapped along with the song. He was in the zone. He fired up a blunt, and drove to one of his spots off Taylor Blvd. to get his windows tinted, and got some customized rims put on his new ride.

ZO hadn't heard from India so he decided to call her, but he got no answer. He decided not to leave a message. ZO was angry, as he talked to himself.

Why the fuck is she not picking up? She has gotten way too comfortable with Coco. I think India got her own agenda. All I know is she better not fuck this shit up for me or she's getting fucked up. I want to step off in Mina's spot so bad tonight for that grand opening, but the time ain't right. Until then, I'm gon' do me and sit back and set this nigga straight up. His entire world is about to crumble. Let that bitch nigga lose his woman while he's locked up. That bitch, Mina, ain't shit, either, she just out for a nigga that's getting paid. She got that nigga, Ty, open. Let me hit my friend up and see if I can slide through before I head in for the night.

ZO made a phone call.

"I'll be there in fifteen minutes. I'm gon' need you to do what you do best, and put this dick in the back of your throat and choke on this fat head for me. Yea, that's what I like to hear. I'll be there shortly, be ready for me." ZO hung up the phone, turned up his music, and made his way down the highway.

Chapter 27
Ty

"Baby, come on, let's go," Ty said to Mina as she applied her makeup. She didn't appreciate him rushing her.

"Damn, Ty, we have plenty of time. What is the rush?"

"I'm trying to do a last walk through and make sure shit is set up the way we asked them to set it up, so come on."

"Look, if you in that big of a hurry, then go ahead without me because what I won't do is rush. I'm not on anyone's time clock I come and go as I please. Ever since that shit happen with your house catching on fire, you've had a fucked up attitude. I know it's something you're not telling me, but I can't worry about that. I'm stressed about this grand opening because it's my first time. I've been there all damn morning and afternoon, trust me shit is the way I want it to be."

He looked her up and down. He felt as though she said too much.

"Alright, I'm not trying to hear that shit. I'll just meet you there." He grabbed his keys and walked out the door.

Shit, Mina is on some bullshit for real. I can't hear all that shit right now. I got too much on my mind and although she isn't to blame, I just ain't trying to hear the shit. That's why I just left because if she would of said shit else, she was about to see another side of me. I know she ain't ready for that and she doesn't deserve that, but damn, baby need to know when to keep her mouth shut.

Ty's phone rang and it was Mina. He hit the reject button and sent her to voicemail. He was tired of arguing, he wanted to clear his mind. Since he was robbed, he tried to figure out who the fuck did it. He hadn't heard of any niggas that had come up all of a sudden, so he was unsure. His connect thought that Ty was hot.

Shit ain't looking good for business at all. When I find out what nigga did this shit, I'm gon' handle that shit. You can believe that.

Ty was almost to the club when he decided to call Mina back. He didn't want them to be up tight at the opening of her new spot. When Ty called he got the voicemail, but left no message. He sent her a text message instead.

Mina, baby, I'm sorry for just leaving like I did. I have a lot of stress on me lately with the new club, the fire, and all that shit is weighing heavy on me. I know it's not your fault, so I want to apologize. I love you, baby, just know that. See you in a few.

Ty sent the message. He knew she was upset with him and he also knew how much that night meant to her. At the time he wasn't concerned, but he calmed down. He knew he fucked up and he felt bad.

Ty pulled up in front of the club.

My baby has out done herself. Ty got out the car and handed his keys to valet. Mina wanted her club to have all the perks. She said, 'what woman really wants to park far away and walk in five inch heels?' My baby spot is just that, the spot, Ty said with a smile on his face.

Chapter 28
Mina

Fuck Ty! Mina screamed!

What the fuck is wrong with him? I can't believe how selfish his ass is acting. He knows how much this means to me. Fuck it! I'm gon' enjoy myself tonight. Hell, I'm proud of my damn self. Ty nor anyone else is going to rain on my parade. I'm looking too good to be arguing with him.

Mina wore a Donna Karan sequined bustier dress with a pair of Jimmy Choo sequin pumps. Her jewelry was diamond studs and watch, and, of course, her beautiful engagement ring. She applied her makeup and while doing that, she listened to music and had a drink.

Damn, I look amazing, I must say. Mina smiled at herself in the mirror. Her makeup was a natural look and her skin glowed. She was on her own high, no weed, just life itself.

God, please, be with me tonight and let my grand opening be a success.

Mina headed to the garage, got in her car, and headed out. When she pulled up, she parked in her reserved spot and she was greeted at the front entrance by Ty. When she walked up to him, he licked his lips as he admired her beauty.

"Damn, baby, you look good. I love you in that dress." He kissed her and embraced her. He whispered in her ear, "I'm sorry, baby."

Mina looked at Ty. "I love you," she said as she kissed him, and then they walked into her club. She was amazed at how beautiful and elegant it looked inside. It had three levels. The top level was VIP. Each level was set up differently and each had a different feel to it, the shit was nice. Mina had out done herself. They did their walk through and were in awe the entire time.

Damn, this is my spot, Mina thought as she approached her office, which was beautiful as well. She took in her entire surroundings with tears in her eyes. She did what she set out to do. "Thank you, Ty, for standing beside me and always believing in me. You are truly the best."

"Baby, you know I got you. Your happiness means the world to me, just like you do. I got you always, Mina."

It was time to officially open the doors to the new spot. Mina greeted everyone as the crowd formed. The turnout was amazing. It was a red carpet event. Mina took picture after picture. Ty was inside holding things down. He made sure everything ran smoothly. He joined Mina back at the front entrance where they took more pictures.

While taking pictures, Coco and India arrived. They looked fabulous. Coco was flawless, as always. She wore loose sequined tee and metallic leather leggings with crystal covered strappy sandals, the shit was sexy.

"I love it, Mina. Club Essence is the place to be," Coco said as she hugged her friend. "I am so happy for you." Coco knew how much that night meant for Mina. She deserved her own spot.

"Damn, this shit is gon' be the talk of the city, bitch." Coco hugged Mina one last time. She was proud of her friend.

"Thank you, Coco."

"Congratulations, Mina, you look amazing and your spot is the shit," India said with much excitement.

"Thank you for coming. You look stunning. I love your dress." India wore a magenta V-neck bandage dress. The dress fit like a glove and her shape was killer.

"Damn, India, you favor Asia a lot." Mina continued to stare at her. She couldn't get past how much they actually resembled one another.

"You know what, people been saying that for a while now. Maybe it's the chinky eyes."

"Shit, maybe, all I know is you too could pass as sisters. Where is Asia ass at, anyway?"

No sooner than the words escaped Mina's mouth, Asia and Big R walked up. "I love your new spot, Mina, this is nice. Give me a hug. You out did yourself. This shit right here is off the hook." They hugged.

Asia looked gorgeous. She wore a chilli Zimmermann silk lace back jumpsuit. The back of the jumpsuit was bad as hell, it was crisscross. Asia's breasts sat up in the jumpsuit perfectly and she looked just like a china doll. The women took plenty of pictures before heading in.

"Who is this pulling up in this brand new 2013 Dodge Viper Charger?" Mina asked as she tried to figure out who it was. When Mina's brother stepped out the car, she smiled.

He made it, she thought. Taye walked up and hugged Mina.

"I am so happy for you, big sis, Congratulations."

"Thank you, Taye. I'm just glad you're here. When did you get that new car? The shit is nice."

"Thanks, sis, I came up on a little something. Your little brother is doing ok these days. I'm following my big sister's footsteps. I love you, Mina, Always know that."

Ty walked out to see Taye standing with Mina.

"You ready to party baby? You are the woman of the hour. You got to make your walk through."

"Alright I'm out. I was just coming through to say congratulations. I ain't here to start trouble." Taye pulled away from Mina.

"What, you not gon' even come in? Fuck what happened awhile back, I want you here tonight. At least walk in and have a drink, please. Give your keys to valet and come party with me."

Taye couldn't tell her no and Ty was pissed. *Where the fuck that nigga get that ride from? Some shit ain't right. I know this nigga ain't the one who got me on,* Ty thought. Mina could tell that he was pissed.

The club was jumping inside. Mina had security all around the club because she didn't want shit popping off. Everyone enjoyed themselves in VIP. Out of nowhere, Michael walked up to Mina.

"Congratulations on Club Essence, Mina." Caught off guard, Mina looked at Michael and he stared back at her in awe of her beauty.

"You look beautiful as ever. Can I get hug?" She was speechless at first.

"Thank you, Michael. I wasn't expecting you to be here."

"Did you think I would miss your grand opening? I will always love you Mina. What about that hug?" She hugged Michael, and he whispered in her ear, "I'm truly happy for you."

Security rushed up on Mina and told her there was a problem downstairs with Ty and her brother. Mina took off quickly with Michael, Asia, Coco, and India right behind. What Mina saw when she got downstairs was Ty kicking Taye ass. Security had nothing on Ty. He was pissed. Mina hollered for Ty to stop, but he was in a rage. She went to stop Ty, but Michael stopped her.

"I got this, baby." Michael pulled Ty off of Taye. "Alright, man that's enough. Cool out!" Ty looked at Michael and told that nigga to raise the fuck up off him. Mina ran to Taye's side and told Coco to call the ambulance.

"Don't call anyone. I'm good. You a bitch ass nigga, Ty, I promise you I'm gon' dead your ass."

"Whatever Taye, get the fuck up out of my spot."

"Nigga, suck my dick. This is my sister's club." When Taye said that shit, Ty launched for him again this time, he damn near knocked Mina on her ass. Big R stepped in, had he not, Michael was about to and the shit would have really gotten ugly. Big R calmed Ty down and he told Michael to go the fuck on. Michael headed out to leave, not because of what Ty said, but because he felt like Mina had been disrespected enough.

"You know what? You're a weak ass nigga, a selfish one as well. It's your woman's grand opening and you in this bitch fighting her brother. You fucked up, nigga. I'll see you around," Michael said as he walked out of the club.

Mina was pissed. Her only concern was her brother, nothing else mattered. *Fuck Ty, I'm tired. What the fuck was this all about?* Mina thought.

"Taye let me take you home, please."

"I'm good, sis, I'm sorry. I told you I should have never come. Your nigga is on some bullshit, real talk."

"Look, Taye, I'm taking you home." Mina insisted.

"I can take Taye home. He's not too far from me," India said.

Taye was cool with India driving him home. Mina tried to enjoy herself the rest of the night, but she couldn't and she stayed away from Ty.

The night was finally over and she was drained. She headed home and all she could think about was Taye. She pulled up to the house and her cell went off. It was a text from Michael.

Hope everything calmed down once I left and if you need a friend to talk to, you know how to reach me, Love Michael. She felt a certain type of way. She was mad and hurt by Ty's actions. She was confused about her feelings for Michael. Before that night, she hadn't thought about him in a long time. He was back on the scene at the wrong time because she was vulnerable. She needed a friend, her fiancée was tripping, and she didn't know who he was anymore, yet Michael was so familiar to her.

Chapter 29
ZO

"Damn get that nut up out of there. Suck this long dick. You know how I like it. Suck that motherfucker."

ZO's phone vibrated. The head he received felt so good that he didn't want to answer the call. He noticed it was India and he had no choice because he was waiting to hear from.

"India, you got anything good to tell me? Alright, then I needed that info baby, good looking out. I'll be heading to you in about thirty minutes. I got some shit I'm in the middle of right now."

ZO was so into getting his dick sucked that he didn't disconnect the call and India heard everything. Once he busted his nut he got himself together, cut out, and headed to India's house.

Damn, this shit is going to work out better than I thought. Yea let me get over here and see what info my baby got for me.

ZO arrived at India's place and used his key to let himself in. India was in her room rolling a blunt.

"Sup, India." ZO kissed her on the lips. "Why you got this fucked up look on your face?" India sat there not saying shit.

"I know you hear me talking to your ass. Look, you said you had some info for me, so speak. What the fuck is up? If you were gon' be on some bullshit, I could have stayed my ass where I was."

"Fuck you, nigga! I heard you getting your dick sucked! Yea motherfucker, you didn't disconnect the fuckin' phone call, stupid ass motherfucker!" ZO smacked the shit out of India.

"I got your stupid motherfucker. Say one more fuckin' word and I'll wipe the floor with your ass! You don't know what the fuck you heard."

"I heard you getting head by some bitch name Ree or Red, nigga! I heard it all! Don't insult me by acting like I didn't hear shit. So, that's what the fuck you out here doing, huh? Getting your dick sucked while I'm hanging with that bitch Coco's stuck up ass. Playing the friend role and getting you information about Ty. Have whoever was sucking your dick do it for you because I'm done."

Again, ZO hit India, but that time with his fist. He punched her in her eye and she fell back off the bed. He stood over India looking like a mad man.

"First of all, India, you gon' do what the fuck I say. As for you calling Coco a bitch, I told you about that shit. That's my daughter's mother. Watch what the fuck you say about her. Is that understood?" ZO waited for India to respond and when she didn't, he back handed her in the mouth.

"What now? You don't have shit to say? Oh, and yea, I was getting my dick sucked. Your ass running around this motherfucker getting your pussy ate by that Rick Ross looking nigga, so shut the fuck up. You claim you not giving him any pussy, but that shit is a lie. That nigga is breaking you off too much loot for you not to be fucking and sucking him. Far as I'm concerned, we even." India cried.

"I'm doing all this for you, damn it! What do you mean, ZO? I love you and this is how you treat me? I can't believe you put your hands on me!" India cried out in pain. Her lip was bleeding and her eye hurt. ZO realized he was wrong. After all, he was the one who didn't hang up his phone. He knew India was crazy about him and he also knew he needed her to finish off his plan, so he apologized. He promised the shit wouldn't happen again. Wanting to believe that he wouldn't do it again, India forgave him. She loved ZO.

He stayed with India to reassure her that he was sorry. She gave him all the info about the party and the details about taking Taye home. She knew he was up to something, but she didn't know what exactly. ZO lay in bed with a smirk on his face. *Soon, I'll make my presence known.*

Chapter 30
Twan

Twan headed back from Detroit. He met up with his new connect who put him on. He had a lot on his mind and the ride gave him time to clear his head.

Yea, from here on out, I got to do my own thing. I got love for my nigga, Ty, but since day one, the nigga has never played fair. He never let me meet his connect and we 'pose to be in this shit together. I'm coming with my half of the money, but can never meet the man in charge. This nigga got robbed and he's making it hot for everyone. I told Ty he's not untouchable. I should have known the nigga was on some other shit by the way he did ZO.

Ty was wrong for leaving the nigga locked up, wouldn't accept any of his calls, and didn't drop shit on his books. If Ty didn't give a fuck about him, who's to say, he would give a fuck about me? Difference is I'm one step ahead. He ain't gon' catch me slipping. Not now, not ever.

"What up doe?" Twan said when he answered his phone. "Shit, baby, I'll be back in the city in about thirty minutes. What, you done playing with a nigga? Asia, you ready to give me some of that good pussy or what? Sounds good to me, I'll see you shortly." Twan hung up the phone and smiled.

Shit, it's been a long time since Asia gave me some ass. I knew she couldn't stay away from this action. Dick too long, plus, I know that nigga Big R ain't making that pussy pop like I was! Bet she miss daddy and I damn sure miss her fine ass.

Twan's phone rang again. This time, it was one of his partners he saw while in Detroit on business. "What it do, Nate?"

"What up, Twan? Shit I forgot to tell you I just got word that the nigga that just got us on a few weeks back is from the Ville. We not for sure who the nigga is, but his license plate was from Kentucky, Jefferson county, or some shit. That nigga made off with some major work and cash. We not letting that shit go that easy. So, if you hear of anything or see that a nigga came up all of a sudden, holler at me."

"I got you, told you what happen to that nigga, Ty. As a matter of fact, the shit happened around the same time. I will keep my ear to the streets. I'm out, holler back. Damn, what the fuck is going on? I got to be extra careful out here in these streets," Twan said out loud as he made his way back to Louisville.

Chapter 31
Ty

Ty was sitting behind his desk at the club finishing up some paper work when his phone vibrated. He looked down and smiled and shook his head. *Man she gone fuck around and get me in trouble,* Ty thought as he continued to read the messages that were still coming through.

I've been thinking about you since our last conversation. I miss you so much Tyrese. I can't get you off my mind, I think about what I want to do to you. First I lay you back on the bed and kiss you OH so passionately starting at your lips and making a trail down your body, I pause once I get to your manhood... admiring it.... taking in its beauty before I gently lick around the tip damn I can't wait to taste you. I then kiss around the head ... I wrap my long tongue around the head moving slowly but with so much passion. I then slowly begin to take you into my mouth.....taking you in more and more each time. I'm so turned on my mouth waters. I part my lips and relax my throat seeing how much of you I can take in at once. I continue to go further and further down, saliva is seeping from the sides of my mouth. Up and down I go as I look at your shiny manhood. The more I take you in my mouth the more I feel him rising growing with each suck and gentle lick of my tongue. You moan as you enjoy the sounds of mouth around your dick. Dick just wet and slippery as I stroke you up and down with my hand as I continue to deep throat you I gag a little which turns you on even more. You grab me by my hair something you know I love. I go all the way down and then back up sucking on the head of your dick as I continue to stroke it. I pick up the speed as I suck all the way down to the shaft and work my way up this time focusing all my attention on the head of the dick. I do my thing with my tongue which drives you crazy. My Star is wetter than wet she is ready to explode only you can make me cum without fucking me, sucking on you pleases me. I look into your eyes and they say a thousand words no need for verbal communication our bodies are in sync we feed off of one another. Our eyes are glued to one another. I continue to engulf you heartily enjoying every moment. I speed up and take you in gagging a little each time. Your eyes begin to roll into the back of your head and I feel your manhood throb as I can feel the nut working up into the head I suck like never before then you explode in my mouth and I eat you up hungrily trying to savor the taste. I suck on you until I can't taste you anymore. Thank you baby is what I say as I watch you tremble. Love your #1. See you soon......

Ty sat behind his desk with a big smile across his face. "Damn she knows how to get to a nigga. She's my addiction I'm trying to stay away because I know once she's in my presence that's it. Yeah I got something for her," Ty grabbed his phone to text her back.

You know what you doing to me right? Yea you know. I just want you to know you got this dick over here rock hard. I miss you T. Let me give you a little sample of what you got to look forward to.... First I'd slowly start playing with Star getting her nice and wet. Then I'd stand up and start kissing your neck. I continue kissing and licking my way down your body long slow licks until I get to where the juice is. I'd then slowly start tasting you licking my lips as I enjoy every drop. I spread your legs while you are standing and she starts to drip. Damn she's wet!!! I catch the drip with my tongue. Then I start sucking on your clit, I lay you down and continue to suck on your clit and tasting your juices, making you continuously cum until you can't take it anymore. You're begging with your eyes for my dick to be inside you. I suck your bottom lip and tell you to assume the position. You smile as you turn over and lay flat on your stomach, I get behind you and slap that dick on your ass and then slide it across that wet pussy before I enter you. You lock your ankles once I'm inside of you. I'm watching as my dick goes in and out of you it's glistening from your wetness. The deeper I go she starts to talk to me and I love it.…….. I know you over there going through it, yea now you know how you got me over here feeling. I'll see you soon baby.

Chapter 32
Mina

Mina ran around the room, rushing. She got her things packed because she and the ladies were going on a mini vacation.

Shit, I need to hurry up and get finished packing. Ty will be here shortly to take me to the airport. Vegas, here I come!

Mina, Coco, Asia and India were going to Vegas for a few days, then to Atlanta for the NCAA Championship game. There was no way Mina was going to miss her Cards play. Michael had texted her as soon as he knew they were in the Final Four and told her he would get tickets for her and the ladies. He knew she would appreciate it.

Mina had a lot of things running through her mind as she packed her luggage. For one, Ty still acted brand new although, he said he was ok, she didn't believe it. She was also still pissed about the fight at her grand opening. Since then, Taye started acting distant. He wasn't calling as much as he used to and that bothered her.

This trip should relax me. Hell, it's going to be fun with Coco, Asia and India coming along as well. I haven't been around India like that so I can't really say how she is, but it's something about her that doesn't sit well with me. I mean, out the blue she and Coco are friends, but I'm going to give her a chance. Coco knows I don't roll with too many females. I have associates outside of Asia and Coco, but I'm not with the drama and bullshit. And as far as Asia, I love her, but the fact that she knew that Rel was still here and never bothered to tell Coco really makes me question her friendship. That was some shady shit and that right there is why I don't fuck with a lot of bitches. Can't trust them, I know Coco, she has always been up front, she is who she is, so if she considers India cool or a friend then I'll respect that, but I will have my eye on her, best believe that shit! Plus, I need to find out just how close India and Taye are. When I stepped to him about it he kind of blew me off, maybe that's the reason he's been so distant.

Mina heard from Asia that Taye and India had been seen out a couple of times since the grand opening. When Mina addressed Taye about it, he told her India was cool and to give her a chance. She asked Taye if they were sleeping together. She let him know to be careful and strap up. She tried to protect her brother. She knew he wasn't ready for a woman like India. She was too much woman for him; Mina knew that India could easily turn her brother out.

While packing, her phone vibrated.

Damn, Michael better stop texting me. Ever since the grand opening, he's been texting and calling. If Ty knew his ass was contacting me, he would fuck Michael up. I haven't forgotten how things went down with Michael. The shit still hurt. At one point he was everything to me, so there will always be feelings attached, but as far as us ever getting back together, I don't think so. I'm very much in love with Ty.

Shit, where is Ty? I, at least, thought we could get in a good quickie before I left. Damn, he always messing something up. Let me call Coco and make sure they are going to be on time to the airport. She packs fifty different outfits and for what? All she gon' end up doing is buying more clothes. Mina laughed as she made the call to Coco and continued to pack.

Chapter 33
India

"Taye, right there, baby, fuck your pussy." Taye gave it to India just the way she liked it. They start fucking around after the grand opening. They had it bad for one another. India loved his bad boy ways, but underneath it all he was a gentleman and what she loved most was that he adored her. He fucked plenty of women, but to him, India was different. It was something about her that made him want to be a better man. He was falling for her.

The night she drove him home was when he made his move. He let her know that he was feeling her and, to his surprise, she said she would like to get to know him a little better. India always thought he had the potential. She was just so gone off of ZO that the thought was just that, a thought. While ZO was locked up, India gave Taye a little attention when she saw him. It was nothing major, just a little flirting. It had finally paid off because they were fucking one another's brains out.

"Fuck, your pussy is wet, India, damn, you throwing that pussy on this dick." Taye was gone just like Mina knew he would be. But, India was also gone off of Taye. He treated her like a woman should be treated. He didn't talk down to her or put his hands on her. With him, she felt safe. She no longer fucked ZO, hell, she hardly talked to him. If he knew that she was fucking Taye, he would have killed them both. ZO wasn't into India like that, but he'd be damn if he would allow her to play him for Taye.

Taye had India's legs all the way bent back. He put his dick in her ass and fucked her slowly, making sure his entire dick was in her asshole.

"Taye, aw, baby. It feels so good. Please, give it all to me, baby."

He went in deeper and deeper. He stroked her faster, and he then put his two fingers in her gushy pussy and played with her clit with another finger. Shit drove her crazy. He loved to hear her moan and say his name.

Taye did his thing as he fucked India. She could no longer take it. The feeling of him in her ass and then playing with her pussy was too much for her to handle. She squirted everywhere. Taye loved it he had no idea that he had her sprung. She took in every moment they spent together.

This nigga got me turned out and just not sexually, but mentally as well. I'm starting to have strong feelings for him. I didn't plan on this happening, it just did.

Taye pounded that ass and smack it at the same time. He grabbed a hold of India's legs still bent all the way back and fucked the shit out of her. He busted all in her ass.

"Fuck! That felt good as hell, India." He kissed her.

"I love you, Taye." India said without any hesitation. *Did I just tell him I love him? Damn, I do, I can't deny that. No man has ever made me feel like he has. I'm not sure what I'm going to do, but I want him to know just where my heart is.*

"You don't have to tell me back. I just want you to know how I feel about you. You make me want to be a better me and for that I love you. I really do."

Taye stared into India's eyes. He didn't say he loved her back, which was fine with India. She didn't want him to say anything that he didn't mean.

"Ok, baby, I got to go. You know I'm going to Vegas with your sister and the girls. If I'm late to the airport, Coco will kill me." India got up and headed for the bathroom to shower and get herself together.

"India, you want me to drop you off? I ain't got to come in. I know they don't know about us. I just want to be with you a little longer. Is that cool?"

"Of course, it is, Taye." They hopped in the shower and started round two. Afterwards, India got her things together for the trip. They rushed like crazy. They got to the airport just in time. Taye got out and helped India with her bags.

"I'm gon' miss you, baby. Make sure you call me," Taye said as they hugged. Taye smacked her ass. "Here's some shopping money. He handed her a stack of money. I know you like to shop, so have fun and win us some money."

"Aw, thank you, baby. You know I'm good on the crap table. I'm gon' get that money." They kissed again and India made her way inside the airport.

Once inside, she met up with the ladies. India looked down at her phone and it was Taye calling her. She answered the phone with excitement in her voice.

"I miss you already and I haven't even left the airport yet. I just want you to know that I enjoy the time we spend together. I want you to be my woman, Indy. And, I also wanted to tell you I love you, too."

India smiled as tears flowed down her face. He loves me, she said to herself.

"Call me as soon as you touch down in Vegas. Have fun." All India could do was smile. She finally found what she longed for, *true love.*

Chapter 34
Rel

Rel took care of business and was ready to head home the next morning.

Shit, can't wait to get back to see Coco. I enjoyed this time I had with my daughter, though. She is getting big, looking just like Ciara. He was there on business, but he made plenty of time for Carman. She was his everything.

Ciara been acting strange since I been here. I don't know what's up with her, but what I won't do is worry about that shit. I told her let Carman come with me for a few months. Ciara's trying to do her own thing she ain't around half the time no way. Hollering about I'm not worried about Carman. I'm too worried about Coco and getting back with her. She needs to get the fuck out of here with the loose rap.

Rel packed his bags. He would be on his flight out at seven a.m. He needed to meet with his father about some things and from the sound of his father's voice, it was urgent. He called Big R and let him know he needed to be picked up from the airport, and he made sure he knew exactly what time the plane landed. His thought was broken when he heard a knock at the door.

"Who is it?" he said in a stern voice. It was after midnight and Rel didn't know who it could be at his door that late. When he looked he saw that it was Ciara.

"What does she want? What's up, Ciara?" He opened the door and Ciara said nothing, she just walked in.

"Damn, you just gon' walk up in my spot like you running shit?"

"Look, I was just coming to let you know face to face that I will be moving to Louisville for a while. Not sure how long, but I will be catching a flight out on Friday."

"What you mean you coming to Louisville for a while? Where you staying and why are you coming?"

"I got a spot, no need for you to worry. I have moved on just like you."

"Look, I don't know what you got going on, but I damn sure don't have time for your games." Rel was pissed.

"I don't care what the fuck you do. What I do know is you're about raise up out of my crib. I'll see you around. You make it hard for me care about you. Your ass does some dumb ass shit." He opened the door and Ciara stood there with a disappointed look on her face.

"Why, you looking sad? You walked in here like you was the shit, so walk out the same way."

Ciara walked out the door and turned to face Rel and just as she did he slam the door in her face.

Chapter 35
ZO

ZO was at his crib smoking a blunt, getting ready for the night.

Tonight is the night. I'm about to set this plan in motion. After tonight, Tyrese Mitchell's life will forever change. I don't give a fuck about none of these nigga in the streets. That nigga left me to rot in prison. Yea ok, he will soon learn that he should have never crossed me. I called India ass today and the bitch sent me to voicemail. Her ass is about to get dismissed as soon as this shit is over. She played her part, now she can go the fuck on. I'm gon' be with Coco and can't a damn person stop that from happening. I need to handle that nigga she be fucking with. From the looks of it, they aren't that serious. Their little trip will be cut short once they get the news about what is about to go down. Soon after that, I will make my presence known.

ZO grabbed his fifty caliber Desert Eagle and placed it in his waist of the back of his pants. He poured another shot of Remy Martin VSOP, sat back, and fired up another blunt. He was a beast in the streets. He didn't give a fuck about anyone or anything besides himself and the two loves of his life, Brandy and Coco. He would end one's life and wouldn't think twice about it.

When ZO was sixteen, his mother died in a car accident, she was hit head on by a drunk driver. His mother was his world and she was the one person that he loved more than life itself. After his mother was killed, he barely graduated. He sold drugs and robbed folks. He went to jail at the age of eighteen. While he was locked up, his father had a massive heart attack and died. That changed him forever. They wouldn't even let him attend the funeral. He loved his father and to not be able to see him laid to rest left him with hate in his heart for any and every one, except for Coco, she was always there when he needed her most.

Let me get out of here so I can get this shit over with. ZO grabbed his keys and out the door he went. He drove all the way to the Eastside and when he got to the condos, he parked directly across the street. Shit, he didn't give a fuck where he parked. His intent was to be in and out. It was two thirty in the morning, and he waited until he saw Taye pull up and park his car. Once Taye was out, he made his move, jumped out the car, and followed him to his door.

Taye was fucked up. He never even heard ZO behind him. He put the key inside the door and had it unlocked when ZO put the gun to the back of his head.

"If you turn around nigga, I'll splatter your brains all over the front of your motherfucking door."

Taye jumped when he heard the voice and felt the gun. Once inside, ZO took the butt of the gun and knocked Taye in the back of the head.

"What the fuck you want from me? If its money, shit, I'll tell you where it is, but this here isn't called for."

"Shut your weak ass up, nigga. I don't want your money. I came here to kill your ass, so turn around and meet your maker." Taye turned around and couldn't believe who it was. Before he could say one more word, ZO put the gun in his mouth.

"You have your sister's fiancé to blame for this." Taye did nothing but close his eyes. He knew his time was up. ZO pulled the trigger and Taye's body fell to the ground with his brains splattered everywhere. ZO had blood all over his face and clothes, but he didn't even bother to wipe the shit off. As he left, ZO left Ty's lighter there at the doorway as if he had dropped it on the way out. It had his initials on it. The night the cops got ZO, he had it in his pocket. Ty let ZO use it and he forgot to hand it back to him. Good that he did because that would work great for setting Ty up.

ZO got into his car and pulled off. He felt good. He lit the blunt and rolled down the windows. He forgot he had blood all over him until he looked in the mirror.

Fuck, let me get the back to the spot, so I can shower, and shit. Now all I have to do is sit back until this shit hit the fan. I'm coming for you, Ty, he said as he drove across town.

Chapter 36
Ty

Ty was in his office having a conversation on the phone. He shook his head because he couldn't believe the news he heard.

"Alright, baby, thanks for the information. I'll see you in a week when you touch down." Ty hung up the phone and took in all that was told to him.

Damn, you can't trust anyone these days. I can't believe that Twan went and got his own connect. He is doing his own thing, which is coo, but damn he couldn't even tell me. My baby got her ears to the street. Good thing she does because if not, I never would have seen this shit coming.

Ty sat there thinking to himself he couldn't understand why Twan would try to play him like that. Whatever the reason was, he would get to the bottom of it. He leaned back in his office chair as he called Twan.

"Twan, I need to holler at you. Where you at? Stop by Mina's spot? All right then. I'll see you shortly." Ty hung up the phone.

I really need to step away from this shit. I own several night clubs. Mina and I aren't hurting for money. The shit isn't the same for real. The game has changed I need to get out before the game catches up with my ass. When Mina gets back I need to tell her everything. I should have never kept this from her. Ty sent Mina a text message while he waited.

Hey, baby, I just wanted to let you know I miss you and can't wait 'til you arrive home. I got something I need to discuss with you when you get back. I love you, enjoy yourself, Ty.

He sent the message and got a shot of Remy VSOP. On his way back to the office, Twan came in, said what's up, and took a seat. Ty got straight to the point.

"What's up, Twan? What's this I hear about you having a supplier in the Detroit? So what, are you doing your own thing now?" Twan sat there with his mouth open. He was caught off guard with the question.

"Damn, is that what you do go behind your partner's back and make your own moves? Shit, you didn't feel the need to let me know what you were trying to do."

Twan sat on the edge of the couch, looking Ty up and down. He felt like Ty was on some tough shit and he wasn't having it.

"Hold up, Ty, shit you coming to me like I owe you some sort of explanation. As far as I see it, I don't have to tell you about shit I'm doing. We were 'pose to be partners, but you never once let me meet your connect. So, what's the difference? I'm fronting my money just like you are. You say we in this together, bullshit, nigga, you all about self. You forgot about me. You always feel the need to try to out shine a nigga. Those days are over. You not gon' fuck me over like you did that nigga ZO."

"What the fuck you mean like I did ZO? You don't know what took place behind that shit. I didn't owe ZO a motherfucking thang therefore, don't speak on business that ain't yours."

Ty was heated. You could see it all over his face. They sat there with nothing said.

"Do you, Twan. Like you said you don't owe me an explanation. Thing is we came up together hustling on the streets. I've always been about my paper, my word is all I got and I always been one hundred with you. This shit you doing is some bitch shit for real, nigga. Take it how you want to, but you know I'm right. I have never tried to play you. As far as my connect, he was only trying to deal with me and me only. As long as you were getting money, that's all that should have mattered. So as far as you saying I'm getting greedy, that would be you. I'm done talking. Nothing more needs to be said. I'll see you around, Twan, be careful out here. These streets are ugly."

Ty stood up to let Twan know it was time to go. Twan looked at Ty with anger in his eyes. He walked out and Ty shook his head.

Chapter 37
Mina

Yes my bed, finally. I've had so much fun. We have been partying like crazy, I love it. I didn't think I would have fun with India, but that bitch is the life of the party.

Mina lay on her bed still fully clothed. She was wasted and couldn't get up. While lying down, she felt something vibrate. She looked down and it was India's phone going off. When she looked down at the phone, she saw a text message from Rel she went to close it but hit the scroll button and saw Taye name and of course she read the message.

Omg! I knew it, damn. I didn't think it was this deep. This chick is really in love with Taye and he is in love with her. Just as she finished the messages, India walked in.

"I was just about to come find your ass. Your phone has been blowing up. Here, take this phone."

Mina handed her the phone; she had a slight grin on her face. She wasn't going to mention anything about the messages. It wasn't her place. Mina knew that Taye would tell her when he was ready.

"Damn, thank you, Mina. I thought I lost my shit until Coco reminded me that I gave it to you to put in your purse."

"No problem. I'm about to take off these clothes and take me a hot shower. You bitches will not have me like this the entire trip."

"Alright, Mina, you need to get some rest because tomorrow we up and out early."

"Tomorrow is today its damn near five a.m. What the hell you mean early?" Mina said. India giggled.

"We're getting our tattoos done!"

"Damn, I forgot about that shit, but, cool, I already know what I'm getting. I'm going to get Taye's name tatted on me. He has my name tatted right on his heart. I love my brother."

She smiled as she expressed to India how she felt about her brother. It was her way, of letting India know that if she fucked him over, then she would have to deal with her.

"Yea, I know what you mean. I love Rel just the same."

They said good bye and India headed to her own room. While Mina took a shower, she had an eerie feeling come over her. She felt as though something was wrong, but she had no clue as to what. Mina got out of the shower, dried herself off, got into bed, and passed straight out. She had a dream about Taye. He was calling for her, but in her dream she couldn't find him. She only heard his voice. She woke up and called Taye, but only got his voicemail.

Damn, that dream seemed real as hell. I need to talk to Taye. Mina sat there in bed for thirty more minutes and continued to call Taye.

Chapter 38
Coco

"Rise and shine, India," Coco said in a cheery mood.

"Coco, take your ass back to sleep. Come on, we just laid down." Coco looked down at her watch.

"No, actually, you have been sleeping for almost six hours. It's time to get up. If you can't hang, then you don't need to drink." Coco laughed as she opened the curtains to allow the sunlight to enter into the dark room.

"You know what, bitch, you really will get on someone's nerves. Do you do this to my brother?" India complained.

"I don't have to, missy. He knows how to handle his liquor when he drinks. We have a full schedule today, so come on! If you don't want to go, that's cool. We'll meet up with you later."

"Kiss my ass, Coco, I'm getting up!"

"Good, now I'll just go wake the other two up. Thirty minutes, India, that's how long you have to get ready." India was about to respond, but Coco was out the door before she could even get a word out.

After waking up everyone Coco headed back to her room to call Rel.

"Good afternoon Rel. What you up to?"

"Shit, I'm headed to the airport as we speak. I was supposed to be on an earlier flight but I over slept. I'm glad you called. You all been going hard, haven't you?"

"Hell, yea, we have. I hate to leave here the day after tomorrow, but we got to head to the ATL for the game. You know we ain't gon' miss the game."

"So, you really think the Cards are going to beat Michigan?"

If Rel could have seen Coco's face, he would have died laughing. She had her face scrunched up and couldn't believe he asked her that.

"You must have lost your mind, Rel. I'm not even gon' answer the question. You know what it is."

"Damn, baby, calm down. Rep your city, I ain't mad at you. But, on the real, Coco, I miss you. I know you all got a long day planned, so I won't hold you up. Tell India I said win some damn money and tell everyone else I said, hello. Be careful, baby, and I'll see you soon."

"I will, Rel." Coco hung up with a smile on her face. She was glad she talked to him.

"Let me guess, that was my brother you were just on the phone with?"

"Yep, it sure was," Coco replied.

"I figured that with that big ass smile on your face." They laughed and headed out to go get Mina and Asia.

They made it to the tattoo shop they already knew what they would get. Mina went first and got Taye's name right above her heart. The other ladies had already got started on theirs as well. Once everyone was finished, they gathered together to show one another what they had gotten. Asia got China Doll tattooed on the back of her neck.

"The damn tattoo artist gon' ask me about my birthmark I got on my neck behind my ear. He said it was very different."

"Where is it at? I want to see," India said.

"What, we about to see is your tattoo," Asia said. "What did you get?"

India got Taye's name in Chinese writing on her arm.

"What is it, your name or what?" Asia asked.

Mina continued to look at the tattoo. She knew what it read. She knew that because Taye had the exact tattoo on the left side of his neck. Mina smiled at India, and said, "I love it."

"Ok, Coco, what did you go get? Don't tell me you went and got Rel's name on you," Asia said.

"Hell naw, you know only name I got on me is my baby, Brandy." Coco had got sexy written on her foot in cursive and the shit was all that. All the women were pleased with their tattoos, so they headed out to shop.

Chapter 39
Ty

Ty was out making moves. He thought long and hard, and decided to get out the game. The events that occurred fucked with him. He knew that shit wouldn't last forever. He had a bad feeling that something was about to go down. He was headed back to the house when he got a call from Mina's mother. All he heard when he picked up the phone was Mrs. Smith screaming into the phone.

"Someone killed my, baby. My son is dead. Taye is dead." Ty couldn't believe what he heard on the other end of the phone.

"What, mama, you have got to calm down. What you mean Taye is dead, what happened?"

"I went to his apartment because I hadn't heard from him in two days. We kept getting his voicemail. I decided to drive over and when I unlocked the door, the smell was horrible, but not as horrible, as seeing my son's brains outside of his head," she hollered.

Ty tried to calm her. He told her he was on his way there.

Damn, this is going to kill Mina when I tell her. Ty pulled up and rushed in the house. Mina's mother ran to Ty and cried in his arms. Mina's father cried as well. They had lost their only son. Ty couldn't believe this was happening. He couldn't imagine what it would do to Mina.

"Mama, why haven't you called Mina?" Ty asked.

"I can't, Ty. I can't tell her that her brother is dead."

She looked at Ty with confusion on her face. She knew that having to tell her the only sibling she had was dead would kill her.

"I'm going to call Mina and tell her it's an emergency and to come back home. She needs to get here ASAP," Ty said.

"Can you call her now, please? I don't want her to hear this from anyone but us. Please, call her."

Ty called Mina and told her to get home because something happened. She was upset with him for not telling her what it was about. She let him know that she would catch the first flight out. There was a knock at the door. Ty opened the door and it was Detective Reynolds, the person handling the homicide investigation.

"I'm Ty, Taye was my soon to be brother-in-law. What happened, detective?"

"It looks like Taye was shot two days ago around three in the morning. Not sure if he knew the person or not, but there wasn't any forced entry. We know he was killed with a 9mm Beretta. Whoever it was put the gun inside his mouth and blew his brains out."

Ty had tears in his eyes. The description alone turned the pit of his stomach.

I know me and Taye had our times, but fuck, I would never wish this on that man, ever, Ty thought.

"Do you have any ideal who may have wanted to hurt, Taye? We found over $200,000.00 in Taye's home. Do you know where he would have gotten that type of money from?" Ty looked puzzled. He didn't respond for a minute.

"Detective Reynolds, if you don't mind, can we do this some other time? You see how hard his parents are taking this."

"I'm done for now, but I will be contacting you all."

Chapter 40
Mina

Mina and the ladies packed their things, tossing shit in suitcases.

"What the hell happened? I need to hurry and get there. It must be something bad if Ty couldn't tell me over the phone. I knew something was wrong. I had that feeling. God, please, let everything be all right with my family."

She needed answers, but she knew she wouldn't get them 'til she was home.

"India, tell me that you have talked to Taye?" Mina insisted.

"I haven't heard from him since the night we arrived. I've tried calling his phone. At first it would just rung, now it goes straight to voicemail. You don't think this has anything to do with him, do you?"

"I'm not sure, let's head to the airport. The flight will be boarding in forty-five minutes." Everyone rode in silence to the airport. It started out as a fun trip and ended in confusion and desperation. No one knew what took place back at home. They had no idea that the death of Taye would affect each of their lives.

Once at the airport, things moved along smoothly and the women boarded the plane. India was scared that something was wrong with Taye. She prayed silently that he was ok. The more she thought about him, the harder she cried. Coco and Asia wondered why India was crying. Mina went over to India, held her hand, and hugged her.

"India, I know about you and Taye." India stared at Mina with tears still streaming down her face.

"I know you love him, that's his name you got tattooed on you. I saw the text messages on your phone. My brother loves you and I'm happy for you two. Don't be sitting here crying. We don't know what has happened. Try to stay calm."

Mina comforted India, she was a nervous wreck. She wanted to believe those words she spoke to India, but in her heart she knew something happened to Taye. Once the plane landed, the women got their luggage and grabbed a cab. Mina gave the cab driver the address.

"You all don't have to go with me. I'm sure everything is all right."

No one spoke a word, they just looked at Mina. She knew they were not leaving her side.

Once the cab pulled up to the house, Mina started shaking. She was nervous and scared. Ty came out the front door and walked over to the cab. He helped Mina out and paid the driver. Ty told them to put their bags in his Range Rover.

"Ok, Ty, I'm here now. What has happened?"

"Mina, as soon as we get inside the house, baby." She wanted to go off, but she stayed calm. She flew in the house. When she walked in, she saw her parents crying.

"What is wrong? What happened? Damn it, what has happened?" Mina was frustrated. Her parents looked at her not saying a word.

"Calm down Mina." Ty said sincerely. Her mother couldn't take it. She broke down making Mina cry even more. Everyone looked at Ty for answers. He had tears in his eyes and couldn't look Mina in the face as he trembled.

"Baby, its Taye." Mina froze as her attention focused on what Ty told her.

"I don't know how to tell you this. Earlier today mama went to Taye's crib and found him dead. He was killed."

Ty caught Mina as she fell to the floor. She let out an agonizing scream a scream that everyone was bound to hear throughout the neighborhood. Asia, Coco, and India couldn't believe what Ty said.

Ty held Mina as she continued to scream over and over,

"Why did this happen? It can't be true, oh my brother!" Ty's heart hurt for her and he didn't know what to say. He held her tight.

Coco cried as she comforted Mrs. Smith and Asia consoled Mr. Smith. India sat on the couch and rocked back in forth. She cried and asked God why? How could God allow this to happen? All of a sudden it hit her.

Oh, my God, Ty said that he was killed. God, please, don't let it be ZO that killed Taye. Oh, God it's my fault. I got to get out of here. I can't stay, but I can't leave my friends, they need me. India thought.

India got off the couch to comfort Mina. She wanted to be there for Mina because she was there for her on the plane. She knelt beside her and Ty, and laid her hand on Mina's hand.

Chapter 41
India

India was in deep thought about Taye as she rode in the back seat of the taxi cab.

I can't believe he's dead. I didn't want to leave Mina, but I figured she needed time to grieve with her family. She isn't talking or anything. She is just in a daze. I keep calling ZO's phone, but all I get his voicemail. I've got to talk to him.

India finally arrived home and the cab driver helped her with her things to the front door. Once India made it inside, she headed back to her bedroom. All she wanted was a hot bath and to relax. She had so much on her mind and the guilt killed her. India felt in her heart that ZO had something to do with Taye being murdered. She gave him too much information about Taye and all that went down at the club with Ty.

Why kill Taye? She kept saying to herself. India couldn't wrap her brain around it. She figured that he didn't have anything ZO could possibly want except for money. He was a greedy motherfucker, but what he really wanted was to fuck up any and every one's world, including India's.

All I know is that Taye is dead and if it was ZO that done this, I am as guilty as he is. How can I ever live with myself knowing I am the reason behind the man I love's death? India talked out loud as if she was waiting for someone to respond.

When India walked into her bedroom and turned on the light, she paused. She had a huge, brown teddy bear on her bed along with a Tiffany box and a card. She sat down on the bed and opened the card. Tears streamed down her pretty face as she read the card. "I love you." That was the front of the card. She opened it. Inside, Taye wrote:

India, babe I would have never thought it was possible to fall in love in such a short time, but I now know that it is. You have made me the happiest I have been in a very long time. You make me want to be a better me. I just want you to know I love you and that you have my heart. When you wear your gift, just keep me close to your heart, Taye.

India read what Taye wrote over and over, crying uncontrollably. She opened the box and gasped as she looked at the beautiful Lock Heart pendant. It was handmade platinum covered with paved diamonds. Inside the box was a small note.

Read the back of the pendant. India turned over the necklace it read; *you have my heart, Love Taye.*

Once again, India cried. I love you, Taye, she repeated over and over again. India finally got up and ran her bath water, got undressed, and stepped into the whirlpool tub. She played Pandora on her phone and relaxed.

She slipped on her night clothes, and then went to pour herself a glass of Riesling. She walked back into her bedroom, took the necklace out of the box, and placed it around her neck. She looked at herself in the mirror and prayed to God. She asked Him to forgive her for all the wrong she did and for all the people who was hurt behind her wrong doings. She told Taye in her prayer that she would always wear her pendant and he would forever have her heart.

I love you, Taye, India said before she closed her eyes and went to sleep.

Chapter 42
Mina

"Mina, baby, it's time to get up," Ty whispered in her ear.

She had slept for twelve hours. Ty knew Mina needed rest, but, at the same time, her family needed her. It was time to talk about the funeral arrangements.

"Ty, please, just leave me alone. I don't want to do shit but lay here, just give me a little more time to rest."

"Baby, I know you're hurt, but your parents need you. You have to stay strong for them."

"How can I? My brother is dead. He's gone and never coming back. I know that may not mean shit to you since the last few times you seen him you were trying to bash his fucking head in, but it matters to me. I lost my only sibling. He was my heart and now he's dead!"

Ty hugged Mina and allowed her to vent. He knew she didn't mean shit she said, or at least he hoped she didn't. She had every right to be angry. He knew how much Taye meant to her.

"Ty, I'm sorry. I know you're not trying to do anything but be here for me and my family."

"You don't owe me an apology, baby. I'm here and I don't plan on going anywhere."

After about thirty more minutes of lying in the bed, Mina got up and Ty started the shower for her. He laid out her clothes and while she showered, he cooked breakfast. Mina stood under the hot water and cried, wondering who killed Taye and why. She knew her brother did some fucked up shit, but he didn't hurt anyone and he certainly didn't deserve to be killed. Her mind raced as she thought about all that happened.

As soon as Taye's funeral is over, I need to talk with Detective Reynolds and see if he has any leads. Someone had to see something. Damn, the thought of my mother walking in and seeing her only son dead, gives me goose bumps. My parents will never be the same without Taye.

Mina slid to the shower floor with water streaming down her face along with tears. Her life had drastically changed within twenty four hours. She wasn't sure how she would pull through this.

Mina got out the shower, got dressed, and grabbed her cell phone to check to see if her parents called. They called and so did everyone else. She knew it wouldn't be long before the news got around. She scrolled through and read her text messages. Everyone offered their condolence and help with anything that her family needed. She thought it was a nice gesture, but didn't want to respond to anyone.

Mina made her way down the steps. Ty had her plate made so she sat at the breakfast bar, but she really didn't have an appetite. She ate, anyway. She knew it would be a long day. Once Mina finished breakfast, she was out the door. The ride to her parents' house was a quiet one. Once she arrived at her parents' house, things would be pretty emotional. Mina's mother greeted her at the door, her eyes were bright red and swollen.

"Mama, have you had any sleep? Have you and daddy been up all night?" She looked at her father and he looked just how her mother did, restless.

"I can't sleep. All I see when I close my eyes is Taye lying there on the floor with his..."
Mina quickly interrupted her mother.

"Mama, please, I don't want to hear about how you found Taye. I'm going to contact A.D. Porter & Sons

Funeral Home in the South East on Bardstown Road. I'm going to schedule to meet with them today sometime. We need to pick out a nice Urn to have Taye's ashes placed in."

"What do you mean his ashes?" Mrs. Smith yelled.

"My baby isn't getting cremated."

"What do you mean he's not getting cremated?" Mina was confused.

"You heard me. My son is not being put in any incinerator." Her mother was pissed.

"You said yourself how Taye looked with his brains blown out his head. Now you want to have him placed in a casket for everyone to see him? Hell naw! Taye would not want that and you know this. He would want everyone to remember him how he was. You really need to get some rest because you are truly tripping. Daddy, you agree with mama? Daddy this is your son as well. You have a say on how you would like things to go."

Mr. Smith looked at his wife.

"Honey, you know Deontaye wouldn't want anyone to see him like that. Please, let Mina handle everything."

Mrs. Smith sobbed. "I'm sorry, Mina, you're right. I just didn't want my son to be cremated, but it's for the best. Do what you think is right. I can't handle this and you knew Taye better than anyone. You know how he would want things."

"Thank you, mama. I'll make sure everything is perfect for Taye's home going."

Chapter 43
Rel

Who would have thought I would come back to the city and learn that Taye was killed? Damn.

Coco called Rel and let him know what happened to Taye. He had been with her ever since he got back in town. Rel was puzzled because he couldn't believe that whoever killed him didn't take the money. He needed to holler at Ty, but he knew the time was all wrong.

Coco got ready to go meet up with Mina to help with the funeral arrangements.

I tried to call India and she isn't picking up her phone. Once I leave here, I will be making my way over there to her. This isn't like her to not respond at all.

Rel was worried about his sister. Seeing what Mina went through losing her brother made him thank God for his sister. If anything were to ever happen to her he would lose it, so it was important to see her and make sure she was ok. His cell phone rang, it was a call he needed to take. He stepped out on the patio just in case Coco came downstairs.

"Hello, yes, I'm trying to get that information now. As soon as I know or hear anything, I will contact you as soon as possible," Rel said to the person on the other end of the phone. He hung up and stepped back inside. Coco came down the steps and Rel hugged her as soon as she hit that last step.

"You ok, baby?" he asked.

"Yea I'm okay. I'm glad you're here with me. It means a lot."

"You don't have to drive me to Mina's parents' house, I can drive myself. She has a lot that she needs to get done. The funeral will be Saturday, she just isn't sure of the time yet."

Coco's eyes watered. Rel put his arms around her waist and told her everything would be okay.

"Baby, you heard from India today?"

"No, I haven't. I've called and texted her several times, but no answer or response. You know once we got the news about Taye, she broke down. I know India and Taye got close here lately. I'm not sure if anything was going on between them. If so, your sister is probably grieving and needs someone. You need to check on her and if you need me, you call me." They kissed and went their separate ways.

Rel pulled up to India's house and both her cars were parked in the driveway. He knocked on the door several times before he decided to use his key and let himself in. He called out for India, but got no answer. He walked to her bedroom. India was in bed her eyes were puffy and red from crying.

"Indy, you ok? What's wrong? Talk to me."

"Please, just leave. I don't feel like talking."

Rel looked at his sister. Coco was right. India had to be dealing with Taye because what else could explain why she was laid up in her room crying her eyes out.

"Indy, I'm not sure what's wrong. I just want you to know I'm here for you. Don't be holding shit in."

India looked up at the ceiling. Nothing Rel said made a difference. She was consumed with guilt.

"I'm sure this has something to do with Taye, but when you ready to talk, I'm here."

She wanted to tell him everything. She knew she could trust her brother, but she was afraid and ashamed. If she told Rel, that meant she would have to tell him about ZO and she wasn't prepared to do that, at least not yet. Rel sat on the bed and India laid her head on his chest.

She thought about ZO and how she allowed herself to ever fall for a man that didn't care shit about her.

A man can change a woman in the worst ways, India thought as she shut her eyes and cried herself to sleep.

Chapter 44
India

India woke up the next morning feeling a little better. She finally opened up to Rel about Taye and their relationship. India told him what she felt she could about everything, but she left out ZO, of course. He told her to keep Taye close to her heart and that he wouldn't want her sitting around depressed. She realized that he was right. Taye wouldn't want her sitting around crying. It was a new day and she was going to get herself together, but first she was gon' get a hold of ZO.

India hopped in the shower and got dressed. She was on her way to ZO's house since he hadn't answered her phone calls.

India got on the block ZO lived on and noticed a familiar car in his driveway, but couldn't think of whose car it was. India decided to park around the corner. She had no ideal on what she may be walking into, so she thought it would be best to park her car where it couldn't be seen. India went around back and used her key to let herself in. She walked through the kitchen and heard moaning coming from down the hall toward ZO's bedroom.

I know his ass isn't in here fucking! India was pissed. Although, she didn't care for ZO like she did it still hurt because she knew that he had no respect for her what so ever.

India continued to make her way back toward the bedroom.

"You are trying to suck the skin off this dick," she heard ZO say.

I finally get to see who this bitch is, India thought.

India stood in the hallway and could see ZO perfectly. She had to see who ZO was fucking with. He repositioned his body. When he did that India saw who it was and she damn near threw up in her mouth.

Bitch nigga! India said under her breath as she headed down the hallway and out the back door. Once outside, she ran as fast as she could to the car. She was disgusted by what she saw.

I can't believe this shit. Who is this nigga that I called myself loving for years? How could I not have known? ZO is gon' pay that is one thing I know for sure.

India had nothing but hate in her heart for ZO. Although, she still didn't know if he was the one who killed Taye she found out something much more.

Chapter 45
Mina

It was twelve thirty in the morning on a Thursday and Mina's cell phone rang. She couldn't imagine who could be calling her. She spoke to Ty about twenty minutes ago he was at the club taking care of things. The phone continued to ring. Mina looked at the number, but didn't recognize it.

"Hello," Mina answered.

"Mina, baby, I am sorry to hear about Taye. I will be in town tomorrow, about noon. I have already talked to mama and pop, so that's where I'll be. You know how I felt about Taye. He was my little brother. I still can't believe he's gone. There's no need for me to ask you how you are because I already know. Taye was your baby brother."

"Michael thanks for calling. Mama and daddy aren't doing well at all. They haven't slept, they barely eating and I just feel helpless."

"You shouldn't say that. Mama told me how you took care of the entire funeral arrangements. You have always been strong and stepped up when your family needed you. Don't try to tell me that shit. You know I was there from the start and as you see, I'm not going anywhere. You all will always be my family, so I will see you tomorrow. I'll be at the house by twelve thirty p.m., so get some rest. I love you."

Michael hung up before Mina could say anything. She knew that he loved her family as much as he loved his own. The Smith's showed him love and support, and always would.

I'm glad Michael called me. I really am. He may have fucked up what we had, but he would forever be a part of my life. Shit, while I'm up, I need to call Asia. She did so much for me these last couple of days. Without her and Coco, I would have lost it by now.

Mina dialed Asia's number, but only got her voicemail. I'll call her in the morning, she said before she hung up. I wonder how India is doing.

I have tried calling her since she left mama's house, but she won't return any of my phone calls. I can't understand that at all. I need to talk to her. I don't want her to be alone. My brother loved her and my family will welcome her with open arms. As soon as I get up in the morning, I'm calling Rel.

Mina lay in bed looking at pictures of her and Taye. She had already chosen the pictures that she would show on the slideshow for the funeral. She also had a picture of Taye and India, which she had gotten from Taye's phone. The picture was cute. They made a nice couple. It was one of Mina's favorites. She had everything the way she knew Taye would want it. She wanted the memory of her brother to never be forgotten.

Chapter 46
Asia

I wonder what it is that Mina wants. I hate that I didn't pick up her phone call, but I don't know what to do with the information that I just heard. I can't believe that it is being said that Ty killed Taye. Shit, should I say something to Mina or not? I don't think Ty is capable of killing Taye, but, then again, who knows. The way Ty fucked Taye up at the grand opening and everyone heard Ty say that he would dead Taye, and that was not the first run in they've had. I'm just gon' leave it alone. I'm not trying to start no bullshit because all that's going to happen is the shit will get flipped back on me. I will be the one to blame, so I rather not say shit. I'm going off of hearsay and Mina has enough going on. I just want her to have Taye's funeral so she can start piecing her life back together, Asia thought.

She wondered if she should call Big R or not. She hadn't heard from him, and last time they talked, he told her he was trying to help Rel track down India. Word got out about India and Taye, which was no surprise to Asia because she already knew. Asia knew a lot, she just never said anything. She actually felt for India because she knew how it felt to be in love and at the snap of a finger, the one you cared about was taken away from you.

Asia was about to call Big R when a text came through on her phone. It was a message from Twan and a smile crept across her face. He wanted to meet and Asia knew exactly what that meant. She told herself that she was done fucking with Twan, but being that Big R was not paying her any attention, she told him she would meet him at the Crown Plaza. She knew that he couldn't come there, but it would be just her luck that Big R would show up. Asia took a quick shower and got dressed; as she applied her makeup she started having second thoughts.

Asia didn't look at Twan the same. She saw how he went behind Ty's back and got his own connect. On top of that, he talked too much. He told her all about Ty and ZO, and how Ty was in the car with ZO the night he got locked up. Asia always knew that Ty was in the streets, hell, the only person that didn't know was Mina. She felt like Mina was engaged to a man she really knew nothing about.

After thinking about it, Asia grabbed her keys and left.

Fuck it, I need some dick. I promise this is going to be my last time fucking with Twan.

Chapter 47
ZO

Why ain't this nigga locked up yet? ZO watched Ty walk in Mina's parents' house. He had been watching him since he had killed Taye. ZO sat there for awhile before he headed out to India's house.

ZO got to India's house and used his key to let himself in. When he walked in, he heard the shower running. He walked in the bathroom and stood there as he watched India rinse off.

Damn, her body is beautiful. Shit I'm gon' miss that pussy. Now that I think about it, India and I haven't fucked in a while. I should hop on in there and get me some pussy real quick, ZO thought.

India jumped as she looked up and saw ZO watching her.

"You act as if you've seen a ghost, damn, you not happy to see your man?" India stared at ZO as she stepped out the shower to dry off.

"Here, let me help you with that, baby." India let him dry her off. He kissed her breasts, but he soon stopped when he saw her necklace.

"Where the fuck you get this from?" ZO looked at India as she stared at him like, 'get the fuck out my face.' "Answer me!"

"Damn, why you tripping? Rel got it for me." India knew if ZO knew it was from Taye or any other man he would wipe the floor with her ass.

"Shit, next time you better speak the fuck up when I ask you something." India stepped away and got dressed.

"Hey, baby, did you hear what happened to Taye?" ZO stared at her.

"Yeah, I took care of that nigga." India grabbed her chest.

"Huh, you killed Taye?" Her eyes watered, but she held back the tears from falling. She knew if she let a tear drop, ZO would snap.

"Hell yea, I killed that nigga. Shit, with the info you gave me it was the perfect set up for Ty to take the fall." India was frozen in one spot, unable, to move, or say shit.

"Why the fuck you looking at me like that, India? Don't tell me you getting soft on me."

"I can't tell that Ty took the fall for it. He isn't locked up yet." India knew she had spoken too soon, the look on ZO face confirmed that.

"What in the fuck are you trying to say? Don't think because that nigga ain't locked up yet that I'm done with his ass. If that plan didn't work, I'll try something else. I may just kill that bitch, Mina, as well. I'll take out that nigga's entire family one by one. Either way, that nigga gon' feel pain."

India looked at ZO with nothing but hatred in her eyes. That look spoke volumes because ZO smacked the shit out of her. He hit her so hard, she fell into the dresser and hit her head on the corner of it.

"I'm sorry, baby. I wasn't saying that at all. I was just thinking if you set him up, why he isn't locked up yet? You never told me that you were setting up Ty."

India was in pain, but she talked to ZO as if nothing happened. She knew one more slip up and he would kick her ass. She wanted him to feel like she was still loyal to him. She needed to know his next move.

"Man, get up and get some ice for your head and lip. You need to watch what the fuck you say. Think about the shit before it escapes your lips."

"I understand, baby. It won't happen again," India said with blood oozing from her lip.

"Are you going to tell me how you set Ty up?"

"Let's just say I left a little something behind that had his name written all over it." ZO had a smirk on his face.

Chapter 48
Mina

Mina pulled up to her parents' house Thursday at about one o'clock in the afternoon. Michael texted her and told her that he had made it.

Mina's phone rang, and she reached inside her Michael Kors purse and saw that it was Ty.

"Good afternoon."

"Baby, damn, you left without even saying goodbye. You ok? Where are you?"

"I just pulled up at my parent's house."

"You didn't want me to come with you?"

"I didn't want to wake you up. You've been by my side this entire time. You need your rest."

"I'm 'pose to be by your side. Shit what you mean? Look, I'm about to jump in the shower I'll be there shortly."

"You don't have to do that. I was just stopping by checking on them. I'm going to leave here and take care of the programs. Plus, Michael just got in town he's here at the house."

Ty sat on the other end of the phone in silence.

"So, is that why you rolled out of here this morning without waking me up?"

"I told you why I didn't wake you up, now if you want to come then come on."

"I'm good. You got who you want there." Ty hung up the phone.

Did this nigga just hang up on me? She tried calling Ty back twice and he sent her straight to voicemail. She knew she was wrong. She knew the reason she didn't wake Ty up was because Michael was in town and truth be told, she wanted to spend time with him alone.

I don't have time for this shit. If Ty wants to be mad, let him, selfish ass tripping over nothing.

Mina got out the car, and as she walked up the driveway Michael walked out the front door and walked toward her. As they reached one another, Mina could see the tears in his eyes. Nothing was said and it didn't need to be. They held one another not caring about who watched or what they thought.

"I'm sorry, Mina. I can't believe Taye is gone. Who in the fuck would have done this shit?"

"I don't know. The police have no leads what so ever. All they said was Taye had a lot of money in his place. I can't understand why someone would kill him and not take the money. That shit has been on my mind ever since I found out. No one on the streets seems to know anything."

"Trust me when I say this, we gon' find out who did this and I'll make sure their mama got her black dress on to attend their funeral." Michael looked Mina in her eyes. The two hugged just as Ty pulled into the driveway. Michael let Mina go. Ty stepped out the car and walked up to Mina.

"Hey, baby, I see you made it." Mina hugged Ty.

"I told you I was coming. What's up, Michael?" Ty placed his arm around Mina's waist and pulled her closer as he kissed her. Michael cleared his throat.

"I'm good. I'm just here to be with my family." They looked at one another. Ty couldn't stand Michael and he couldn't stand Ty. Mina could feel the tension.

"Are you ready to go in?" She grabbed Ty's hand and they walked into the house with Michael following.

Mina and her parents went over the final arrangements for the funeral. Everything would be on

Saturday at noon. There wasn't going to be a wake being that there was no body to view, but there would be a ceremony that no one would ever forget. Mina had asked everyone who attended to wear white. She didn't want anyone to mourn her brother's death, although, his life ended the way it did. She wanted to celebrate the life he had in a way that only Taye would want it.

Chapter 49
Rel

"Here Indy goes with this shit, not picking up the phone. Mina called me twice asking have I been in touch with her. I'm just gon' have to pop in on her again. She can't continue to do this shit. I know my sister is mourning, but she can't shut those out that care," Rel said as he talked to Coco on the phone.

Coco called to let him know what time the funeral was on Saturday. He told her about what went on with India, being that Coco still hadn't talk to her. He told Coco he would let her know how India was once he saw her.

Rel drove to India's place and all he thought about was his baby sister. When he arrived, he saw a blue Charger drive off. It was the same as hers. The side view of the person looked familiar, but he couldn't really figure out who it was. *Who the fuck was that?* Rel knocked on the door first and, got know answer. He knocked again and decided to use his key to let himself in.

"Indy, where are you?" He heard the music on down the hall near her bedroom. When he walked in the room, he saw her standing in the bathroom putting on her makeup.

"Turn that shit down. You can't hear shit with that loud ass music," Rel shouted to India.

India damn near jumped out her skin.

"Damn, Rel! Why didn't you knock? You scared the shit out of me."

"I did knock! I knocked twice. Turn that music down and maybe you could hear. Why haven't you been returning my calls? Mina has been trying to get in touch with you. How you just not gon' answer her phone calls knowing she just lost her brother?" India had tears in her eyes.

"I'm not trying to come down on you, but damn, baby girl, when you gon' stop thinking about yourself and think about others? I know you going through your thing as well, missing Taye, but think about his family."

India knew Rel was right. She was being selfish. Rel walked closer to her and that was when he noticed that her lip was busted.

"What the fuck happened to your lip?" Rel grabbed her by the chin as he looked closely.

Damn I forgot about my damn lip, India thought.

"Indy, I know you heard what I said! What happened to your lip?"

"Damn, Rel, it just happened when I got out the shower. I slipped and hit my lip on the damn faucet. Shit, you acting like I got my ass beat." Rel looked at India as to say, 'you a damn lie.' But, he left it alone.

"Alright, put some ice on that shit and call Mina, please. You want me to come by and get you Saturday morning for the funeral?"

"You need to be with Coco. She will need you as well."

"I'm worried about you. I'll be here to get you unless you want to just stay over at my house."

"Yea, I think I rather stay the night. I'll see you then. I'm going to call Mina. Thanks for checking on me. What would I do without my big brother?" India hugged him.

"You know you can tell me anything, right? You don't have to go through anything alone. Just know that, ok? I'll always have your back no matter what." Rel kissed her on the cheek. He knew she wasn't being upfront with him.

"I love you, Rel".

Rel drove home thinking that something wasn't right with India, but he didn't know what.

India and I used to be so close. Now, she will hardly open up to me as if she's scared and I know she isn't scared of me. I love her to death, something or someone got her shook up.

Chapter 50
India

Once Rel left, India wondered how she ever allowed herself to fall for someone like ZO.

I can't believe I allowed this nigga to put his hands on me once again. I can't stand ZO. I used to think he was The One. How wrong I was. Look at my damn lip. I can't believe I allowed myself to get caught up in this damn mess.

India looked at herself in the mirror. She looked restless. She had spent most of her nights crying the guilt she felt was weighing heavy on her heart and mind. She wanted to tell Rel, but didn't want to drag him into her mess. She figured she got herself into it and she would get herself out of it. Her real reason for not wanting to tell him was that she knew he would kill ZO.

India applied her makeup and finished getting ready, then texted Mina to ask if it was ok if she stopped by to talk. Mina replied back fast, saying yes. India drove directly to her house and sat in her car awhile before she got out.

God, please, give me the strength to go in here. Just as India said her silent prayer, her phone rang. She looked down and it was ZO. She knew if she didn't answer he would continue to blow her phone up, so she did.

First thing he asked was where she was. India wanted to lie and say at home, but she was afraid he may want to come over so she told him the truth. ZO didn't like the fact that she was anywhere around Mina. He asked her why she was still hanging with her and India let him know that she was trying to be there because Mina asked her to be. ZO didn't like that answer, so she played her role and told him that she was still trying to stay close, so she could find out any info he may need to know. He liked that idea. Mina needed to be watched at all times.

The hate India had for ZO grew more and more each day. She hated the fact that he thought he was playing her. She was about to flip the script. She would no longer be his punching bag and he damn sure would never get any more pussy. Not after what she had witnessed a few days before. That image made her want to vomit.

India got out of her car and walked up to the front door where she was greeted by Mina.

"Give me a hug. Why haven't you been answering my calls?"

"I'm sorry Mina. I should have been here for you. I was just going through my own grief and kind of shut everyone off. I truly am sorry. I should have put aside my own feelings and thought about yours."

"I just didn't know what was wrong. We could have grieved together, but you're here now and that's all that matters. Well, I got everything ready and taken care of for tomorrow. I hope you don't mind, but Taye had some pictures of you two and I included them in the slide show for tomorrow." India sat there in a daze and her eyes began to water.

"I'm sorry, India, I should have asked you first, but I couldn't get a hold to you and I really thought you wouldn't mind. I can take the photos out if you want me to."

"No, don't do that! I'm not upset. I'm happy that you are including me in all of this," India said with tears running down her face.

"My brother loved you, all the small changes he was starting to make within himself, I now know was because of you. At least he was able to experience what love truly felt like even if it was just for a moment, you made a difference in his life," Mina said as she noticed her necklace.

"That's a beautiful necklace."

"Thank you. It's from Taye. When I arrived home after we got the news about his death, this was in my room."

Mina smiled as she looked at the necklace.

They chatted while, enjoying their time with each other.

"Where did the time go? I have been here for over three hours. Let me get ready to leave. Tomorrow will be a long day."

"India would you like to ride with us to the funeral?"

"Thanks for asking but I plan on staying with Rel tonight I need him right by my side tomorrow."

India said goodbye and headed home. On her way home, ZO called and, she sent him to voicemail.

I can't stand ZO, but I got something planned for his ass. I'm going to change my locks or I may just move. I don't want to have any dealings with his ass at all.

India made it home and got her clothes together to head to Rel's house. She didn't want to be in the house alone. She didn't feel safe knowing, ZO could show up at any time.

Chapter 51
Mina

It was the day of the funeral. Mina was up at seven that morning and Ty was sound asleep. Mina checked her phone and had a miss call from Michael. She called him back and they talked for a few minutes before Michael offered to take her out to breakfast. At first she said no, but then she told him she would meet him at Crackle Barrel in thirty minutes.

Mina got up, took a quick shower, and threw on a jogging suit. She left Ty a note saying she stepped out and would be back shortly. During the drive, she thought about the events of the day and actually felt good. She knew that day would be hard on her parents she needed to be strong for them.

When she pulled up, Michael was sitting in one of the rocking chairs outside. He walked to the car and helped Mina out. He gave her a hug and a kiss on the cheek. They headed into the restaurant and were seated quickly.

"How are you doing, Mina?" Mina stared at Michael.

Umm, he looks handsome. I shouldn't even be here. Although, it's breakfast, I still shouldn't be here. Ty is going to lose it, she thought.

"I am actually ok. I am more concerned about mama and daddy. Hopefully, after today they can rest knowing that Taye is finally resting in peace. Although, I can't rest until I find out who killed my brother."

"Yea, about that, have you heard from Detective Reynolds anymore?"

"As a matter of fact, I haven't heard from him. He advised us when he got any new information he let us know. I been so busy with the funeral arrangements that I hadn't even thought about it, but you can best believe on Monday I will be make a trip to the police station."

"I can go with you. I'll be here for the next month to help out in any way."

"You don't have to do that Michael ."

"Come on, now, don't do that. We're not together anymore, but that has nothing to do with me wanting to be here and help out. I'm doing this because I have always done it. Taye was my little brother as well. This isn't about us, so stop thinking I'm trying to make a move on you or some shit. That's the furthest thing from my mind. Just like you want to know who killed Taye, so do I," he said with a little tone of attitude.

Mina sat there in silence. They ate their meal, and then went their separate ways. Mina walked in the house to find Ty cooking breakfast.

"Good morning, where did you run off to?" Ty kissed Mina.

"I just needed to get out and clear my head, that's all," she lied. She didn't want Ty to know she had breakfast with Michael.

"Well, I made you some breakfast. Are you hungry?"

"No, I'm really not all that hungry, but since you cooked I'll try to eat a little something."

She ate what she could and headed upstairs to get ready.

"Mina decided to text Michael, while Ty was in the shower.

I just wanted to apologize from earlier. I know you love Taye. Sorry I thought you're intentions were otherwise. I'm also glad you will be here a little longer. Having you here has made a difference, Love you.

Chapter 52
Coco

Coco was up early because she had a lot on her mind. The night before, she got a phone call from some guy letting her know that ZO would be home soon. The man didn't say anything else. She didn't know whether to believe him or not. Her first question to him was why wasn't ZO calling and, the man said he was just told to make the call.

Coco was about to run her bath water when her phone rang.

"Why are you calling me this early, Xavier?"

"Damn, no good morning? I was calling to see if you wanted to go have breakfast, with your smart ass."

"I was actually getting ready to cook something to eat," Coco said.

"I know you ain't cooking shit," Xavier hollered.

"Shut up! I cook sometimes. You're more than welcomed to join me. Just bring your shit over here and get dressed."

"I'll see you in about twenty minutes, plus, what you cooking?"

"Don't worry about all that. I know what you like. Come on because we got to be there by eleven fifteen a.m."

Coco hung up the phone and laughed. She loved Xavier and was happy that he would be by her side.

Coco started cooking and decided to make all meat omelets with toast. Just as she set the table, Xavier knocked on the door before he unlocked it.

"You got some clothes on, Coco?" Xavier walked up the hallway headed to the kitchen.

"Get your ass in here. Like you never seen me."
Coco laughed.

Xavier stepped into the kitchen and gave Coco a
kiss on the cheek.

"What's up? You got it smelling good in here and
you even set the table."

"Shut up and sit down so we can eat." Coco fixed
his plate and poured him a glass of fruit punch.

"Listen to this shit. I get a call from some guy
saying that ZO will be home soon. I asked if he could
give me a date. He said it will be sooner than ZO thought.
I don't know what to think of that. I haven't heard from
him since, shit, it's been months. I can't understand why
he didn't call himself. Hell, I can't even tell Brandy that
he is coming because I don't have a date."

"Are you surprised? That nigga is a lame and you
know this. That's your daughter's father, but he has
always been fucked up. That nigga ain't gon' never
change."

Although, Xavier was right, Coco was a little
upset and didn't like the fact that Xavier was talking
about ZO. She could, but in her eyes he couldn't.

"You mad now, Coco? Look I'm just speaking the
truth. Don't get all sensitive and shit. You know as well
as I do that he should have let you know he was getting
out soon. How he gon' have a nigga call you who you
don't even know? He's a weak ass motherfucker."

They sat there eating and Coco seemed as though
she had an attitude.

*Shit, Coco is tripping when it comes to that weak
ass motherfucker. That nigga mind ain't right. She can be
mad if she wants to, but she knows he's fucked up.*

"You're right, I'm not mad. I know you're
speaking the truth." Coco hugged him. He always had her
back and always kept it real.

"Okay, we got to start getting ready. It's about that time and I have to be there on time to help Mina in anyway."

"Are you going to be, ok? I know you want to be there for Mina, but hell Taye was like the brother you never had."

Xavier was right, a tear slid down her face and Xavier put his arms around her. He let her know he would be by her side the entire time.

Chapter 53
India

India was up early and ready for the day. She just knew everything would be perfect for Taye's home going. She got out what she would wear to the funeral. She picked out an all-white stretch satin suit by Albert Nipon, a pair of all white Swan Embellished Satin pump by Manolo Blahnik with a jeweled satin clutch bag. She picked out simple diamond earrings with a watch to match and her necklace that Taye got her.

This look is perfect, India thought. She knew Taye would love her look.

India's phone rang. She grabbed it and answered without checking to see who it was.

"Why the fuck haven't you answered any of my calls?" ZO screamed into the phone.

"ZO, what are you talking about? You only called me once yesterday and I told you I was going to be over Mina's house. I was there for over three hours."

"Yea, ok, you been acting real strange since you been back from Vegas. What you not down for your man anymore? What happened to the loyalty you were so willing to show me? Let me tell you like this, bitch, if you decide you want to go get a conscious, remember, your ass is just as guilty as I am."

"Fuck you, ZO. You can go eat a dick, you weak motherfucker! I'm tired of your shit!"

"What the fuck did you just say to me, bitch?" ZO couldn't believe she talked back to him like that. Did she not know what he was capable of?

"You heard me, nigga, and if you didn't I'll repeat it! Go eat a dick! I'm sure that's right up your ally or, better yet, up your ass, bitch nigga. Let me give you something to think about, I saw what you were doing a few days ago. Yea, you heard me correct. I know you don't want that shit to leak out, so miss me with the threats. Lose my fuckin' number."

India hung up the phone before he could say shit else. She was fed up and felt guilty enough without having his ass throwing shit in her face.

India felt better knowing that ZO no longer had the upper hand. If he wanted to play, then she was game.

"Indy, you dressed?"

"Yea, come on in!" India shouted.

"What's wrong with you? Why you sounding like that?" Rel wondered about the hoarseness in her voice.

"I'm okay, Rel, I just had a fucked up conversation with someone, but I'm good now."

"Indy, you can't let anyone fuck up today for you or any day, for that matter." India ran her bath water while listening to Rel.

"Shit, I see you got your wardrobe put together. That shit is nice, Indy."

"Thanks Rel, when you plan on getting ready? We have to head out at eleven okay?"

"I'll be ready."

India applied her makeup she had a natural look going on. She looked in the mirror as she looked over herself.

Taye if you're listening and I know that you are, please can you forgive me. I am so sorry. I never meant for you to get hurt. I had no idea what ZO was up to. How can I make it through today at your funeral knowing that I'm part of the reason why you're dead? India cried as she continued to talk to Taye. Give me a sign to let me know that you forgive me. I love you, Taye, and again, I am sorry.

India wiped the tears off her face, turned on the radio, and when she did, Marvin Sapp's *Never Would Have Made It* played. Taye shared with her that he loved that song. If it wasn't for God, he would have never made it because he had done so much wrong in his life and that no matter what, God forgives. "Thank you, Taye." India smiled as she headed down the steps.

"Indy you look like an angel in all that white."

"Thank you, Rel. You look handsome. White has always looks great on you."

Rel grabbed India's hand. "I'll be right here for you, sis."

Chapter 54
Mina

Mina finished getting dressed when Ty walked in and just stared at her.

"Do I look ok baby?" Mina asked

"You're breathtaking." Ty continued to admire her.

Mina looked angelic. She had on a white cotton piquet tunic dress by A. McQueen, a pair of leather ankle boots by Tibi with a white leather clutch. She also wore simple diamond studs.

"Thanks, Ty you look good as well."

"Baby, it's time to go. The limo is here."

Mina took a deep breath.

Lord, please, be with me today and give me the strength to make it through.

They arrived to Mina's parents' house. They looked very nice and relaxed. Michael entered the limo last. He looked very handsome in all white and Mina couldn't help but to stare. When they arrived at the funeral home, it was set up so beautifully. Everything in the room was white and it didn't even look like a funeral. It looked like something you saw in a magazine. It was definitely something that Taye would have loved. As soon as you walked in, there was a huge picture of Taye to greet you. On the right side of the room, there was a picture of Taye, Mina, and their parents. On the left side was a picture of him and India. The entire set up was breathtaking.

Mina spotted India and Rel. When India made her way up front, she smiled when she saw the picture.

"This is beautiful, Mina. I love the picture. Thank you."

Mina took India to meet her parents. As soon as Mrs. Smith saw India, she hugged her.

"You look beautiful, India. I can see why my son loved you. I just want you to know you're part of our family always. I know Taye is no longer with us, but you were a part of his life, therefore, you're apart of ours."

India was speechless, they had lost their loved one and they were showing her love like she had been around for years.

It was ten minutes to twelve and the funeral home was packed. Mr. and Mrs. Smith couldn't believe the turn out. Taye was truly loved by a lot of people. Asia sang *The Battle's Not Yours* by Yolanda Adams. She had everyone shouting because her voice was beautiful. Mina smiled as Michael got up and said goodbye to Taye. The funeral was just about over and the last song was about to be sung. It was Marvin Sapp's *He Saw the Best in Me*. It was church inside the funeral home as Taye's friend sang the song. Rel held on to India while she cried as the slideshow played.

At the end of the funeral, everyone formed a line, said goodbye to Taye, and give their condolences to the family. One by one, people walked up and hugged the family. Out of nowhere, a man in an all-black suit walked up. Heads turned as he approached Mina.

"Mina, I'm sorry to hear about Taye." Mina looked shocked by the man that was standing in front of her.

"ZO, I didn't know you got out, give me a hug, and thank you for paying your respect to my brother. That means a lot."

"Word got around while I was locked up that Taye was killed. That shit saddened me. I felt like we were once family. I wanted to pay my respect. I didn't know it was all-white affair. No disrespect intended."

"You're fine, thanks you for attending."

Ty thanked the pastor for all that he did. He had no idea that ZO was there. Everyone said their goodbyes as the funeral home cleared. Mina was the last one to exit. She had a private moment alone in the room surrounded with pictures of Taye.

She spoke to him.

"Rest in peace Taye, I'll love you always and forever."

Chapter 55
Coco

"The service was nice, Xavier."

"Yea, it was. You held it together well." He hugged her and out of nowhere, ZO walked up.

"Hello." Coco jumped as she recognized the voice. She turned to her right and her eyes grew wider as she stared at ZO.

"I got you jumpy like that. Can I get some love, Coco?"

Coco stepped back away from Xavier.

"Brandon, when did you get out?" Coco gave him a hug, he held her tight in his arms.

"Damn, ma you calling me by my government now?"

Xavier laughed. He thought Coco was trying to be funny. She knew he didn't like to be called by his first name, everyone called him ZO.

"I got out today. I heard what happen to Taye, so here I am. Sorry, I wanted to surprise you and Brandy. Damn, you look good."

Xavier stood off to the side, not believing that ZO was out of prison and that he was at the funeral.

"I'm glad you're out, Brandon, oh my fault I mean, ZO."

"So, when can I see my daughter? I know she's over my sister's house. I want to be at the house when she comes home. Is that cool with you?"

"Yep, that sounds good," Coco said.

Xavier stood right there, the two men didn't exchange any words, they just stared the other down. ZO gave a look to Xavier that said, 'Yea, I'm out, nigga'

Coco knew they couldn't stand one another. Just as Coco was about to say something, Rel and India walked up. You would have thought India saw a ghost the way she stared at ZO.

"India, you look beautiful." Coco gave her a hug.

"Baby, you look gorgeous, you okay?" Rel gave Coco a hug and kiss. ZO stood there with a mean mug on his face. *Look at this bitch and her weak as brother*, he thought.

"Rel and India, I want you to meet Brandy's father, ZO."

ZO had a smirk on his face as he said to Rel, "What's up?" He extended his hand out to India. She looked him dead in the face and said hello with an attitude. Rel looked at India strange, but didn't say anything.

"Alright, ZO, I take it I'll see you a little later. I'm about to find Mina and see if there is anything she needs."

"Can I talk to you alone real quick, Coco?" ZO asked. They walked away from everyone else so they could talk.

"Damn, why the brush off? A nigga just got out of jail and you acting like you could give two fucks." Coco stared at ZO with confusion all over her face.

"What you talking about? How am I supposed to react? I haven't heard from you in the last few months, and then out of nowhere here you are."

"Okay, I hear what you saying, but damn, I missed you and I want to see our daughter. You can't go tell Mina goodbye so we can leave?"

"My closest friend lost her brother! No, I'm not leaving! I'm sorry, but had you let me know you were going to be here today, I could have worked something out. Being that you didn't, this is what you have to deal with. Shit isn't always on your time."

"Fuck you mean, Coco? What, you brand new because of Xavier and that nigga, Rel? What the fuck you been out here doing since I was locked down?" Coco was pissed because he crossed the line.

"Look, I'm not your woman anymore, so whatever the fuck I been doing is my business. I'm glad you back home, but you pissing me off. Call me later." Coco turned and walked away.

Chapter 56
Ty

The service was nice, Ty thought. He was headed outside when he saw a familiar face. He thought maybe his sight was fooling him.

"Mitch Wassup?" ZO said as he walked toward Ty.

"You tell me, nigga, when they let you out?"

"I got out today. Just thought I come pay my respect to Taye. You didn't think I would be out this soon, huh?" ZO smirked.

"As a matter of fact, I didn't." Ty smirked back.

"Guess you wouldn't know being that you never accepted any of my phone calls. Damn, and to think we were 'pose to be partners."

"Fuck you mean? What did you expect me to do? Shit, the way I seen it, nigga, I didn't owe you anything. We did business together, nothing more, nothing less. Don't come to me on some shit as if I left you for dead while you were doing your bid."

Ty was pissed and you could always tell when he was upset because his jaw locked up. Xavier and Rel looked from a distance and could tell the conversation was getting heated, so they walked over.

"Nigga, why is you here? I heard you say you came to pay your respect. You've done that, you need to step." ZO sized Ty up. He rubbed his hands together and laughed a little.

"Fuck you, make me leave."

Ty was about to get in ZO's ass, but Rel got in between them.

"Hold up! This is a funeral. This isn't the time or place for this shit." Rel stood between them to keep them apart.

"Fuck you, Rel. You don't know me, nigga. Don't say shit to me and back the fuck up." Rel chuckled a little.

"Yea, it's clear that you don't know me, but let me tell you like this, keep talking that shit and it's gon' be you laid up here in this funeral home."

Rel stood face to face with ZO, neither backed down. Rel wanted him to do something because he was going to show ZO he wasn't to be fucked with.

"Shit, what we got here? ZO, what you doing out? Give me some love. Y'all look like y'all was about to go at it. Not today. Don't disrespect Mina and her parents like that." They all looked at Twan, wondering where the fuck did he come from.

"You right, Twan." ZO gave him a dab.

"I'm out of here. Just know this shit ain't over I'm back and ain't shit none of you motherfuckers can do about it."

"Alright, come on, ZO." Twan and ZO walked off.

"Put my number in your phone and hit me up so we can talk about doing some business together." Twan said.

"I'm not fucking with Mitch on that level."

"This doesn't have shit to do with Ty. I'm doing my own shit, so get at me." He took Twan's number as Ty watched.

"That nigga Twan be on some bullshit." Rel looked at Ty in agreement.

"Yea, he is. Ty you need to watch that nigga, for real." Rel shook his head.

"How's the saying go, Rel? Keep your friends close, but your enemies closer. In this case, my enemy may damn well just be my friend. You can't trust anyone."

"Why was ZO here?" Twan asked as he walked up.

"What you mean? I'm just surprised as you were." Ty was pissed off.

"Look, I don't know shit about the hot headed nigga, but what I do know is he better stay the fuck away from me," Rel said.

"Shit, that's Coco's daughter's father. ZO ain't going anywhere." Twan laughed as he made that comment.

"What, you his co-signer?" Rel asked.

"Fuck you talking about, Rel? All I'm saying is the nigga gon' be around, so deal with it. He in love with Coco and he ain't gon' stop 'til he gets her back. You take this shit how you want. These two niggas here can tell you the exact same shit. ZO ain't going anywhere."

Ty and Xavier shook their heads.

"Rel, don't even worry about that shit. ZO is a lame ass nigga," Xavier said.

"Like I was saying, he ain't going anywhere. I'm out of here. Ty, tell Mina I said goodbye. I'll holler at you niggas later." Twan walked off laughing.

Ty headed back inside to get Mina and her parents so they could leave. He told Xavier and Rel not to mention what went down to Coco because he didn't want Mina finding out shit.

Chapter 57
ZO

ZO made his way back across town. He had an appointment at two thirty to take a look at a duplex on the Eastside. When he arrived, he walked in, the receptionist told him to have a seat, and that they would be with him soon. While he waited, all he thought about was how Coco acted toward him.

"Mr. Carter, would you like anything to drink while you wait?"

"No, thank you, sweetheart. I'm ok." The receptionist blushed.

ZO was a ladies' man and he had charm, believe it or not. He knew how to manipulate women into anything. That was his gift and he used it to his full advantage. The office door opened and out walked one of the prettiest women ZO seen in a while, besides Coco and India.

Damn, who is that? ZO thought.

"Miss Jones, we hope to hear from you soon."

"Please, call me, Ciara, and I will be in touch very soon."

"Excuse me, how are you doing? My name is Brandon." Ciara turned around and looked.

"Excuse me, are you talking to me?" Ciara said with a smile.

"Yes, I'm talking to you. Do you have a second to spare? I'm new in this area. I wanted to get your take on the duplex." ZO was running game. He knew that area, hell, he knew the entire city.

"My name is Ciara. I can't really tell you much because I'm not from around here, either. I just moved here from Cali. Sorry I can't be of any help to you, Brandon." Ciara turned and walk out the door.

"I'm sorry; I'm going to have to reschedule my appointment." ZO walked out the door to catch up with Ciara.

"Miss Jones," Ciara heard ZO say, so she turned around with a smile on her face.

"The name is Ciara, or did you forget that quickly?"

"No, I didn't forget anything. I'm trying to get to know you. Let me show you around town once you get settled in."

"I thought you weren't from here?"

"Naw, you misheard me, sweetheart, I said I was new to this area, just meaning this part of town. I just always stayed closer to the south and west area." Ciara smiled. She liked how he stepped to her. She most definitely wanted to get to know him.

"Hmmm, so you want to get to know me, you say? Well, I guess that sounds good. How about you give me your number and when I'm free, I'll call you."

"Come on now, Ciara, how about we both exchange numbers being that you're new in town. I'm sure you have a busy schedule getting things together, you may forget to call me and I don't want that to happen." ZO looked at her with his light brown eyes and licked his lips. Ciara smiled and they exchanged numbers.

Damn, she was fine and she's not from around here. Someone new, just what I need. Let me call Coco and see when she will be home.

ZO called Coco and she told him to be at the house in two hours. He had some time to kill, so he bought Brandy a necklace that read *Daddy's Girl*. He loved his daughter more than his own life. She was the one person who truly loved him no matter what. She had no ideal her father was a monster on the inside.

What the fuck Coco thinking, having these niggas around my daughter? Xavier and that new nigga, Rel, fuck them both. That motherfucker talking about I'm gon' be laying up there in that funeral home if I keep talking shit. That nigga don't know me at all. He will soon find out, ZO thought as he headed to Coco's.

Chapter 58
Asia

"The service was nice, Big R. I wish you were there with me. I needed you, but I managed to hold it together. Baby, when you gon' be back in town? You said you'd be here damn near two days ago. You got you a woman there in Atlanta?"

"There you go with that shit, Asia. You know a nigga taking care of business. Fuck I need with another woman when I got your sexy ass?"

Asia smiled. She missed him. He had been gone for a week and she desperately needed to see him because she was horny as hell.

"I'm sorry, baby it's just that I miss you so much. Plus, I'm about to explode. I need some of that good dick."

"I miss you, too, baby. I'll be back Tuesday morning."

Asia turned her face up as she looked at the phone. "Tuesday morning? Damn, it's Saturday! You mean to tell me I have to wait 'til then to get some dick?"

"Come on, Asia, you really got an attitude? Send me a video of you playing with it."

"I'm not trying to make no video. That shit ain't about to help me."

"You heard what I said, play with that pussy and send me a video of you doing it. Matter of fact, Face Time me. Show me exactly how much you missing your man."

Asia hung up the phone and did like he asked her to do. She Face timed him. Asia didn't waste any time getting started. She had on a pretty hot pink bra and panties set from Victoria's secret . She set the phone up on her own personal stand and laid back on her king sized mattress with her black silk sheets. Asia slid her panties down and undone her bra, exposing her pretty breasts.

She stimulated her clit with the bullet and right off top she came. She then slid her finger in her pussy, she suck her secretions off her finger. Big R loved it as he stroked his dick. Asia was doing her thing. She knew what her man liked and she aimed to please him any way necessary. Asia went inside her toy box and pulled out a ten inch black dildo that she called Black Dingo.

Her legs were cocked wide open and with one hand, she plunged the dildo inside her pussy. With the other hand, she played with her clit. The sight of it was beautiful. Big R stroked his dick faster and faster as he heard moans escape Asia's lips. Just as he was about to cum, Asia did what she did best making her pussy squirt. The shit looked like a sprinkler going off. He had nut dripping from his hand as he continued to jack his dick as he watched her.

"Damn, I can't wait to get home and get in my pussy. You know what the fuck you doing. You know after seeing that, I'll be there on Monday, hell, it may even be tomorrow."

They laughed, but he was serious. He was gone off Asia and everyone knew it.

"Alright, baby. I hope you enjoyed your preshow. Once you get home, I'll put on a show you will never forget."

Asia was ready to get him off the phone because she was about to get her some real dick. She meant what she said when she said preshow because she was about to meet up with Twan and get what she longed for, a big dick.

"Ok, baby. I'm about to take shower so I can meet up with Coco." *Why the fuck did I just say Coco, hell ,all he got to do is ask Rel. Too late to change it up now. I'll deal with that when it comes up.*

"Call me tomorrow, Asia. I love you, babe."

"I love you, too." Asia hung up the phone, hopped in the shower, and smiled as she thought about how much she cared about Big R.

I love him, but not like that. He's just someone I can kick it with. Plus, he isn't giving me enough time. I mean, between him kicking it with Rel and in and out of town. That's the reason I still fuck Twan from time to time. But, I'm about to leave his ass alone as well. He on some other shit, the streets got him tripping. I mean, he don't even have to be in these streets like that, he chooses to. Thinking that's what bitches like, he ain't even trying to be low key about his shit, just out there being careless. That's why he must go after tonight. Hell, really, I don't even want to meet up with him at all. As a matter of fact, I'm gon' shoot him a text letting him know I can't do shit tonight. I don't want this shit to back fire on me cause if Big R had some bitch on the side, I would be pissed, so I'm just gon' chill out. I may just stop by Coco's house for real because I can't believe ZO is back in town. Some shit is sure to pop off. I wonder what went down with him and Ty. Fuck, I got to call Twan because he's worse than a bitch. He will tell me all I need to know about what happened outside the funeral home.

Asia was in deep thought as she dialed the number she told him that she was exhausted from the funeral. When she said that, he ran it. He told her all about ZO, Ty, and Rel. He told her that the situation was only going to get worse. After Twan gave up the 411, Asia let him go and called her girlfriend named Dee.

She told her to meet her at the shop because it was Dee's birthday and since she had been busy all week, she promised her she would definitely do her hair later.

Besides, Dee knew the 411 on what happened in the city. If anyone knew anything, it would be her.

Wow, this shit with ZO being back in town is going to be something else. Yea, I wonder what Coco's going to do now that the big bad wolf is out.

Chapter 59
Coco

Coco was headed home after picking up Brandy. She was nervous and decided not to tell Brandy anything. She wanted to see the expression on her face when ZO came in.

"Mommy, was Uncle Taye's funeral sad?" Brandy was seated in the back seat looking at her mother, waiting for her to respond. Coco continued to drive. She didn't know where that question came from.

"The funeral was beautiful. But, there were people that were sad."

"Were you sad, mommy?"

"At first I was sad, but now I am happy because I know Taye is in heaven with God, your Granny, and Grandpa." Her eyes watered as she thought of both her parents being deceased. It had been almost three years since they were in a terrible car accident.

"Mommy, did I make you cry?"

"No, baby, I'm crying because I miss your grandparents."

"I miss them, too. I cry sometimes because I don't have any grandparents. Daddy's parents are in heaven and daddy is gone. I miss him, mommy. Why hasn't he called me in so long?"

"Baby, I'm not sure why daddy hasn't been calling, but I'm sure he is ok."

"Ok, mommy, I love you."

"I love you, too, Brandy." Coco pulled into her driveway and she saw a blue Charger parked across the street.

"Damn, that looks like India's car," Coco said underneath her breath.

When Coco and Brandy walked through the door, there stood ZO with the living room filled with clothes, toys, and shoes. Any and everything you could imagine a little girl would want, he bought. Brandy's eyes lit up as she cried. ZO picked her up, hugged her, and kissed all over her. That day was the second time Coco ever seen ZO cry.

The first time was the birth of Brandy. She never had seen him shed a single tear, even when his parents died. Of all the things Coco was certain of, it was the love ZO had for his daughter. Brandy was his life.

"Mommy, come and give daddy a hug." ZO smiled. He knew Brandy put her on the spot.

"Yea, Coco, come give daddy a hug." ZO smiled from ear to ear. That was just what he wanted, his family back. Coco rolled her eyes at him. *Nigga is making me sick*, she thought as she walked over and hugged him.

"Yay, we're one big, happy family again, right, daddy?"

"No, Brandy, remember, mommy and daddy aren't together anymore. We are friends," Coco said to her daughter.

Brandy looked disappointed.

"Damn, Coco it's like that? You just done gave up on us completely?" ZO was upset and crushed.

"Brandy, sweetheart, go look at the things daddy got you while your mother and I talk."

"Okay, daddy, but promise me you're not going to leave?"

"Daddy isn't going anywhere. I'll be in there shortly."

"Look, ZO, I ain't for the dumb shit. You just got out and you already trying to start shit."

"You are so fucking selfish. I just got out and you can't even act like you're happy to see me. You and Brandy are all I thought about the entire time. I told you I wanted us to be a family again."

"Is that what the fuck we were, a family?" Coco laughed and that pissed ZO off.

"Is something funny?"

"Yep, you're funny! Your ass has the nerve to stand in my face and call me selfish when all you did the entire time we were together was cheat. So, as far as us being a family, that's a negative! I did what I had to do, which was pretend to be all happy and shit for the sake of our child. But, now I no longer have to do that. She understands were not together, so don't start putting shit in her head."

"Get the fuck outta here with that shit. You too busy worried about your own happiness. Worry about our daughter's. Running around here fucking that nigga Xavier and Rel, both those niggas can suck my dick."

"You can get the fuck out of my house. I don't have to deal with this shit at all. I'll pack Brandy an overnight bag and she can stay with you. Do something with her instead of worrying about me."

"You don't have to pack her shit. I'll get her whatever she needs. I'll take her to school on Monday. Brandy, come on, you going home with daddy. How does that sound?" When Brandy ran back into the family room, she was so happy that she was going to be with her daddy. ZO's entire demeanor changed when she entered the room. He was back to being Mr. Nice Guy. That shit frustrated Coco, she just rolled her eyes.

"Daddy, I love you, let's go." Brandy hugged Coco goodbye. ZO stared at her as he shook his head and walked out the door.

I can't believe him! He truly has issues. I need a drink after dealing with that nigga. I'm going to call India and see if she wants to meet up. Coco called India, and India told her to come over and to bring a bottle of Hennessey. On the way out the door, Coco got a text from ZO.

This shit ain't over, understand you gon' always be my woman. Coco deleted the message as soon as she read it. She knew that he was gon' make her life a living hell.

Chapter 60
Rel

Rel was headed home after dropping off India. He thought about the conversation they had. He asked her what that look was about when she was introduced to ZO. He wanted to know if she knew him. When he asked her she got defensive, and he couldn't understand why.

He pulled into his driveway. Whose car is that? He didn't have many people just show up at his crib. He grabbed his nine from underneath his front seat. He never took any chances, he wasn't about to get caught slipping. He got to the front door to unlock it and as soon as he did, he heard Carman's voice shouting that daddy's home. Rel quickly tucked the gun away.

"Daddy," Carman screamed as she ran into his arms. Ciara came from around the corner with a smile on her face. Rel gave her a look as to say, 'what the fuck you doing in my crib?'

"Hey, baby girl, you surprised, daddy." He looked at Ciara, who stood there with her arms crossed and a smirk on her face.

"I saw that you weren't here, so I let myself in with the key I have."

"Why you ain't call me and let me know you were coming, C?" Rel was sick of Ciara's bullshit and the fact that she just came into his crib without any notice pissed him off.

"I told you last time I saw you that I was moving down here. What you thought I was bullshitting? I'm not here trying to cause any trouble. I just want Carman to be closer to you. Plus, I need a change of scenery."

"What you mean you need a change of scenery? If that's the case, take a vacation. How you just gon' up and move? What the fuck are you thinking? That's just it, you never think, and you do dumb shit on an impulse. Fuck everyone else, you gon' do what the hell you want to do. Where you plan on staying? Carman can stay here with me, but you can't."

"So, you just gon' say fuck me huh Rel?" Ciara was hurt because she didn't expect him to react the way he did.

"What is it that I've done to you Rel? You really don't give two fucks about me do you?"

"Don't ask me to answer a question you really don't want to know the answer to."

Ciara didn't say anything else. She grabbed her purse, keys, and kissed Carman goodbye. She walked toward the door when Rel told her to leave the key. She stood there with a blank stare on her face. She couldn't believe he wanted his key back. She took the key off her key ring with tears in her eyes, sat it on the mantle, and walked out the door with her head hung low.

"So, Carman, what do you want to eat for dinner and don't say McDonalds." Rel didn't seem to give a damn about Ciara. He acted as if he hadn't made her feel like shit once again.

"Daddy, how did you know I was going to say that?"

Rel tickled his daughter as he picked her up and gave her a big kiss. He was happy she was there. She was his world. He enjoyed his time with Carman they went to Gattiland.

After they spent hours there, they finally made it home. He gave her a bath and read her a book before she headed off to bed. He sat there watching her sleep. She looked so much like Ciara. He wanted nothing more than to have his daughter close. He just hoped that Ciara wasn't there to start no shit.

Chapter 61
India

I'm glad I'm home. The phone call from Coco was just in time. Rel was on his interrogation shit.

India unlocked her front door and when she walked in, her shit was trashed. The furniture had been tossed over and glass was shattered everywhere. She couldn't believe what she walked into. She didn't have to guess who done it, she knew it was ZO.

When India made her way to her bedroom, she thought she would pass the fuck out. Her room was destroyed. All of her clothes, jewelry, and everything ruined. She walked into her bathroom connected to her bedroom. When she walked inside, there was writing all over the walls that read: *Bitch, slut, whore, eat a dick, and all sorts of shit.*

ZO is a bitch ass. What nigga you know write all over the fucken' walls? India was annoyed and she was sick of his shit. She went back in the bedroom and stood in the middle of the room in disbelief. She glanced at the bed and noticed that there was a dead rat lying on her pillow with a note.

He's has lost his mind. Lord, I need to get this nigga out of my life.

India grabbed the note and read it. *You can be a rat if you like. I will dead your ass just like I did your man. Bitch, yea, I found your card and pictures of you and that dead nigga. You ain't shit.*

India tore the note to pieces. She ran to her dresser and saw her card and pictures burned up. She went to pick it up, but the shit was wet. ZO had pissed on the pictures after he lit them on fire. India was devastated. She walked through the rest of the condo and saw everything was ruined, nothing could be saved, nothing.

I can't call Rel, he will be pissed and ask a thousand questions. What the fuck? I knew I should have changed my locks.

India's thoughts were interrupted when she heard someone knock on her door. Shit, Coco's ass. India went to the door to let her in.

"What took you so long to answer the door?" Coco said as she stepped in.

"Bitch, what the fuck happened in here? Were you robbed?" India shook her head. "India, you okay? Say something, please. I'm about to call Rel."

"No, Coco, please, do not mention this shit to Rel or anyone else for that matter." Coco looked puzzled.

"Look, India, what is going on? Do you know who did this?"

India walked back to her bedroom and Coco followed. She was in disbelief walking through India's place. When she reached India's bedroom, she lost it.

"Who in the fuck would do some shit like this? Who did you piss off? Better yet, what type of niggas do you fuck with?"

Your fucked up ex man is who did this shit, India thought.

"I think I know who it is, Coco, but I'm not for sure, so I'm going to move."

"Yea, that would be the best thing to do. I mean, damn, whoever did this shit was not playing."

She knew that India wasn't telling her everything, but she didn't want to upset her any more than she already was. She observed India's bedroom and saw the dead rat.

"What the hell is that? Is that a fucken rat, bitch? India, you need to call the police and report this shit!"

"No, Coco, I have got to get out of here. Please, can I stay with you for the night?"

"Of course, you can stay with me for however long you need. Just leave this shit. Have you checked to see if it's anything in here that you can keep?"

India looked at Coco and shook her head. She was tired, and all she wanted to do was get the hell away from that house and even farther away from ZO.

Chapter 62
ZO

"Wake up, daddy!" Brandy said as she jumped up and down on the bed where ZO slept.

"Brandy, why you up so early? You're not gon' let daddy sleep in for at least thirty more minutes?"

"No, daddy, you said we were getting up early to go to breakfast before my hair appointment. Please, get up, daddy."

ZO was tired as hell, but he could never tell Brandy no, so he got up and they went to take showers and got dressed. He looked handsome that morning, wearing Polo from head to toe.

"Daddy, you look nice."

"Princess, you look beautiful, as always."

"I know I do, daddy. Can we go now?" ZO laughed to himself. *She gets that honest from me*, he thought.

They headed out of the door. Brandy had an eleven a.m. hair appointment and it was eight. They arrived at Bob Evans and were seated. While they were waiting on their food, ZO's phone rang he answered it with a smile on his face.

"Good morning, sexy," he said when he picked up the phone.

"I'm good, Ciara, just having breakfast with my daughter. If you're not busy later on, we should get together and catch a movie or just go out to eat. How does that sound? Aright then, I'll see you later this evening."

He had been seeing Ciara and was feeling her a little bit. They still hadn't fucked yet, which was cool with him. He was getting pussy from other women, so he wasn't sweating it. Ciara was different, she was sexy as fuck and knew her place. She never questioned shit he said or did, she just let him take the lead and that was what he liked.

"Daddy, do you have a girlfriend?" Brandy was curious of who her father was on the phone with.

"Princess no, daddy just has a friend."

"Is that who you were talking to? I thought you said you would always love mommy no matter what?"

ZO stared at Brandy. He didn't know how to tell his only daughter that although he loved her mother to death, they would never be a couple ever again. Coco made that clear and since the funeral, she didn't have much to say to him. She allowed him to get their daughter and that was about it. He wasn't trying to hear it or accept it at first, but he really had no choice because every time he got Brandy that nigga Rel was there, which pissed him off.

"Daddy, did you hear me?"

"Yes, I heard you. I will always love your mommy, but mommy has Rel, so we can no longer be together. Do you understand that, Brandy?"

"Yes, daddy, I do. I just wish we could all be together again." He didn't say anything else. He knew his daughter was hurt and there was nothing he could do to change it.

They finished eating and headed to the hair salon. Brandy said goodbye as he kissed her before she walked into the salon. He had plans to meet up with Twan that afternoon. Shit was working out in his favor. He was getting paid and that was all that mattered. He still wasn't content and he wanted to know who Twan's connect was, but like Ty, he kept that shit on the low.

Let me hit this nigga and make sure he knows that I'm coming to the spot at noon. Twan be on some lazy shit. All that nigga keep on his mind is pussy. Yea, he likes to make his money, but that man will drop whatever for some pussy. Twan don't fuck with that nigga Ty, at all. As a matter of fact, Ty been kind of off the scene for real, but I'm still gon' handle him when he least expects it.

Just as ZO was about to make a call to Twan, he got a text from Brandy saying that she left her bag in his car. He wasn't too far away from the shop, so he busted a U turn and made it to the shop within ten minutes.

He walked inside the shop and every head turned in the direction of the tall, handsome man standing before them.

"Asia, where's my baby?"

"Damn, hello to you, too. She's in the back getting her hair shampooed. You can just leave her bag. I'll make sure she doesn't forget it."

"Naw, I want to see her. You know she will be mad knowing I came in here and didn't let her know. Hello ladies." Every woman in there smiled and said hello. ZO laughed, *these whores are thirsty*, he thought. Brandy ran from the back with a plastic bag on her head and hugged him tight.

"Daddy, thanks for bringing my bag to me. I love you." Everyone in the salon watched as ZO kissed Brandy on the cheek.

"Daddy loves you, too. I'll see you tomorrow." As he walked out the door, he saw India pull into the parking lot. *Look at this bitch right here. She's a nothing ass whore.*

ZO got in his car. He didn't have time to fuck with her. He needed to be at Twan's to conduct business.

Chapter 63
Twan

Fuck, this shit can't be happening right now. Twan got off the phone with Nate, who let him know that his connect just got hit by the FEDs.

Twan was fucked. He knew no dope meant no money would be made. He had no other connects and he hadn't spoken to Ty since the funeral. He knew that he had to get in contact with him. At that moment, Twan thought about how shit went down with them. He knew it was fucked up of him to be doing business with ZO, but that was just what it was, business.

Twan made the decision to call Ty, so he dialed his number and got the voicemail. He was desperate, so he jumped in his car and decided to go see him. He drove to Ty's nightclub that was located on Broadway. He didn't see Ty's truck, so he rode to his next spot, which was on Main Street, and that was where he saw Ty's truck parked. He walked in the spot calm and cool.

"Russ, what it do, nigga?" Twan said to the bouncer at the club. The bouncer looked at Twan as to say, 'Why the fuck is you here?'

"Shit, nigga, Wassup, Twan? Where the fuck you been?"

"Shit, maintaining and doing me. So where's your boss?" Russ gave a shitty grin.

"You know where he's at. I'll let him know you're here."

"Damn, it's like that? I'm a stranger now?"

The bouncer looked Twan dead in his eyes. "Yea, you are. You haven't been around nor have you been fucking with Ty. So again, I'll let him know you're here.

"He said he'll be out in a minute. Shit, get you a drink, Twan, relax, nigga."

Twan went to the bar and had the bartender make him a double shot of Henny. His phone rang and it was ZO. He forgot that he was coming through to meet him.

"When you coming through ZO?"

"Shit, nigga, thought I told you I was coming through at twelve."

"I'm out handling something. We need to meet up soon. Some shit went down with my supplier in Detroit. Shit's looking bad, but I'm trying to make some moves right now, so I'll hit you in a few."

Twan hung up and downed his shot, he was about to signal for the bartender to make him another drink when he heard Ty's voice.

"Twan, what brings you to see me this afternoon?" Ty looked like the boss that he was. "What you need?"

"What you mean what I need?"

"Shit, what other reason would you be here for? Let me guess, I'm assuming you here to fuck with me because your supplier got them FEDs on his ass. Yeah, nigga, news travels fast."

Twan stood there speechless and wondered how in the hell Ty found that out or, better yet, who in the fuck was his source.

"I can't believe you even had the balls to come here, but since you here, shit, holler at me." Ty stood there with a smile on his face. He knew why Twan was there, shit, he knew Twan had no supplier now that his people got busted.

Why in the fuck did I come here? This nigga still think he run shit, Twan thought.

"Ty, I'm here because I need you to put me on, shit, we had our differences and shit, but this is business."

"Correction, this is personal for me, fuck you! I ain't fucking with you, Twan, and nigga, you need money. Not me. I'm good and gon' continue to be good. So, only thing you can do right now is get the fuck up out of my club." Ty stood there, jaws locked. All of the brotherly love he had for Twan was gone. Twan was a bitch in his eyes. Greed took over and he could never fuck with him on any level.

"Fuck that, Ty. I was loyal to you, nigga, and now you gon' play me like this?"

"Twan, what you know about being loyal? So, you gon' stand here in my face and tell me you been a loyal?"

"If you ain't got shit to say, you need to step. Loyalty given will be loyalty returned, remember that the next time you decide you want to fuck over a real nigga."

Ty turned and walked away. Twan left out the club heated. "Fuck Ty!" Twan kept saying as he drove to his spot to meet ZO.

Chapter 64
India

"Congratulations! You are pregnant. You are three months along," the doctor said. India sat there with tears in her eyes. *I can't believe this*, she thought. For the last month she felt sick. Every morning like clockwork, she would throw up. She thought nothing of it because she still had her period. Once she started having a lot of tenderness in her breasts and heartburn she finally decided to make a doctor's appointment.

India was excited and sad all at the same time. She got dressed and the doctor gave her some prescriptions to get filled. She got into her car, sat there, and cried. She talked to Taye and told him that she was having his child and that she wished that he was still alive to see their first child born. India felt better after that. She thought about Mina and her parents. They would love to know that Taye would have a child.

I want Rel to be the first person I tell, India said to herself. India called Rel and got no answer. As soon as she was about to call him again, her phone rang and to her surprise, it was Rel calling back.

"Hey, Rel, where are you at?"

"I'm at home, Indy, you ok?"

"Yes, I am. I'm on my way over there. Is that ok? I have some good news."

"Yea, come on over and use your key because I may be in the shower."

"Ok, I'll see you shortly."

India made her way across town to Rel's. Once she got there, she let herself in.

"Rel, I'm here!" she yelled throughout the house.

"Damn, Indy, I told you I was gon' be taking a shower. Your ass hollering, you wake up Carman and you gone take her home with you for the night." Rel came down the hallway with some basketball shorts on and a wife beater.

"I'm sorry, I didn't know my niece was here, and if she wakes up, I have no problem taking her home with me." Rel followed India into the TV room.

"Give me a hug. You look beautiful as always. So what you have to tell me?" India stood back and smiled.

"You're going to be an uncle." Rel smiled and hugged his sister again.

"Congratulations, Indy."

"Thank you. I wanted you to be the first person I told." He held on to India. He was happy for his sister.

"So, how far along are you?"

"I'm three months. I'm so happy, although, Taye is no longer here, he will have a child that will carry out his name. At first I was sad, but I know this baby is a blessing not only to me, but to his family as well."

"I'm happy for you, sis, and just know I'm here for you always. When you going to tell Mina and her family?"

"I plan on telling them soon. I have to call Mina and set up a time I can tell them all together."

"Shit, when you gon' tell your own parents?"

"You mean when am going to tell our parents? I guess when they get back in town."

"Shit, you got somewhere you need to be? I need a favor can you watch Carman for me, please? I need to go take care of a few things."

"Of course I will watch her. I'll just stay. I don't want to wake her up."

"Thanks. I just ordered some Chinese if you want some. I'm gon' get dressed and then I am leaving out. I'll be gone no more than two hours."

"Damn, Rel, just go. I ain't got shit else to do. Plus, you my brother and there is nothing I wouldn't do for you."

Rel kissed India on the cheek and headed upstairs to get dressed. She fixed a plate of the Chinese food. She loved sweet n sour chicken. Damn, I forgot to call Mina. Let me call her before I forget again. India called Mina, but got her voicemail. She didn't bother to leave a message. She hung up and sent her a text saying that she wanted to get together as soon as she could. She couldn't wait to tell Mina and her parents. India's phone went off and it was Mina saying that they could meet sometime that week. India agreed and sat back and thought that things were starting to fall into place for her. She had a new house and was pregnant. Life, indeed, was turning around in her favor.

Chapter 65
Rel

I wonder what the fuck is going on with that nigga, Twan. Ty called me saying we need to talk and he mentioned that nigga. I told Ty he couldn't trust him.

Rel pulled up to Big R's house and blew his horn. He came out the house and hopped in the car with Rel.

"Wassup Rel?"

"Shit, that's what I'm trying to figure out. Ty called me talking about some shit about Twan. These niggas here don't know the meaning of loyalty. Niggas will double cross you in a minute. Yea, when I saw ZO and Twan together, that shit surprised me."

Big R nodded his head in agreement. "Man, on a brighter note, I'm about to become an uncle. India told me today she's three months pregnant by Taye."

Big R sat there with a blank expression on his face.

"Damn, no congrats? What's wrong with you?"

"Congrats man my fault. How is India doing?"

"She's happy, man. You know Indy, she loves kids and to be able to have the man's child that she loved is a blessing to her."

"Tell India I said congratulations for me." Big R was in a foul mood after that but he played it off.

Rel drove to Mina's club, which was where Ty was for the night. When they walked in, the spot was crowed.

"Rel, what's up?" Ty asked. "Big R, good seeing you, partner."

They made their way back upstairs into a private VIP area.

"What are y'all drinking on tonight?" The waitress stood there looking sexy as hell as she took their orders.

"Give me a Remy on the rocks," Ty said.

"Give me the same with a bottle of Corona with lime," Big R said.

"And, for you, handsome, what would you like?" The waitress licked her lips as she looked Rel up and down. He looked at the waitress and smiled.

"Give me a double shot of Patron."

The waitress brought the drinks back as she handed Rel his glass, she slid him her number and winked at him.

"My name is Channel. Give me a call." Ty looked at Rel.

"Man, she's dangerous. You better watch out for that one. I heard she got that killer. You know what that means niggas will kill to get a shot of that pussy."

They laughed as Rel stuck the card in his pocket.

"So, Ty, what do you want to holler at us about?" Rel wanted to get down to business.

"Twan stopped by, unannounced of course, wanting me to put him on." Rel looked at Ty with a confused look.

"Yea, same look you giving me is what I gave him. His connect got popped by the FEDs and now the nigga need some work."

"Fuck Twan, man, I hope you put his grimy ass out your spot, Ty."

"Big R, who you think I am? Twan talking about that loyalty shit to me. Man, his ass can't spell loyalty. Just keep your ears open to the streets. I don't trust him or ZO. Twan's ass is up to no good. I got a bad feeling about this shit. I got a bad vibe period. Some shit ain't sitting right with me." Ty was dead serious as he talked to Rel and Big R.

"Yeah, I plan on laying low and letting Big R handle shit. I don't need any motherfucker making my shit hot. Ty, you need to handle that nigga, Twan, before I do."

Rel was pissed. He had been Ty's connect all that time and no one knew, and that was how he wanted to keep it. He didn't need all the extra attention and bullshit. Rel was slick with his shit and he had the perfect cover up. They discussed business and agreed to keep their ears to the streets.

Chapter 66
Mina

It was seven a.m. and Mina was jogging. She had fallen off of her work out. She was back to her regular routine and she was focused on business and, most importantly, Ty.

I wonder what India has to tell me. I can't wait to see her. It's been too damn long. Honestly, I haven't seen anyone. Coco calls me, but we always miss one another and as far as Asia, she's been kind of distant since the funeral, which is cool. She's been funny since New Year's. I love her to death, but she is on some shady ass shit. Mina had so many thoughts on her mind as she jogged back to her house.

Mina was so busy running she wasn't aware of her surroundings. From the time she started running someone had been following her, but not close enough for her to notice. Once she made it to the house, the man hopped into a car and drove off.

"Ty, I'm back," Mina hollered as she went into the kitchen to get a cold bottle of water. Ty walked into the kitchen with just some sweat pants on.

My baby is looking good this morning. I love that man. Mina had a smile on her face.

"What you smiling about Mina?" Ty kissed her and pinned her back on the breakfast bar, and his dick was rock hard. He wanted some loving.

"You want some of this pussy for breakfast?" Ty didn't say shit. He pulled down Mina's yoga pants and panties, and lifted her ass up on the counter.

He sucked on her neck, which she loved. As he did that, he moved down her stomach, placing kisses all over her body. He pulled her ass all the way to the end of the counter to devour her pussy. He sucked on her clit as he played with her pussy. His fingers were deep inside her. Mina enjoyed every tongue flicker. Her moaning let Ty know that he was pleasing her and not to stop. That turned Ty on. He ate her pussy as if the shit was his meal for that morning.

He finally came up for air. Ty picked her up and he slid his dick in her warm pussy.

"Damn, baby, your pussy got a grip on this dick, keep on pulling me in."

Mina rode his dick as he walked around the kitchen with her bouncing up and down. He was built and had no problem carrying her around the entire house if that was what she wanted. They made their way into the family room where he sat her ass on the edge of the pool table and continued to fuck her long and hard then, nice and slow. The shit was fire and she loved it.

"Tell me how you want daddy to give it to you."

Mina looked at Ty and he knew exactly how she wanted it. Mina assumed the position. She was bent over with her ass in the air. No words needed to be said. He went deep inside of her and she pulled him in with her pussy muscles.

"Open up that pussy, baby. Let me feel that pussy cum on my dick again." Just as he said that, she came. The feel of the warm wetness on his dick made him cum as well.

"You ready for round two, Mina? I'll just give you a sample. How does that sound?"

"Sounds like you can't get enough!" She said teasingly.

"You damn right I can't get enough. Now, get your sexy ass back to the bedroom so I can blow your mind." Ty smacked her ass and they made their way to the bedroom for round two.

Chapter 67
Coco

Coco was up and ready to start her day. She had new inventory in and she knew that her day would be a busy one. That evening, she had a flight out to see Toni in Detroit. She had a fashion show and Coco would be there to support her friend. She needed a break and some time away from home. ZO was constantly on some bullshit and Rel was beginning to act brand new again.

Rel had been distant for a few weeks and Coco wondered what was going on being that they were on a good page. Honestly, Coco didn't care, she wasn't about to chase after Rel. At one point she thought they could have something, but after how he did her the last time, she really couldn't get over that.

They would always be friends, but she felt like if something was meant to be, it would be. She didn't have to force it shit would just happen. So far, nothing happened between them. They were better off as friends in her eyes. They still hadn't had sex and that was Coco's first sign she wasn't into him like that anymore. They had great chemistry, but that wasn't enough.

Coco's phone rang as she stepped out the shower. *Fuck, who is calling this early?* She looked down at the incoming call and it was ZO.

What the hell does he want so early in the morning?

"Hello!" She had an attitude. She wasn't in the mood for him that morning. She had too much that needed to be done.

"What is it, ZO? I'm in a hurry this morning!" She had an appointment for a manicure and pedicure. She still wasn't dressed and didn't have time to talk.

"I was just checking to see when you were leaving. You are going to see your daughter before you leave to go out of town, right?"

"Bye, ZO." Coco hung up.

He's got some nerve calling me, questioning if I'm going to see Brandy before I leave. He better kiss my ass. She got dressed and sat her bags at the door. She was already packed and just wanted to get it all together so once it was time to leave, she could just grab her things and go.

Coco drove to the nail shop and decided to call Asia. She hadn't really talked to her. She still let Asia do her hair, but they hadn't kicked it since Vegas. Coco dialed the number only to get Asia's voicemail. She left a message letting her know that she was on her way to the nail shop and she wanted to see if she could join her. Asia doesn't ever pick up her phone. I need to talk to her. Plus, I heard her and Keisha have gotten real close. That's messed up because Asia was just fucking her husband, now she turns around and befriends the wife. That bitch knows she ain't right.

Asia thought she was slick, and hiding the fact that she and Twan were messing around. Hell, they made the shit so obvious, always flirting and sneaking off, thinking no one would notice.

Coco made it to the nail salon and to her surprise, when she pulled up Asia pulled up as well. Coco got out the car and waited for Asia to get out. They hugged one another and stepped inside. They relaxed while they got a pedicure.

"So, Asia, how you been? I hear you and Keisha are real cool now, what's up with that?"

"What you mean what's up with that? Shit, she's cool. You bitches got brand-new, so I've been doing me."

"Who's brand-new? Kill the attitude I just asked you a question."

"And, again, Coco, I told you she's cool and we have fun together."

"Asia, weren't you just having fun with her husband?"

Asia gave Coco a look that said 'fuck you bitch', but Coco didn't care. She wanted to hear what Asia had to say.

"What is that suppose to mean?"

"Come on now, Asia, that's that bullshit. I know you not gon' deny the shit to me about you and Twan. I've been on to you two. What you thought your shit was on the low. It never was." Asia sat there not saying shit.

"Look, I really don't feel like talking about that shit and I could care less what you think about me."

"Hold up, I just think it's fucked up that you were just fucking Twan, now you friends with his wife, but whatever, you do you, China Doll."

The rest of the time Asia really didn't say much. Coco knew she had pissed her off. They said goodbye and Coco headed to the boutique. She was parking her truck when she saw the most handsome man she had seen in a while. *Damn, who is that fine ass man?* Coco got her purse, got out the truck, and walked toward the boutique.

"Excuse me," Coco heard.

"Excuse me, sweetheart," Coco turned around.

Damn, Coco thought as she looked into the eyes of the man she saw when she pulled up.

"Yes, is there something I can help you with?"

"Do you happen to know what time this boutique opens? The sign says ten a.m., but as we see its ten thirty and still not open." Damn, *he is fine as wine.*

"The boutique is about to open up now. I'm the owner and my name is Cori Matthews, but everyone calls me Coco. I'm sorry. I was running behind this morning." Coco extended her hand out to shake his hand. "Nice meeting you. I'm Kahlee but I go by King."

"So, Kahlee sorry I mean King, is there anything particular that you are looking for?"

Ummm, Kahlee, his name rolls off my tongue just perfect. Yea, he could get it, and the fact that he's about six foot is a plus. I can't help but stare his chocolate skin covered with tattoos is sexy. Where did he come from looking like an action figure, he must stay in the gym... He's the shit, look at his face clear and smooth goatee perfect and his hair is nice and wavy. I wonder if he's mixed with something with those hypnotizing small chinky eyes and long eye lashes and dark eye brows that lay down smoothly. He's perfect his entire swagger is a complete turn on. Plus the grill in his mouth topped it off I love me a thug, again he could indeed get it, Coco thought as she giggled a little.

He was like a cool breeze that blew in. Coco admired his appearance. She paid attention to every detail about the man. She noticed his manicured fingers and also the fact that he wasn't wearing a ring, so he wasn't married. But, she was positive he had a woman, a man that fine had to.

"I'm looking to get my woman something for her birthday. I heard about your spot, so I decided to come check it out."

"Well, you came to the right boutique. Look around and let me know if there is anything I can assist you with." *Shit, I knew his fine ass would have a woman, damn.*

"Excuse me." Coco turned around to see what it was that King needed.

"Yes, how can I help you?" King stood there smiling.

She is beautiful, Damn, if I was single, he thought.

"If I needed this in another size, could you order it and if so, how long would it take?"

"Let me see what you got here." Coco looked at the outfit. "Okay, you got great taste, I see."

"Yea, I stay fly, therefore, my woman has to stay that way as well."

"I totally agree with you, King, so what size did you need?"

"I need the shirt in an extra-large. Really a one X if it comes in that size."

"Let me check for you. I'm sure that won't be a problem," Coco looked in the database for the item.

"Yes I can get that for you, when do you need it by?"

"Tomorrow, if that's possible." King stood with his hands behind his back.

"Okay, that is no problem. It will be here for you to pick up by noon. I like the outfit, but you going to need shoes and accessories. Let me get you together real quick." Coco did her thing, completing the outfit.

"Thanks, Coco, my baby is going to love this."

"You're welcome. Just make sure you come back and shop and be here tomorrow at noon, no later than five p.m., please. The boutique is closing early. I'm headed out of town tonight, so my assistant will get you together."

"That's cool, so where you headed to? You don't mind me asking, do you?" King smiled.

"I have no problem at all with that. I'm going to Detroit."

"I got some people in the D. Make sure you're careful. The men gon' love seeing you come." Coco smiled as she handed King a business card as she bagged up his items before he left out.

Shit, he smelled good. King just doesn't know I'm looking forward to seeing his ass again. Coco continued her work day. She was busy all day long, but for some reason she couldn't get King off her mind.

I need to get some extra help up in here. Today was busy. Coco gathered her things and locked up the boutique for the day.

Chapter 68
Asia

"Morning everyone," Asia said dryly as she walked into the shop. She had a mean mug on her face.

"What's wrong with you, Asia?" Mina said as they hugged.

", I just left from meeting up with Coco at the nail shop and she is on some bullshit. I love her, but she needs to mind her damn business." Mina laughed at Asia's comment.

"What happened? Coco and you are always getting into it. The thing is you two are too much alike."

"We ain't shit alike." Asia rolled her eyes.

"So, what happened?"

"Well, she said I've been acting brand new. She then went on to comment on why I have been hanging out with Keisha. Asked me how I can fuck with her like that."

"So, Asia, why you think Coco asks you that?" Mina knew all about Asia and Twan, she just wanted to see if Asia would tell her the truth or not.

"She said it because at one point I was fucking Twan." Asia was pissed and had a straight attitude.

"Asia, what are you upset about? I've known about you and Twan, it was no secret. Just like you knew Rel was still in town that was some fucked up shit not telling Coco." Asia looked at Mina.

Damn, here she goes. I should have never said shit. All Mina gon' do is side with Coco.

"All I'm saying is that shit with Rel was fucked up. As far as Twan, that isn't any of my business. I don't know Keisha, but Coco is like your sister, so for you to hold on to some info like that made me question you as a person, a friend, and all of that shit." Mina wanted to let Asia know how she felt and she did just that.

"You know what, Mina, yes I knew about Rel. I didn't know what to say, so I just left it alone."

"Do you understand how you sound, Asia? Let's say the tables were turned and it was Coco who hid something from you. Bitch, you would cut her off, no questions asked." Asia knew that Mina was right.

"Look, I really don't care about that shit anymore. Coco and Rel are good now, so why are you even bringing this old shit up?"

"Regardless if the two are talking again, you were still wrong and you wrong for hanging with Keisha as well." Mina laughed, but Asia found nothing funny.

"Give me a hug. I love you, but you know I'm gon' keep it real. I do Coco the same way, so don't take this shit the wrong way."

Asia took it personal, what other way could she have taken it? She knew that Mina wasn't judging her, but her conscious was getting to her about her not telling Coco about Rel and about her still fucking Twan. She befriended his wife and she was cheating on Big R. Asia had too much going on and the shit was weighing heavy on her.

Asia was done in the shop early that day. All she wanted was to go home and relax. As she walked to the car, she stopped, and couldn't believe her eyes. She smiled as she stared at William Turner a.k.a Willie, her first love. Willie had been locked up for seven years in the federal joint for interstate trafficking cocaine. They called it one of the largest drugs raids ever and they tried to get him on several counts of murder, but nothing stuck. Had they stuck, Willie would have never stepped foot out of prison.

He was about his money and a man that stuck by his word, so if he told you if you don't have my money by this time and date you're dead, then that was what you were, dead. No second chances. His name was the only name you heard in the streets when he was out.

Asia stood there with tears in her eyes because she hadn't seen Willie in two years. She never thought he would make parole. The prosecutor and media made him out to be a monster. The first few years she rode with him, being faithful and saw him on a regular. Willie saw the stress it put on Asia. He loved her enough to let her go.

Asia was his best friend. He wanted her to be happy regardless if they were together or not. She visited him one day as she always did and he told her not to come anymore. He wanted her to live her life and that when he got out, they would take it from there. She didn't want that, truth be told, she would have continued to wait on him. After that day, he no longer called or wrote her. It killed him, but he had to make sure that door was closed. She deserved better and he knew that therefore, he did what he thought was best.

Willie walked up to Asia and smiled as he wiped the tears off her face.

"I hope those are happy tears, Asia." She was speechless. She couldn't stop looking at him.

"Yes, they are! I can't believe you are standing here in front of me right now." She hugged him as tight as she could and couldn't stop crying.

"I have dreamed about the day I would be able to hold you in my arms again, Willie."

"Stop crying Asia I'm here now I don't plan on going anywhere."

Chapter 69
Mina

Mina was headed out to meet India at her house. On the ride over, Mina thought about the conversation she and Asia had.

I hope Asia didn't think I was judging her. I was just trying to get her to see that she was wrong about the way she handled things. It was fucked up. There is no other way to put it. And, being friends with a man's wife that she's fucking is deadly. That bitch ain't thinking straight. Honestly, I think Asia is looking for love in all the wrong places. When Willie got sent away up state that's when things changed for Asia. Then, on top of that, he left her alone. I understood why and I have the utmost respect for him, that shit was real. Not too many men would give up the love of their life, so she could be happy and actually live her life. Real men do real things. I know if Asia was still with Willie she wouldn't be messing around with any of these other men. She's just looking for someone to fill that void.

Mina pulled up to India's new house and loved it. *Damn, India's ass lives too damn far. What in the hell made her move out to Mt. Washington?* Mina got out of the car, walked to the door, and rang the bell.

A few seconds later, India opened the door with a smile on her face and hugged Mina.

"I am so happy to see you. You're beautiful. I love your hair Mina."

"I'm glad you invited me over. It's been too damn long. I love this house. When are you going to have that housewarming party I keep asking you about?"

"I may have it soon, but it's not like I have many people to invite and honestly, I don't want a lot of folks to

know where I live, but you can get me a gift if you like."
They both laughed.

"Make yourself at home. Lunch is almost ready. I
made some chicken Alfredo and a salad. I know you on
your workout shit, so you just gon' have to work off this
pasta. I have been craving it, so that's what I decided to
make."

"I'll eat whatever you cooked. I'm just happy to
see you. Look at you with this glow."

India put the bread in the oven. She was indeed
glowing. Her pregnancy made her look radiant. India
went into the kitchen drawer, pulled out the ultrasound
pictures, and she sat them down in front of Mina. All you
heard was Mina screaming. She jumped up and hugged
India with tears streaming down her face.

"When did you find this out?"

"It was earlier last week," India responded.

"And, you're waiting 'til now to tell me? Wait 'til
I tell mama and daddy. This is the best news you could
have given me. I'm going to be an auntie! We have a lot
of planning to do, so it says here you're almost eighteen
weeks along."

India couldn't get a word in and she didn't care,
just seeing Mina happy made her happy. They sat, ate,
and talked about how they would decorate the baby's
room and when to have the baby shower. Mina let her
know not to worry about anything, that she loved her, and
would be there at each doctor visit.

She made India promise that she wouldn't get in
her moods and shut her out, and India agreed. They called
her parents and told them the news over the phone. They
were so happy. Mina was about to leave when India
broke down crying.

"What's wrong, India?"

"I'm just emotional, that's all. I can't believe I'm having Taye's baby."

"I can that baby was made out of love. Although, he isn't with us anymore, he will forever live on through his child." Mina hugged India and headed home to share the news with Ty.

Chapter 70
ZO

So, this is where the bitch moved to. ZO sat parked a few houses down from India's. He followed Mina and, he knew eventually she would lead him to India and he was right. ZO tried to find out her whereabouts for a while. He needed to make sure India didn't decide to get a conscious and tell Mina or anyone that he was the one who killed Taye.

He saw all he needed to see. He would pay India a visit soon. He pulled off and headed back across town where he was meeting Ciara at the airport. They were headed to Atlantic City for a few days.

He was feeling her, although, he still hadn't told her much about himself. He only wanted her to know certain shit. After the shit with India, he knew he couldn't trust a bitch, even the love he had for Coco changed. She was no longer a thought to him and he knew he had no chance. She made that clear each and every time she saw or spoke to him.

The only love he had was for his daughter, the love of his life. He still had love for Coco, but he wasn't interested in trying to get back together. She rejected him too many times and he was not one to beg, so he said fuck it and decided to let her be.

Once at the airport, ZO parked his car and got his bag out. He didn't pack much he planned on shopping. Everyone knew he loved to stay fly, so shopping was his thing.

Fuck, look at all that ass in those jeans, ZO thought. He spotted Ciara looking good. She wore a pair of all white Roberto Cavalli jeans and they hugged in all the right places. She wore a matching white wife beater with five and half inch heels by Ruthie Davis. They were the Bond Glitter stud pumps and she had a matching clutch to set it off. Her hair was down in a beautiful flat wrap.

ZO walked up behind Ciara and kissed the back of her neck. She could feel his dick on her ass. He was rock hard.

"You see what you to do to me every time I see you?" He whispered in her ear. She turned around and kissed him. He loved the attention she gave him. She was very affectionate.

"You are looking good, baby. Those jeans are looking good on you. I can't wait to get your ass up out of them, you know this, right?"

Ciara gave ZO a sexy smile. For the first time in a long time, she was happy again. She never thought she would find a man that made her feel just as happy as Rel, but she had.

Before they boarded the plane, Twan called ZO to let him know they needed to talk. ZO let him know he was headed out of town and would be back in a few days. Twan wasn't trying to hear that, but what he could say? He told ZO to hit him as soon as he got back in town.

"ZO, are you ready to focus your attention on me?" Ciara put her arms around his neck and kissed him.

"Yea, baby, I'm sorry. I had to take that call. You have my undivided attention. Now let's go have some fun in Atlantic City."

Chapter 71
Big R

"Baby, can you give me a massage?"

Chanel smiled as Big R massaged her back. He had been fucking her for a couple of weeks. He went back later that night to Mina's club and pushed up on her even though he knew that she was checking for Rel.

She had him wide open like all the other women that he fucked with. He was a sucker for a fine woman.

"What's with the nonstop vibrating of the phone? Thought you said you had your bitches in check!"

"Please, don't fuck up my high with that nagging shit," he said, irritated.

"Nigga, what's fucking up the high is your phone going off."

"Chanel, don't start. Plus, why you worried about it, you still fucking with Rel. What, you think I didn't know? The nigga is like my brother. He tells me damn near everything!"

"He's your brother, but, yet, you went behind his back to fuck me knowing that it was him I was checking for." Big R was pissed.

"Fuck you mean by that, bitch? You didn't have a problem giving me the digits or the pussy."

"You know what, fuck you weak motherfucker, I got your bitch. Let me fill you in on a little something. First of all, I never really liked your ass. You are good for one thing and one thing only, tricking your money." Chanel jumped up and continued to talk shit as she put her clothes on. She was happy that Big R said what he said so she could leave his ass alone for good.

"Oh, and *FYI,* nigga, you ain't got shit on Rel. The nigga's dick is long and his paper is longer. You could never be on his level. You see Asia dumped your ass you were just something for her to do while her man was locked up. Aw, what, you didn't know? You thought you were playing her by fucking with me on the side and all along she been playing you." Chanel laughed as she walked out the door, leaving him standing there looking silly.

Big R stood there with a look of hate in his eyes. He wanted to grab Chanel up and choke the shit out of her.

I can't believe this bitch, Asia. I got something for that bitch, though.

Big R was hurt the shit Chanel had said bruised his ego, especially the part about him never being on Rel's level. He was jealous of Rel and had been since they were kids. He always wanted to be the man, but Rel always out shined him. Rel didn't have to trick money on women to get their attention, but Big R did, that was his thing. He had too much on his mind and he was tired of being Rel's flunky.

Shit, I need something to calm my nerves. Big R went to his drawer, opened it, and pulled out a syringe. He picked up a bad habit and used heroin. It didn't matter what it was, he would shoot it up or smoke it. He needed a fast and quick fix. He hid his drug problem from everyone. One would never know he was a heroin addict, but that would soon change. It had become a daily habit that he couldn't shake.

Big R was tired of Rel and him calling all the shots, something had to be done. Big R was up to no good; he had something up his sleeve. He was about to cross the one person that always had his back.

Chapter 72
Coco

Coco was at the boutique and India was there helping out. Her little belly was noticeable. Coco really didn't want her to do much at the boutique but sit behind the counter and look pretty.

"India, you ok over there? I thought I told you not to touch shit. Your ass better not lift any of those boxes." India knew not to do anything too strenuous because Coco would yell at her every time.

"I'm not going to pick up the damn box! You and Mina don't have to babysit me, damn."

"First of all, I'm not babysitting you at all. I call myself being a friend and looking out, but you can take it how you want. All I know is that you better not lift shit." India noticed that Coco kept looking at her watch.

"Damn, that man will be here shortly. You got like twenty minutes." India laughed.

"What you talking about, India? Shit I'm just checking to see what time it was, so I can leave out for lunch."

"Who you think your fooling, Coco, you're waiting on King. His ass is 'pose to be here in the next twenty minutes to pick up yet another dress for his woman. I don't think he has a woman. He just comes in here to see your ass."

"I wish his fine ass was single. Every time he comes in here he's on point."

King would come in the store at least twice a week either to buy something or just to say hi. Coco couldn't understand why he never brought his woman with him.

"Tell me something, Coco, why doesn't King just bring his woman with him to pick out her own shit? I'm telling you, his ass is only coming up here to see you." Coco smiled; she wished that was the reason behind King's weekly visits.

"India, he is not coming in here just to see me, although, I wish he were."

"Have you talked to my brother? I can't believe you two just decided to be friends."

"I felt like it was best. I put my all into Rel and the fact that he cut me off like he did changed shit. I knew that things would never be the same. I love him, but not enough to try again. I have never been in love, yes, I loved ZO, but that was it, I wasn't in love with him. I want to find Mr. Right. I want God to send me the right man. I know my time will come, so I'm going to be patient."

Just as Coco finished her statement, King walked in.

"What's up, ladies?"

"Hey, King, you made it on time I see." King walked up to Coco and gave her a hug.

"You look good today, Coco."

"Thanks, you're looking good, too."

"Why you so quiet over there, Ms. Glowworm? I see you starting to show. When do you find out the sex of the baby?"

"You're funny with your glow worm comment. I find out next Friday and I can't wait, either. I'll let you know. I'm sure I'll see you next Friday."

King smiled. "So, what were you ladies talking about when I walked in?"

"We were talking about Coco not having a man and finding true love." Coco looked at India as if to say, 'bitch, you talk too much.'

"Is that true, Coco? You're tired of being single? What's the rush? Never rush into anything, baby. The right man will come at the right time and when he does, you will know."

"King you ready for your package? I'll go get it from the back." *India ass talks too much.*

Coco came back up front with King's packages.

"Thanks, I appreciate you putting a rush on these items for me. My sister is going on a cruise and she saw your items online, so I told her I'd take care of it for her."

"I thought these things were for your woman. I was wondering why the sizes were different. I was gon' ask you, but I didn't want to be all in your business."

"You good, you can ask me anything. A matter of fact let me take you to lunch so I can answer any questions you might have for me."

King stood there with his hands behind his back, nodding his head up in down, waiting on Coco to say something.

Without hesitation, she said, "Sounds good."

India was all smiles. "So, you two not gon' feed a pregnant woman right?"

"India, you're more than welcome to join us," King said.

"I'm good. Mina is bringing me lunch."

"Are you going to be ok here by yourself?" Coco asked.

"Bye, Coco, go on with that shit." Coco didn't say anything else. She grabbed her purse and was headed out the door with King.

"Oh, and, Coco, I was right. Enjoy your lunch date. I'll see you later." India said, laughing.

Chapter 73
Rel

It was Sunday morning and Rel was up early. He had some business to take care of. For a couple of months, Big R was really moving some weight. He told Rel he had a new buyer and that dude only wanted to fuck with him, so Rel didn't question it. He let Big R handle shit and why not, he was his partner.

Rel got a phone call the week before from Ty that they needed to have a meeting, so that was where Rel was headed to.

"Chanel, baby. I'm about to head out. What you got planned for the day?"

'Nothing, how long do you think you will be?"

"I can't give you a time, but I will hit you when I get back in."

Chanel was spoiled; she wanted all of Rel's time and attention. She had practically moved in. Rel didn't mind because he was feeling her. What man wouldn't? She was breathtaking. He could never understand why she was ever working at the club as a waitress. He told her that if she was to ever be his woman, she would need to let that job go and that's exactly what she did. She still wasn't his *woman,* although, he treated her like she was.

"Don't look at me like that. I told you yesterday that I may be gone half of the day."

"I know, I be missing you. You're always on the go lately, like, more than usual is all I'm saying."

"Look, I'll be back later."

Rel kissed Chanel and was out the door. On the drive to Ty's house, Rel thought about Chanel. He was really into her, but he wasn't ready to make her his woman. He knew she had men chasing her, but he wasn't worried. Chanel was beautiful and no one could deny that. She was light skinned with long, coal black hair, and her smile would melt one's heart. She had dark almond shaped eyes.

Chanel had one flaw that Rel didn't like and that was her mouth. She said whatever and she didn't think before she spoke. That shit was irritating. He let her know how he felt about that. He told her about Ciara and how she talked crazy. Chanel got the picture real quick. She wasn't trying to lose him. He kind of wished she was more like Coco. He missed her. They talked on and off, and he usually seen her when he saw India at the boutique. Coco knew that Rel moved on and was happy for him. You couldn't say the same about Rel when he found out about King. He wasn't very pleased, but he didn't let it show.

Rel pulled into Ty's driveway, got out, and knocked on the door.

"What you up to, Rel?"

"Shit, slow motion, just been lying low."

They made their way into Ty's office where he shut the door; although, Mina wasn't there he still made sure if she came in that she couldn't hear anything.

"So, what's going on, Ty?

"Let me ask you something, Rel. Who is your man Big R conducting business with?"

"What you mean, Ty?"

"Is that nigga doing business with Twan?"

"Fuck no, he isn't! What made you ask me that?"

"Because for the last couple months, Twan and ZO been doing their thing and its right around the time you said Big R came to you saying he had someone that needed some heavy weight."

Rel sat there puzzled. He couldn't believe Ty would think his partner would be fucking with Twan.

"Big R wouldn't do any shit like that, so get that shit out your head!"

"I know you and your man go way back when, but like you told me, that shit don't matter in this game. Muthafuckers will cross you no matter what."

Rel sat there pissed the fuck off at the thought that Big R would go behind his back and do some disloyal shit like that. From the beginning it was Rel and Big R. They swore never to let money, bitches, or anything come between them and, so far, nothing like that had. Rel trusted him and he never gave him a reason not to.

"Rel, that's not all I wanted to talk to you about. The reason I asked you over is to let you know I'm done. I'm out the game. I told you I been having an uneasy feeling. I'm giving myself three months, and then I'm done. I just thought I should let you know."

"Damn, I wasn't expecting you to say this shit, but I feel you, Ty. Man, do what is best for you. I'm going to have a conversation with Big R. Hopefully, this nigga hasn't crossed the line and fucked with that nigga, Twan. Now I got to look over my shoulder, damn, sometimes the person you'd take a bullet for ends up being the one behind the gun."

They talked a little longer and then Rel headed out. He had a lot of shit on his mind. He needed to talk to the man in charge to get his input on shit.

Damn, you can't trust anyone, he thought as he drove home.

Chapter 74
Asia

"I wish he would stop calling me!" Asia said out loud. Big R called Asia's phone all damn day long. Since she cut him off he had been on some bullshit. He called her a low down dirty bitch and said she wasn't shit. She wasn't stressing over it and that pissed him off. He wanted her to hurt physically and emotionally. She up and left him as soon as Willie came back in the picture.

When Asia cut Big R loose she let him know she wanted her things that were at his house, but he refused to give them back to her. She could have replaced the items, but she was like why should she. One night she decided she would use her key and let herself in when he wasn't home. She walked in to find his ass getting high. Asia couldn't believe it. She was disgusted.

He told her to get the fuck out his crib and to never come back. Asia jetted up out of there, still not able to get her belongings. That night, she waited until he left out. After sitting for damn near two hours, she finally saw him exit the building. To her surprise, Twan pulled up and Big R got in the car with him. Asia didn't know what that was all about and really didn't care. She didn't know how long he would be gone, so she rushed out the car and into the crib.

Once she was inside, she looked around the living room and there was nothing but money and dope everywhere. She gathered her belongings and made sure she left nothing behind. Asia left his key on the way out the door. As she was leaving she saw a picture of Big R and some chic. At that moment Asia realized that Big R wasn't shit. She decided to look around and see what else she would find. She found some naked pictures of India. Asia couldn't believe that he had been with India as well. She had seen enough she grabbed her things, locked the bottom lock, and left.

She got a call later that night from Big R cussing her out saying when he saw her, he would beat her ass. He knew Asia had been in his crib and he knew she went through his shit.. He would call her phone at odd hours of the night. It got to the point where she turned her phone off after midnight. The man Asia once knew was gone. She figured it had to be the drugs making him the way he was. She planned on staying away from him.

Asia was running late she had to be at the shop. Mina, India, and Coco were coming to get their hair done.

Asia made it to the salon and the women were already there, they hugged and greeted each other. While Asia rolled India's hair, Willie walked in the shop with two dozen of assorted colored roses. Asia smiled when she saw him come in. Her face lit up like a Christmas tree. The two hugged and she introduced him to India, who had never met Willie, but heard about him.

"Damn, you two look alike." Willie said to Asia and India.

"Baby, everyone says that," Asia said.

"So, you mean to tell me you two don't think you look alike?"

"Yea, Asia and I favor a little, but that's about it."

"Shit, fuck that, you look identical, real talk." Willie still couldn't believe the resemblance between Asia and India.

"Asia, I'm about to head out. Call me when you get done and don't forget I have something planned for you this evening."

Asia smiled because she was happy. She loved Willie and always would. She now felt complete. She shared with Willies about what she had been into the last two years. Asia told him about Big R, Twan, and whomever else she had dealt with. She admitted to him that she was lonely and she fucked around with them niggas to fill the void of him not being in her life. He told her that she should have never put herself out there like that but he also let her know that the past was the past.

As soon as Willie left the shop, the women starting asking Asia questions.

"Are you and Willie together again?" India asked.

"When were they ever apart? Asia and Willie gon' always have something going. Asia was just doing her the last couple of years just to have something to do. She wasn't really into them other men like Big R and definitely not Twan. They were her play things." Mina said.

Asia knew that Mina was right. She hated that she always knew her so well.

"You are right, I hate to admit it, but you are. And, India, yes, we are back together. It's like we just picked up where we left off. Willie has grown a lot. He is not the same man he was before he got locked up. His mind set is different. His plans are to open up a barbershop, and we're thinking about possibly adding to this building or finding something close by."

"So, he got bread?" India asked. The ladies laughed because they all knew that Willie stayed paid before he got locked up.

"What's funny?" India asked.

"Nothing, you just had to know him. The man was all about his paper chase then, and I'm sure now."

"So, the FEDs didn't touch his money?" Asia looked at India as if she had just asked the dumbest question.

"They didn't see a penny of that money. Willie knew the FEDs were on to him, hell, they watched him for damn near two years before they busted him. By then, shit, we had a plan already together and the money, well, let me just say it's safe and secure."

"When you say money, Asia, how much money are you talking about?"

"Let's just say I could retire and never have to worry about money."

Chapter 75
ZO

ZO was rolling on I-65 rapping to Young Jezzy's song, *Everythang*. He loved that song and kept that shit on repeat. He was making money and feeling good. He was on his way to meet Ciara for lunch when he decided to stop off and get her a bouquet of flowers. Things between them were good, better than he had expected. He looked down at his phone and saw he had a text message.

You fag wait 'til motherfuckers really find out about your bitch ass. What you think your new woman gon' say about what I have to tell her? Your shit is about to be put on blast.

I'm gon' kill that bitch! Who, in the fuck does this, bitch, India, think she is fucking with? I told her ass... I'm gon' have to show her.

The message had him infuriated and all he saw was red in his eyes.

I should have killed that bitch, he thought. He got to the restaurant and as soon as he saw Ciara, his entire attitude changed. He made his way to the table and kissed the back of her neck. He gave her the bouquet of flowers.

"Aw, baby, I love them." Ciara smelled the flowers and gave him a smile that lit up the room.

"I figured you would. So how's my woman doing today?"

"I'm doing fine now that you're here. Today has really been a busy day for me. I had a test today and the shit was hard."

"Baby, I'm sure you did fine. Just think in two years, you will be a nurse. Keep staying on the right track and think positive."

"You always say just what I need to hear thank you ZO." They had lunch and agreed to meet up later that evening to have dinner and catch a movie.

"Thanks again, for the flowers. I'll see you later." Ciara kissed him goodbye.

ZO texted Twan to let him know he was on his way to his crib. Big R had some shit he wanted to discuss with them.

I wonder what the fuck this nigga want to holler at us about. Shit, long as he getting that money, there's nothing really to discuss. He's a clown ass nigga. Him and Twan fucking with that gold diggin ass bitch Asia. She was playing both they ass, now she got ghost on them since Willie got out the penitentiary.

ZO's plan was to get close to Big R and let him know all along that Twan was fucking Asia, and she was the one who told Twan that Big R was in the streets. He knew that the shit was a lie, but he figured the nigga would believe anything, being that he was off on that heroin. ZO noticed the track mark on his arm one day. Plus, there were several times he caught him nodding off. He figured that Big R would cut Twan straight off. Then, ZO planned on robbing him for dope and money, and then kill him.

ZO pulled up to Twan's place. He finished his blunt before he got out the car.

Both these niggas deserve what they have coming to them. First lesson they should have learned is never do business with a nigga you hardly know, ZO thought as he got out his car.

Chapter 76
Rel

Rel was headed to Big R's house. He called him all morning and was pissed that he hadn't returned his phone calls. He decided he would drop by his crib.

What in the hell has been going on with Big R for the last few weeks? Ever since Ty came to him about Big R possibly being Twan's connect. The shit was weighing heavy on his mind. He couldn't shake the shit and, needed to talk to Big R. That was what he planned on doing. Rel knew he couldn't go to his head man that was supplying him unless he knew for sure Big R had crossed them.

On the way over, Rel's phone vibrated. He looked down and saw that it was India calling.

"Indy, you're alright?" Rel said as soon as he picked up the phone.

"Yes, I'm okay, just had a quick question, that's all. Are you bringing Chanel with you to the baby shower?" Rel hesitated for a moment before answering.

"Yea, she's coming with me. Is that going to be a problem?"

"What you talking about? Why would it be a problem?"

"I know you and Coco are close. Wasn't sure how she may feel about seeing me with someone else."

"Coco is good. She could care less about who you bring. That's all I needed to know bye." Rel began to say something else, but India already hung up.

What the fuck was that about?

While Rel was at the stop sign waiting to turn on to Big R's street, he saw him walking out his front door with a large duffle bag. He watched as Big R placed the bag in the trunk of his car and returned back inside the house. He came out with another large bag and put it in his trunk.

What the fuck this nigga doing! The large bags that Big R was placing in his trunk were the same ones Rel had just given him two weeks ago with the dope in them. He got inside the car and pulled off. Rel decided to follow him to see just exactly where he was headed. Rel appeared to be calm, but in the back of his mind he was freaking out. He knew his partner wouldn't cross him. At least, that was what he thought until he pulled over to the side of the road and watched his friend of fifteen years get out of his car and walk to the door. Twan opened it before Big R could even knock on it. Rel was furious.

I ought to go up in this motherfucker and kill both those niggas.

Rel saw a blue Charger pull up and before ZO could get out, Rel already knew it was him.

Rel couldn't even see straight. He needed to get the fuck away from there. He made a phone call and headed out. He had seen enough. The one man he would take a bullet for had crossed him. Words couldn't describe how Rel felt.

Chapter 77
Mina

"Ty, wake up, baby. I'm about to head out to get my hair done. You want to meet up later and have lunch?"

"Sounds good what time?"

"I'm not sure just yet. I'll call you once I get done because I have a few errands to run. I'm trying to get everything I need for the baby shower."

"Shit, you gon' be all day. Your ass went baby crazy." Ty smiled at Mina and pulled her on top of him as he kissed her.

"There you go. You know I don't play about my hair appointment." She gave him a kiss and got up.

She made her way to the salon. She was looking forward to seeing Asia, Coco, and India.

"Good morning, ladies," Mina said when she walked into the salon.

"Morning, Mina," Coco said.

"Hey, Mina, I'll be ready for you shortly. You know Coco has me doing extra shit this morning."

"Take your time, where is India? She usually makes it here before I do." Mina pulled out her phone to call Mina and before she could dial the number, she came strolling in.

"Good morning, all," India said as she walked through the door with a box of bagels.

"I was just about to call you."

"Well, as you see, I'm here in the flesh. So what's up?"

"You know her ass is tripping and shit. I can't wait 'til you give birth to my god daughter so this bitch can stop acting like she's your bodyguard."

"I agree with you on that, Coco."

"Coco, whatever, that's my niece she is carrying. I'm going to harass her ass 'til she has her." India walked over and gave Mina a hug.

"I love you, but you need to stop worrying so much. So, do you have everything for the baby shower?"

"I told you to let me handle this. You don't have to worry about shit, I got this."

India smiled because she knew Mina had everything together. It wouldn't be her if she didn't. She was always on her shit and taking care of everything.

"I'm mailing off the invitations tomorrow."

"Okay, so enough talk about the baby shower. So Coco what's going on with you and Kahlee?" Asia wanted to know all the details.

Coco smiled from ear to ear. "Nothing is up with me and King. We're just cool, that's all."

"Bitch, you're a damn lie! The way you just smiled, please, now what's the deal? Is he still with his woman?"

"Asia, your ass is nosey, but yea as far as I know he is. I don't really bring her up. Like I said, we just cool. We kick it and catch a movie or go out to eat, but nothing more."

"So you telling me you haven't given his ass any pussy?" Asia looked at Coco while she waited for her to respond.

Coco laughed. "Asia, we haven't even kissed."

"All I'm saying is you haven't had any dick in a few months, damn, I know your poor clitoris is swollen. Your ass is killing it with that damn silver bullet."

They all laughed because they knew how Coco loved her sex toys.

"You're real funny, China Doll, but you're right. I haven't fucked in nine months. I started to call Xavier a few times, but I changed my mind."

"I don't know why you didn't call his ass. I know he still be hitting that from time to time. Your ass isn't fooling me." Asia didn't believe a word Coco said.

"Whatever, Asia, you know if that was the case, I would have told you all but when I do get some dick, you will be the first to know. Now, let's talk about something else besides my sex life."

Asia finished India's hair and afterwards, they planned on going out to eat. The women were dolled up Asia had rocked their hair as usual. They hopped in Coco's truck, not noticing that Big R was parked across the street watching their every move.

Chapter 78
Big R

Look at these gold digging whores. All of them ain't shit.

Big R watched as Coco pulled out the parking lot, he then pulled up to the shop. It was still early and there weren't many people out. He flattened every tire on Asia's new 2013 Audi S8 that Willie got for her.

Gold digging ass bitch fuck her, her man, and this fucking car! Big R thought.

He was pissed and the fact that it was broad daylight meant nothing to him. He didn't give a fuck, he busted out all of her windows, and took out a can of spray paint and wrote gold digger on the hood of the car, and on both sides of the car.

Bitch, won't be driving this mother fucker any time soon, trick ass bitch. He headed back to his car and lit a blunt. He wanted to sit there and wait until Asia got back to the shop so he could see the expression on her face, but he had business to conduct so he jetted out of there before someone did notice his ass.

"Twan, what it do?" Big R said as he walked into to Twan's crib.

"Shit, I'm good."

Big R had a smirk on his face. "So, did you holler at your peeps in Detroit?"

"Yea, I got all that shit taken care of, Big R. Told you I was gon' handle it."

"Shit, how much work they need?"

"My nigga, Nate, is talking about twenty bricks. I told the nigga if you want that type of work, I want my bread off top. He said he was cool with that, so shit that's what it is."

"What price did you quote him?"

"I told him he can give me twenty eight, five for each one, so shit, that's $570,000.00 and what I'm taking off top is seventy thousand being that the price is twenty five thousand."

"Okay, Twan, do your thang. I got what you asked for. Where's the bread? So, you gon' hit ZO off some of the extra cash you making?

Twan got the money, brought it back, and tossed the bag.

"I made the deal, they my people, he gon' get his money, but ain't no extras I'm running this shit."

He listened to Twan talk shit like he was the man and in reality, the nigga wasn't shit.

"So, how much work you got left?"

"I'm good on my end Twan."

Fuck his ass worried about what I got? This nigga ain't to be trusted at all. I'm gone make sure I let ZO know about Twan's ass fucking him over with them niggas in Detroit. I'm gon' make sure these two bitch niggas don't trust the other.

"So, you still fuck your partner's woman? Don't give me that look, nigga. Shit, you still fucking Chanel?" Big R gave Twan a look that let him know he was not the one.

"What the fuck you need to know for, Twan? But, to answer your question, naw, that bitch ain't shit. Talking about she loves that nigga, Rel, yea ok. She was just fucking my ass a few weeks back, now she loves that nigga."

"Rel be having bitches falling in love." Twan laughed his ass off. He knew he was getting to Big R.

"Get the fuck out of here, with that shit Twan."

"Damn, the pussy got you like that?"

"Twan, you can't judge me. Look at how you played Ty. You ain't any different or better than I am."

"Yea, you right about that, but I ain't going behind my nigga's back and fucking his woman, either. Not only that, you fucking with ZO. All I'm saying is prepare for the worst 'cause when Rel finds out, it's going down."

"Do I look fuckin worried to you? Twan, look, like I said, I don't give a fuck about Rel! I'm out, hit me when you need some more work. And, why you talking shit about Rel and what he gon' do. Shit, you need to be worried about ZO and what he gon' do once he find out you playing him on that Detroit shit."

Big R walked out the door before Twan could respond.

That snake motherfucker act like he's sucking Rel's dick or some shit. Note to self, watch that nigga carefully, He's up to something.

Chapter 79
Asia

"Damn, that shit was good. I love Wild Eggs."

"Asia, you crazy, you always get the same damn thing, that fuckin hot brown. Switch up sometimes, damn."

"Coco, you worry about what you eat and I'll worry about what I eat. Plus, why are you complaining? Your greedy ass ate off all our plates."

"Yea, well, this greedy chic is putting you out her ride." Coco pulled up to the shop. The ladies were too busy talking to notice that Asia's car was fucked up.

"Hold up, Coco, pull up to my car."

Before Coco pulled all the way up, she already saw that her car had been fucked up. Asia jumped out the truck and couldn't believe that her new ride was fucked up.

"Who in the hell did this shit?" she screamed as she walked around the car, assessing the damage.

"China Doll, give me your phone. I'm about to call Willie."

"Hell naw, he is going to go the fuck off. I don't need him doing shit crazy. Hell, he just got out."

"Forget what you talking about, I'm calling his ass. Asia, I know you aren't still dealing with Twan? Don't give me that look. I'm just asking. Maybe Keisha did this shit."

"No, I just talked to her last night, she has an appointment. Plus, she doesn't suspect shit."

"Ok, I was just asking." Asia wondered who could have done this, and then it hit her. *Big R.*

"Alright, Willie is on his way and he is pissed."

"Damn, Coco, I knew I shouldn't have let you to call him."

"Whatever, he's on his way and that's that!"

"I know who done this shit, that weak ass Big R."

"Asia, what makes you suspect it was him?"

"Mina, because his ass been talking shit to me since Willie been back. I went over to his crib and got my things. The nigga is on drugs, he be talking reckless saying I'm a gold digging ass bitch and all kinds of shit. Hell, the nigga scared me. I went in his crib when he wasn't there and I found pictures of a female he 'pose to be fucking with. Then, I found some other photos as well of some other female. That nigga is crazy, let's just say that."

When Asia mentioned the pictures she found, India had a strange look on her face.

"Oh, shit, Willie is pulling up. What are you going to tell him, Asia?"

"Coco, I'm not sure. Willie will hurt Big R. That's if Rel doesn't first." India looked at Asia when she mentioned Rel's name.

"What does my brother have to do with this?"

"Well, when I was waiting for Big R to leave, Twan came over and picked him up. I know it was about business. What else could it have been? Plus, inside the house he had keys of cocaine all over the place and cash. Look, India, don't repeat this shit back to Rel because I'm sure he knows by now that his ass is a bitch."

Willie walked up and everyone got quiet.

"Asia, if you need anything, hit us up, ok."

"I will, Coco, thanks for calming me down. I love you all."

Once the women were gone, Willie started with the questions and Asia felt like she was being interrogated.

"Damn, baby, I don't know who did this shit. We went to breakfast and when we got back my shit was fucked up. You're hollering at me like I know who did it."

"I'll get to the bottom of this. Call the insurance company and if you want, we can go get you something new tomorrow."

Asia hugged Willie and thought, *now, that's how a boss does it. Fuck that nigga, Big R.*

Chapter 80
Rel

Rel couldn't believe the information that was shared with him. His whole world was turned upside down in a couple of weeks. He still couldn't believe Big R and all the shit he did behind his back and now after meeting his boss, he found out some shit that he wasn't even prepared for.

Damn, I can't wrap my head around this shit, but I'm glad I know.

What I learned today is that loyalty runs deep. It ain't some shit that you earn in a day. You earn that shit day by day.

He knew what was next. He knew that Big R would be contacting him as soon as he needed more work. You could tell the situation was fucking with Rel. Did he want to kill his friend, of course not, but the point was he had to. He crossed him and thought he could get away with it. Rel had to live by the code of if you fuck me over, you die, no questions asked.

Rel's phone vibrated.

"Indy, what's up? You ok?"

Yea, I'm okay. Rel, have you seen Big R lately?"

"I saw his ass a couple weeks ago. Why are you asking me that, Indy? What you need with him?"

"I'm asking because today while I was at the shop Asia's new car got fucked up."

"What you talking about?"

"Her tires were slit, windows kicked out, and all that shit. She thinks it was Big R. She says he's on drugs real bad and that he is fucking with that nigga, Twan."

Rel held the phone.

"Did you hear me? Is any of this true?"

"Stop stressing over this shit, your brother knows what's going on. Trust me, but stay away from that nigga. He's on some bullshit. Trust me, he will get dealt with."

"Look, Asia told me not to say shit to you, but I had to let you know. You're my big brother."

"Don't worry about me, and thanks for letting me know. I love you, sis."

Rel hung up the phone. He was pissed about Big R, but he had other shit on his mind. He still couldn't get the conversation off his mind that he had earlier that day.

Keeping this from India is going to be hard, Rel thought. The news was fucking with him. He knew that it wasn't his place to say shit to her about what he learned. He felt like what if the shit was reversed she'd tell him, but he gave his word and his word was all he had. Therefore, he couldn't and wouldn't say anything.

Man, let me call Ty's ass and let him know what is going on. Also, I need to get at that nigga, Willie, before he gets at Big R.

"Baby, where are you?" Chanel said as she walked into the house.

"I'm in the family room."

Chanel walked in the room looking good as hell. She had on a pair of Juicy Couture, foil coated skinny denim in silver. The pants look like they were painted on.

"Baby, you can't be walking in here looking as good as you do." She smiled as she walked to him and gave him a kiss. He smacked her ass.

"Model for me real quick, let me watch that ass bounce as your strut your shit around this room for your man."

"You like what you see, Rel? I think you would enjoy it even more if I were naked." Rel smiled as he palmed her ass.

"Sounds good, baby, you gon' have to save that for later. I got some shit I need to take care of and before you say shit, it's important because if it wasn't, I would have your ass bent over and fucking the shit out of you."

He kissed her bye and headed out to Ty's spot.

Chapter 81
ZO

Let her ass, send me one more message, I'm gon' stomp that baby out her ass. She is fuckin with the wrong one. What makes India think she's untouchable? ZO sat there as he read the text message he received thinking he would love to kill her on the spot. He got messages damn near every day and he was fed up.

ZO was on his way to pick up Brandy from Coco's house. He pulled into the driveway and was about to get out the car when his phone vibrated.

"Big R, what's good? Oh yea, okay, good looking out. I'll most definitely be meeting up with you later today." ZO hung up the phone, pissed off.

So, Twan's playing dirty? Shit, that nigga gon' learn I don't always play.

Big R had let him know that Twan was charging them Detroit niggas a higher price from what they agreed and that he was keeping the extra.

ZO rung the door bell and waited for Coco to answer.

"Damn, Coco, what the fuck took you so long?" ZO was still fuming about what Big R told him.

"Hold the fuck on, Brandon! Don't come up in here trying to disrespect!"

"Damn, my fault, Coco."

"What is wrong with you? Who pissed you off?" He thought about telling Coco, truth was that he missed talking to her. Hell, he missed her period.

"I just got some shit on my mind, that's all."

"Let me ask you something ZO. You do business with Big R or Twan?" ZO looked puzzled.

Why the fuck she asking me this shit?

"Why you want to know who I associate with? I don't ask you who you fuck with, so stay out my business."

Coco didn't get upset. She rolled her eyes and called Brandy to come down.

"What time you going be home Sunday so I can know when to bring her home."

"What you mean Sunday? You always keep her 'til Monday and take her to school."

"I got some shit I got to handle. This ain't a good weekend."

"Well, I don't give a fuck what you got to handle. That's your daughter, so you figure the shit out. Just like you just said about me being in your business, I need to mind my own, well cool, I don't give a shit about whatever you got going on. Figure the shit out yourself, call your sister, smart ass motherfucker. You know what, don't. I'll pick her up Sunday have her ready by nine a.m."

"Here lately your mouth been real slick. What you bitter about that nigga Rel moving on with his new bitch?" Coco stood directly in ZO's face.

"Let me tell you this, first of all, I cut shit off with Rel, nigga, not the other way around! My mouth being slick ain't got shit to do with him. Thing is, you just get on my fucking nerves. The sight of you makes my stomach turn. Your ass wants to come over here and talk shit, trying to disrespect me. If I remember correctly, you were all up my ass, begging for me to take you back. Newsflash, I didn't want you then and I don't want you now. What I do want is for you to get the fuck out my house."

Right before ZO could respond, Brandy walked in the room and hugged him. He grabbed her bags and they left out the door. Coco hurt ZO's feelings. He loved Coco no matter what, but the shit she said cut him deep.

Chapter 82
Rel

It was Monday morning and Rel was up early as usual. He had to meet up with Big R, he needed more work. Yea, this nigga just don't know he ain't getting shit else from me. I'm gon' throw that nigga a few bricks just to hold him over. Rel had a planned worked out for Big R, but he wasn't ready to set that shit in motion. That weekend was India's baby shower and he didn't want shit to fuck up her weekend. He decided he would hold off on what needed to be taken care of.

He got dressed and headed down stairs. He was on his way out the door when his phone rang, it was Ciara.

"Hey, C, what's going on?"

"Hey, Rel, sorry to call so early, but can you watch Carman Friday night? I can get her when I come to the baby shower Saturday, is that ok?"

"I don't mind just call me Friday when you headed this way."

He hung up, and thought, Shit really been okay between me and Ciara. I thought she was gon' be on some bullshit, but she proved me wrong.

Ciara didn't have much time to be pissed at Rel. She was over that situation and on to something new. She was so gone off of ZO that she could care less about Rel. She was in a good place, she met a man that she cared about, and Carman was happy that she was able to be around her father. Everything was perfect.

Let me get the fuck out of here and head over to this nigga's crib. When Rel got to Big R's crib, he took his time before he got out the car. How in the hell can I walk up in here and act like ain't shit wrong when all I really want to do is fuck this motherfucker up?

Rel calmed down and knocked on the door. Big R let him in.

"Rel, seems like I haven't seen you in minute. You don't check on your partner or nothing?"

"Whatever, nigga, you the one had been missing in action. Only time I hear from you is when your ass need some work. But, I'm here now, so what's good?"

Rel stared at Big R and he looked him over. He had, indeed, changed. His entire appearance was of a nigga who just didn't give a fuck. The man dropped at least twenty pounds and one would notice being that he was a big nigga. Big R looked old in the face the drugs definitely had a hold on him.

"Damn, what you been doing? Shit, you on a diet or some shit? Looks like you dropped a few pounds or more."

Big R looked nervous, as if he had been found out. It wasn't hard to tell that he was on drugs. He stayed so high he hardly had an appetite. On top of the shit he did to Asia's car, he was paranoid about what Willie would to do to him. To make things completely worse, he crossed the one person that had always had his back. No matter how high he got, he couldn't escape his demons.

"I'm good, hell, you know I can stand to lose a few pounds," Big R said with a nervous tone.

"Okay, just make sure you don't overdo it. One may think you on something the way you dropping this weight off."

Rel pulled out the six bricks. "This is it for now. My people's is getting they hands on some more shit."

"Damn, Rel, I needed more than this, but shit, that's cool. These niggas will just have to wait. So, what's up with you and Chanel? You still fuck with her?"

"She practically lives at the house, that's my baby."

Big R's attitude changed and Rel took notice. "Shit, you and Asia still kickin it?"

"Man, fuck Asia. She can suck my dick, gold digging ass bitch!" Big R was hot at the mention of her name.

"Damn, it's like that?" He was fucking with Big R and it worked.

"That bitch back with her ex. Some nigga named Willie." Big R was steaming at that point.

"Yea, I heard about Willie. He was the man in these streets from what I heard."

"Fuck that, I don't give a fuck about either one of them."

"Alright, well, I'm gon' head out and I'll hit you when I hear from my people."

Rel left out the door. He couldn't believe that Big R was fucked up like he was.

Damn, why is it that I didn't see this shit coming? Big R was like my brother.

Chapter 83
Mina

A few more days 'til the baby shower and I have a lot more to do, Mina thought.

"Ty, wake up, baby. I'm about to run to mama's house and visit before I get my morning started."

"Alright, baby, be careful and tell the family I said hello." He rolled back over. She grabbed her purse, and left out the door.

"Good morning," Mina said as she walked into her parent's house, "Daddy, where is mama?"

Her father told her that her mother went to the grocery store.

"Well, I'm here to get the baby pictures of Taye." Mina went into her mother's bedroom and looked in the dresser draw for the pictures. She found what she was looking for, but right before she closed the drawer she spotted the lighter she had gave to Ty when they first start talking.

I haven't seen this lighter in forever. Why does mama have this? Mina thought. As soon as Mina said that, her mother walked in the room and had a strange look on her face when she saw that Mina had the lighter.

"Mama, why do you have Ty's lighter?" Her mother was quiet and stood there with a blank expression on her face. She closed the bedroom door and continued to look at Mina.

"I have to tell you where I found this lighter." Mrs. Smith was shaking. Mina sat down on her parents' bed as she listened to her mother tell her the details of the morning she found her brother dead in his apartment.

"Mama, so you telling me this lighter was by the door?

Mina's mother told her how she picked up the lighter and kept it. Mina's mind raced. She didn't want to think Ty had anything to do with her brother's murder.

"I'm gon' get to the bottom of this mama, first let me take care of India's baby shower."

She agreed and, although, Mina said she wasn't going to worry about it until after the weekend that was all she thought about. Mina left and took the lighter. She put it away and would show Ty in due time to get to the bottom of it. She was on her way to pick up India to take her to her doctor's appointment.

Damn, I can't wait 'til this weekend is over. I have to find out the details behind this fuckin' lighter, Mina thought as she pulled up to India's house.

Chapter 84
Coco

Thank goodness today is the baby shower. I didn't think this day would ever come, Coco thought as she got dressed.

She was headed to see Asia's so she could get her hair done. Mina and India were on their way as well. The ladies were at the shop having small talk. They had shit on their minds. Asia was worried about what Willie would do to Big R. He promised Asia he wouldn't do shit, but she knew him. Even if he didn't do it himself, he would make sure someone took care of Big R. She was afraid that if Willie did do anything that he would take the chance of going back to prison. She just got him back and wasn't ready to lose him again.

Mina was in deep thought about Ty. She wondered if it was possible that Ty had something to do with Taye being killed.

India was torn. She was full of emotions and knew that her world would change. She was about to have a baby, she knew that her daughter would never know her father, and she was part to blame for that. She knew eventually what was done in the dark would come to light. She was in way too deep and there was nothing she could do. India lived in fear of ZO.

"India, what's wrong? Why the sad face?" Coco asked.

"I'm okay I didn't get much rest last night. Your god daughter was kicking my ass. Let me pull it together. Today is my baby shower and Mina has gone through a lot to make this day special for me."

India had tears in her eyes. She continued to think about all that had happen in those last few months.

God, I wish Taye was here. It's all going to catch up with me. All the secrets and the lies I've told that one day will come out. The love I shared with Taye will be questioned and the bond I grew to have with these women will be destroyed. Lies, love, and loyalty, India thought as a tear escaped her left eye.

"Coco, you're awfully happy this morning. Did you finally give Kahlee some loving?"

"Asia, there you go, bitch I told you when I do give King some you would be the first to know. We are meeting up after the baby shower, so tonight just may be the night."

Coco had a smile on her face. She was really feeling him and it had been a long time since she was happy.

"That reminds me, India can Brandy still stay the night after the baby shower?"

"Why are you asking me that? I told you I was keeping her and Carman. It will be fun. They can help me with the baby room."

"Coco, you ain't playing, are you? You plan on getting some dick tonight. It's throbbing and wet right now aint it? Hello kitty, just need some loving. If you need to go to the bathroom and handle that, go right ahead, we won't judge you."

Asia had everyone cracking up.

"First off my pussy aint no hello kitty bitch told you to Google me my shit is a tiger/panther."

The women couldn't stop laughing. "On the real, though, I'm feeling King. I like everything about him. The way he looks at me as if I'm the prettiest woman he's ever seen. He treats me like no other. Don't get me wrong, Rel was a pure gentleman, always opening the car door, catering to my every need, he was great, but he let me down. It's like this, if he can walk out on me once, what's to say he won't do it again? I'm looking for something real and someone real. That's why I like King because from the start he was up front. We didn't start going on dates until he was out of his relationship. I respect that about him."

They all listened to Coco as she poured out her heart. Her friends were happy for her. They knew what she went through Rel had hurt her deeply, so to see her back out and dating was a big step.

Chapter 85
India

India looked around at her gifts. She was happy and felt very blessed. The turnout was great; she truly had family and friends that loved her. Everyone got along fine. Rel brought Chanel along and she got along with everyone.

When the shower ended and every one left, Coco straightened up. Mina and Ty left because India told them to go home and rest. They did so much to make everything just right.

Coco rushed to get everything cleaned up. For one, she had a date and secondly, she felt awkward being around Ciara. She was there as well helping to get India's house back in order. Ciara tried to make small talk with Coco, but she wasn't having it. She wasn't trying to befriend anyone new, especially not Rel's ex.

Asia also left right after Mina and Ty. She had some things she needed to take care of.

"Okay, India, I'm about to head out. You need to get some rest and don't be doing too much. If you need anything else, leave it for tomorrow. I'll get it when I pick up Brandy. Let me go tell my baby girl bye and that I love her. Then, I'm off for my date." Coco smiled as she made her way up to the guest room to tell Brandy goodbye for the night.

"Hey, sleepy head, I caught you dozing off. Are you ok?"

"Yes, mommy, are you about to go on your date with Mr. King? I hope you have fun, mommy. Tell him I said hello."

"Yes, baby, I'm going on my date, and I will make sure I tell him you said hi. You need to get up and get ready for bed. Miss. Ciara is going to run you some bath water. Make sure you brush your teeth and say your prayers before you go to bed, okay?"

"I will, mommy. I'll see you in the morning, right?"

"Yep, I'll be here bright and early. Give me a big hug and kiss. I love you, Brandy."

"I love you, too, mommy." They hugged one more time before she left.

Ciara gave both girls a bath and tucked them in bed in the guest room.

"Ciara, can you do me a favor, please? Would you be able to stay here with the girls for about an hour while I go run somewhere?" India asked

"I don't mind, but what is it that you have to go do? Your ass doesn't need to be out doing shit. You know what the doctor said, India."

"Don't start. I already heard that shit from Rel and Mina. I'll be back shortly."

India made sure the girls were tucked in good. Ciara got in India's bed. She was exhausted, so she put in a movie to watch.

"Alright, I'm about to leave. I know your ass is going to fall asleep. I'll wake you up when I get back."

"Bye, India, and be careful."

India was headed in town when she realized she hadn't turned her cell phone on. She powered it on and automatically got alerts saying she had new voicemail. When she listened to her messages, she gasped for air. She felt her heart literally skip a beat. ZO left her threatening messages. She damn near ran off the road when he repeated her home address and said he was gon' kill her and her unborn child. He said that her baby would never take a breath. India knew that ZO was capable of anything. She couldn't understand why he was calling her leaving the threats.

How in the hell does he know where I live? India thought as she made a U-turn to head back home.

Chapter 86
ZO

ZO turned onto India's street and the neighborhood was quiet. He planned on being in an out.

If her ass didn't live so far out I would torture that bitch.

ZO had all kinds of shit running through his mind. He thought about how he once cared about India. Although, she started off as a jump off, over time he developed feelings for her, but those feelings were gone. He couldn't have anyone holding shit over his head, he had to deal with her and that meant he had to silence her forever. India had become a problem. He thought she would just leave the shit alone he was tired of all the text messages.

Fuck India, I told that bitch to fall back. Of all people, she knows what I am capable of. Why would she want to try me?

ZO thought about Brandy and how she had hugged him goodbye when he had dropped her off earlier at home. She kept telling him how much she loved him. For a split second he thought about India's unborn child, but shook that off as soon as it entered his mind. He thought about what it would cost him in the long run if anyone was to ever find out about all his secrets. He couldn't risk that, so he was gon' do what he did best and that was put his murder game down.

ZO entered the house through the back door. India was such in a hurry to get out the house that she forgot to set the alarm. Once inside the house, he made his way through the family room and toward the steps. He saw all the gifts that India got earlier that day.

Spoiled bitch, too bad none of this shit will never be used. Once upstairs, he made his way back to the master bedroom, the door was open and the TV was loud. ZO stood in the doorway.

This is going to go smoothly. She won't even see me coming. Dumb bitch sleeping like a baby with that comforter pulled over her head.

ZO moved fast as he reached for a pillow and placed it over what he thought was India's head. He pulled out his Beretta and placed it to the back of the head. Before Ciara could attempt to fight back, ZO pulled the trigger. He grabbed the gasoline can that he had brought with him and poured the shit all over the bed and the entire room. He then left out of the room and poured gasoline throughout the house. ZO made his way down the stairs, poured gasoline in each room, lit the match, and ran out of the burning house, not once looking back.

ZO sped off quickly.

Damn, am I tripping or did I hear a child scream before I got in the car?

His adrenaline was pumping. He went seventy miles per hour in a thirty five mile per hour lane. He was high off the whole situation and very pleased with himself. He went around the curve and lost control of his car. As he swerved into the other lane, he watched as the car in front of him tried to avoid hitting him. The other car swerved and crashed into a utility pole.

ZO continued to drive, he couldn't stop. He committed two crimes, so his only concern was getting home.

Chapter 87
India

India drove back to her house, hoping she wouldn't find ZO there. She tried to get a hold of Ciara, but got no answer. She was in a panic mode and didn't know what to do. She decided to call Rel.

A tragedy was about to occur. She never thought the tragedy would be her in a car wrapped around a utility pole. She never thought that ZO would actually come after her all the way out in Mt. Washington. Hell, he shot Taye in cold blood. Why wouldn't he take her down, too?

India tried calling Rel several times, he never answered. On her way back to her house, a car approached her head on. She saw the car and knew it was ZO. Fear crept upon her like a snake. India tried to call Rel one last time and decided to leave a voicemail.

"Oh, my God, it's him! I can't believe it is him." That was the only thing left on the message to Rel. She tried to swerve in the opposite direction to miss the accident, but ZO drove too fast. The last thing she saw was the head lights of ZO's car coming toward her.

India couldn't open her eyes. She tried so hard to open them just a little, but it was impossible. She felt pain all over. It was the kind of pain that made your skin crawl. She had never felt anything like that before. She tried to scream for help, but nothing came out.

India thought, oh, my God, I am going to die. I can't die. I have a baby that needs me. I have Taye's unborn child that needs me to be its mother.

She tried to scream again, but again no sounds escaped from her mouth. India drifted off to sounds of sirens coming toward her.

The scene looked like it was Christmas with all the lights. The ambulance arrived and everyone thought there was no way anyone would survive a crash like that. The crew worked for forty-five minutes to get India out of the car. The EMT couldn't believe it when he found a faint pulse on her. When the EMT worked on her, he soon realized there was another heartbeat.

"I need this woman to be rushed to the hospital! Someone call and give them a heads up! She has to be the number one priority!" the EMT said as he wheeled the stretcher into the ambulance. He never dreamed that she would actually make it alive to the hospital.

The ambulance ran the stretcher into the emergency room. It seemed like every medical staff in the hospital was there to help save her life. A nurse took a phone from the EMT. It was the only belongings they could salvage from the wreck. The nurse dialed the last number called by India, which was Rel.

Chapter 88
Rel

Rel and Chanel had made it home from the baby shower.

Damn, Mina did her thing. The baby shower was one to remember, he thought.

"Chanel, baby, did you enjoy yourself?"

"You know what, Rel, I did. That was the best baby shower I have ever attended. India has some great friends that love her."

He thought about the statement and she was right. India did have some great friends, something she had never had. She had friends and so much more. Rel was happy for his sister. She changed so much and now in a couple of months she would be a mother.

"So, how did it feel being in the room with two of your exes and your new woman?"

"What you talking about? Shit, I was cool and so were they."

"So, you knew your two ex-women would be there?"

"Yea, I knew."

"So, why wouldn't you tell me ahead of time?"

"Man, don't start any shit. I didn't say shit because wasn't no reason to, so kill the noise."

"You know what, I'm just gon' leave and I'll holler at you some other time." Chanel grabbed her purse and was headed for the door.

"I'm lost, what's wrong?"

"Naw, nigga, what you 'bout to do is lose me." Rel looked at Chanel with confusion all over his face.

She must not know who she fucking with, Rel thought.

"Yea, maybe it would be best if you left, then. Get your mind right then holler at me."

Rel walked to the front door and held it open for Chanel. That was her queue to leave. Once she was gone, he was about to get comfortable when his cell phone rang. He looked at the number, but didn't recognize it. He picked up the phone and said hello. He was frozen as he listened to the voice on the other end. He couldn't believe what he heard. It was like he was in a dream, but really more like a nightmare. Rel grabbed his shoes and the lady on the other end was still talking as he headed out the door.

"I'm on my way!" Rel yelled as he hung up the phone.

Rel drove as fast as he could to India's house. The phone call he had gotten from India's neighbor saying there had been a fire had him on edge. He tried not to think the worse, but once he turned onto the street and saw the house, panic and fear took over. He felt like his muscles were tightening up and not letting him move or breath. He couldn't get all the way through the street because of all the fire trucks and police on the scene. He parked his car and ran up the street to the house. He tried to run to the front door, but the officers stopped him.

"This is my sister's house. My daughter is in there!" Rel screamed. "Get the fuck off of me."

One of the officers finally calmed him down as he explained to him that the firemen were doing all they could to put the fire out.

"How did this happen?" Rel asked.

"We're not sure how the fire started, sir."

"What the fuck do you all know? My sister, my daughter, and another child are inside that house. You have got to get them out of there, please."

Rel stood there feeling helpless as tears swelled up in his eyes. A fire fighter walked up to him and said they had contained the fire and that they would bring down two kids, but it didn't look good. He watched as the paramedics brought out the girls on the gurneys. He ran over to them and broke down as he saw his little girl barely breathing.

"Carman, daddy is here, baby," Rel said as they lifted her to place her inside the ambulance. He went over to Brandy and she had burns on her arms and legs. She was unconscious.

"Is she going to be okay?" Rel asked the paramedic.

"She seems to be a fighter. She was on top the smaller little girl with a blanket as if she were shielding her when we found them in the downstairs bathroom."

He had tears streaming down his face as he ran and got into the ambulance with his daughter. He attempted to call Coco, but got no answer. He called several more times, but still the same. He made several calls to his parents and also to Mina.

"Do you know if the woman inside the house made it?" Rel asked

The man looked at Rel, and said, "No, she didn't."

Chapter 89
The Present

When Coco opened her eyes, she thought everything that took place was all a bad dream. That was, until she looked around her surroundings and realized that she was in a living nightmare. She jumped up and saw Mina and King.

"Where is Brandy? Mina, where is my daughter?" Mina grabbed Coco and hugged her.

"Calm down I'll go get the doctor so she can let you know what is going on."

"No, fuck that. Take me to my daughter. Where is she?" Coco raced out the door and went to the nurses' station.

"Can you please tell me what room my daughter is in, please?"

The nurse didn't know what to say. She looked at Coco with sympathy in her eyes. Just as Coco was about to say something, ZO rushed in.

"Coco, where is Brandy, what is going on?" Just as Coco was about to speak, the doctor walked in.

"Mr. and Mrs. Carter?" the doctor said as Coco turned around.

"How is Brandy? When can I see her?"

"What the fuck is going on? What happen to Brandy?" ZO was getting aggravated at the fact that no one had told him shit.

"Someone better tell me what in the hell is going on before I lose it up in this damn hospital."

The doctor looked nervous as she spoke.

"Brandy is on a breathing machine, which is the only thing keeping her alive. Your daughter has severe burns over half of her lower body, she inhaled too much of the smoke, and she lost oxygen for too long. I'm afraid to tell you this, but she is brain dead."

An agonizing feeling came over ZO, who stood there in disbelief. It finally hit him that his daughter was in the house he set fire to. The screaming he heard from the burning house was his very own daughter. A sense of death and shame overwhelmed him. He couldn't comprehend that he was the reason his baby girl would never talk, laugh, cry, or smile at him again. Coco screamed and fell to her knees.

"It can't be true I just saw her a few hours ago. She's my only child I can't live without my daughter. Please do something doctor I'm begging you please help my baby."

The doctor tried to explain to Coco that there was nothing that could be done you could see the empathy in her eyes as she watched Coco and ZO cry.

"What about the other little girl Carman Vincent is she okay?"

The doctor looked at Mina and explained to her that Carman didn't make it. Coco dropped to her knees and screamed "WHY!"

She couldn't believe that two precious lives were taken so easily. Hearing the news about her daughter and also that Carman died was more than she could take. ZO stood there as he took in what the doctor said. He was filled with guilt. He hurt his only child and killed another one, it tore him up inside. That didn't stop him from being mad at the world. It didn't stop his anger. Yes, he would never get to have another good memory with his daughter, but he wasn't to blame, India was.

"I want to see my daughter", Coco said.

"She is in the ICU. Only two can go back at a time. You may go see her."

ZO grabbed a hold to Coco's hand as they followed the doctor to ICU. When they walked inside, ZO broke down as he saw his only child hooked up to all kinds of tubes and machines. He stood on the side of her bed where he knelt down and kissed her forehead. Words couldn't describe what he felt. His malicious ways cost his daughter her life.

"I'm sorry," he kept repeating over and over as he held his daughter's hand.

Coco couldn't believe her eyes as she watched her daughter lay there lifeless. She wanted to pick her up and kiss her. She wanted to bring her back to life and let her play, run, and jump. She wanted one last kiss, one last hug, one last goodbye.

"God, why would you take the most important person from me? Brandy is my reason for living."

Finally able to move, she stood on the other side of the bed as she kissed on Brandy's face. She didn't want to let her go. She didn't want to leave her side. She wanted hope and time, time to kiss her daughter, and dream of what could have been.

"Brandy, mommy is here now. You don't have to be afraid. I'm sorry I wasn't there to save you, baby. I'm so sorry."

Rel stood outside the door and listened. He had lost his daughter and his sister. His whole world was upside down, but he knew he had to be strong. His parents were on their way to the hospital and he tried several times to get in contact with Ciara, but had no luck. Coco glanced up and saw Rel, and signaled for him to come in. He walked over to her and hugged her as she cried in his arms. She was about to say something to him, but he stopped her.

"Coco, you don't have to say anything. I just want you to know you have a strong and brave daughter. They told me when I went to the house that Brandy protected

Carman when they found them. She covered Carman up with a blanket and lay over top of her. She protected my baby. Carman didn't suffer from any burns, but the smoke she inhaled was too much for her small lungs to take."

ZO was on the other side of the bed still holding Brandy's hand. He didn't want to let go. He wished that it was him lying in the bed and not his daughter. He wished he was the one that suffered the burns, not his baby. He burned his little girl and he couldn't take it back.

Rel bent down and whispered in Brandy's ear, and then placed a kiss on her cheek. He then walked over to ZO, placed his hand on his shoulders, and told him that he knew what he was going through and told him if he needed to talk, he could get in touch with him.

"Coco, call me if you need anything." He kissed her forehead and walked out the room.

Chapter 90
Rel

Rel didn't know what to do. He had so much going on around him. The news of his daughter and sister was too much. He had a thousand things running through his head. He was nervous and calm at the same time. Reality hadn't hit him and the thought had not sunk in that his daughter was gone forever. He couldn't understand why Ciara wasn't answering her phone.

"Hello."

"I'm calling from University of Louisville Hospital. Am I speaking to the brother of India Vincent?"

"Yes, this is her brother."

"Sir, we just brought your sister into ER. We retrieved your number from her cell phone. She was in a car accident and we need for a family member to be here."

"Excuse me, what are you talking about? I'm afraid you have the wrong person." Rel was about to hang up.

"Excuse me the woman we brought in is pregnant. Is that your sister?" Rel couldn't believe his ears. His first thought was if India was there, who was that in the fire?

It hit Rel at that moment that the body in the fire was Ciara's. That was why he couldn't get ahold to her. He told the nurse that he would be on his way. He hung up the phone and went to the waiting room to tell Mina what was going on. Mina told Rel she was riding with him she then called her parents and told them to meet her at hospital.

On their way out the hospital, Ty and Toni arrive.

"Mina, where is Coco? Is Brandy okay? What is going on?" Toni waited for Mina to respond.

"Coco is in the ICU with Brandy. I can't stay and talk. I have to go." Toni gave Mina a strange look. She couldn't understand why she was leaving when Coco was there and she needed her friends.

"Mina, where are you headed to?" Mina explained to them what Rel found out. She told Ty they were going to the hospital, and told Toni that she would check on Coco and Brandy shortly.

Toni headed back to the nurses' station when she saw Asia walking toward her. They hugged one another and Toni explained to her what Mina told her. Asia couldn't believe that Mina would just leave. Yea, India was pregnant with her brother's baby, but Coco was her friend and needed their support, and not to mention Brandy was like her niece.

Rel arrived in the ER and let the receptionist know he received a call saying that his sister was there. The receptionist let him know she would get the doctor or nurse.

"Hello, I'm Dr. Snyder and I'm taking care of your sister. She just arrived. We're about to perform an emergency C-section to try to save the baby. Your sister lost a lot of blood. I'm afraid to tell you that she has slipped into a coma, so we have to operate fast. I will keep you posted."

"Please, save my sister and the baby."

"We plan on it, just stay close by. We may need you to donate blood. Your sister is a rare type, O." Rel had a look on his face when the doctor mentioned that he may have to give blood.

"I'm not going anywhere. I'll be right here waiting."

Just as he said that, his parents walked in. "How is India?" Rel's mother asked.

Rel explained to his parents what the doctor stated and when he told them she would more than likely need blood, they looked at one another puzzled.

He thought, *what am I going to do if they need blood*? At that moment, he knew that the secret he found out would soon come out.

Chapter 91
Coco

Coco wouldn't leave Brandy's side. She knew what she had to do, but she wanted to spend a little more time with her daughter before she sent her home to heaven. She didn't want to move, she couldn't move.

"ZO, we have to do this. I won't let my daughter live like this on a breathing machine, brain dead."

"Fuck that, we can get a second opinion."

ZO loved Brandy more than anything in the world and he wanted to take back the events that occurred, but he couldn't. It was too late, the damage was done. He thought back to when Brandy was first born. He felt like the luckiest man in the world to have a daughter. Most men wanted a son, not him he wanted a daughter that he could protect. He was supposed to protect her from danger, instead, he was the danger and he couldn't protect his baby girl over his revenge.

He felt like his entire world collapsed in front of him. ZO's life would never be the same and he was empty. He felt nothing, he heard no one, and it was like he was in his own lonely world. He was to blame and no matter how bad he wanted to hate everyone around him, he hated himself-more. He walked out the room because he needed to get some air. The thought of taking his daughter off life support was something he didn't want to do, but he knew he had to.

Toni went in after ZO left out. When Coco saw her best friend, she hugged her. Toni comforted her the best way she knew how. She hadn't expected to walk in and see her god daughter the way she was. She was used to seeing her happy, always smiling, and asking a thousand questions. Toni wished that she could wake up at that very moment. She wanted to play with her and hug her.

"Coco, I love you. I can't believe this has happened."

Toni couldn't get her words out. She had a child of her own so she knew there was nothing anyone could say to a mother who was about to lose their child.

"I'm sorry, Coco. I can't stay in here. I can't look at Brandy like this." Before Toni left the room, she took Brandy's hand.

"Brandy, it's me, God Mommy Toni. I love you and I always will."

Toni broke down and couldn't say anything more. She kissed Brandy's cheek and walked out the room.

Asia watched as Toni walked out in tears. She took a deep breath as she walked in the room. Coco was still in the same spot sitting on the side of the bed, holding her daughter's hand and talking to her as if she could hear her.

Asia looked at Brandy and thought about how earlier that day she was running around helping her out with the baby shower. Now here she was hooked up to a machine that was breathing for her. She stood by Coco and grabbed her hand.

"Everything will be ok. God knows best and Brandy will always be with you. She will be God's special little angel."

"Asia, why would God allow this to happen to my baby? What am I going to do without my daughter? How will I ever be able to live without her? This isn't fair and God shouldn't have let this happen."

Asia didn't know what to say. She didn't have any kids, but she loved Brandy like she was hers as well. She thought about how much she would miss seeing her every week to get her hair done and how she always made her feel like the best aunt ever. She was so busy trying to comfort Coco that she realized she needed someone to comfort her as well.

"Coco, I can't tell you why things happen the way they do. What I can tell you is that God loves you and He will see you through this."

Asia stayed awhile longer and said goodbye to Brandy.

"Coco, is it okay if King comes in? He wanted to see Brandy and you."

"King is still here after all this time?"

"Yes, he's still here. He said he wasn't going anywhere unless you tell him to." Asia left the room and King walked in.

"Damn, if I could trade places with Brandy, I wouldn't hesitate. I wish I could take your pain away and make this all disappear."

King leaned over with tears in his eyes and softly spoke to Brandy.

"I'm going to miss seeing your pretty face. I love you." King kissed her forehead, and then looked at Coco and hugged her tightly.

"I want you to know that I'm here for you. I couldn't and wouldn't let you go through this alone."

"Thank you, King. It means a lot to me to know that you're here for me."

He told her he would be in the waiting area. She told him not to wait and that she would call him soon. He agreed. He hugged her one last time and left the room.

ZO stood in the door way to the hospital room as he watched Coco talk to their daughter. He knew he had to let Brandy go, but he didn't want to. He was so ashamed of what he did. His only hope was letting his daughter die peacefully he somehow thought that would give him peace of mind, but ultimately knew that it wouldn't.

ZO and Coco knew keeping her alive with machines and watching her little body waste away was not what they wanted. They wanted to remember their daughter healthy and happy. They agreed that they wanted to hold her without all the tubes and machines.

They stood hand and hand as they watched the respiratory therapist remove Brandy's breathing tube and the nurse unhook the IVs. They clinched their hands a little tighter, both knowing that this would be the last time they would see their daughter breathing. The emotion in the room was thick. It was hard for them to breath. The only noise was that of the machines taking the final breaths for their precious baby girl.

The nurse wrapped Brandy up in a blanket and let Coco take her in her arms. She sat down with Brandy in her arms and rocked her as she talked to her and reflected back to when she was first born up until that moment. Tears streamed down Coco's face as she watched her only child take her last breaths. ZO knelt down beside the two and rubbed his child's head. All was silent in the room when Brandy took that final breath of her life. They both cried as they held their daughter's hands a little while longer. Coco laid Brandy on the bed and got in with her. All she could do in that moment was hold her lifeless child and cry.

ZO watched Coco talk to their daughter. He wished that he could just take back the last five hours, but he couldn't. He couldn't change the monster he was. He couldn't take the pain away that he caused. He never thought it would be like that. Neither of them would have ever thought they would lose their daughter at such a young age. Coco continued to rock back and forth on her side with Brandy lying peacefully next to her. She kissed her cheek and looked down at her daughter and thought, *my life will never be the same.*

Chapter 92
Rel

Rel, his parents, Mina, and her parents waited for what seemed like forever. The doctor had not been back out; it had been forty five minutes since he said they were performing a C-section to deliver the baby.

What is taking them so long? I can't take this. I need to know something. I can't sit here and wait. I need to see my sister. I need answers, Rel thought.

"Shit, I'm gon' go find out what is taking so long."

Just as Rel was about to walk away, his phone rang. It was Toni. She called to let Rel know that Coco took Brandy of the machine and she was no longer alive. Rel couldn't speak. He handed Mina the phone. She then gasped and whimpered.

"No, she can't be gone. I wasn't even there to say goodbye." Ty ran to Mina's side and consoled her.

"Damn, this shit is fucked up we need some fucking answers." Rel was furious.

"Mr. Vincent, I'm Officer Thomas. I was here regarding the fire at your sister's house. It seems as though traces of gasoline were throughout the entire house. Looks as if someone broke in through the back door and killed the woman that was there, but we haven't yet identified her. Do you know who the woman was at your sister's house?" Rel was caught off guard.

"What do you mean, Ciara was killed?"

"So, Ciara is the victim's name that was murdered tonight? She had a single gunshot to the back of her head."

Rel couldn't believe what he heard.

"So, you telling me someone murdered the mother of my child, my daughter, and my friend's daughter."

Rel was pissed, he went off and snapped. He screamed and kicked anything in sight. Everyone could see the fire in his eyes. He was at peace thinking it was an accident, but knowing that his family had been killed was the last thing he ever thought. The officer told him he would be in touch. Rel explained to Ty what he found out, and had Ty get some of his partners in the street to find out if anyone knew or heard anything.

Rel stepped away from everyone and made a phone call.

"Something happened to India," Rel told the person on the other end of the phone. Rel explained everything that went on.

"Ok, I'll see you tomorrow and I'll let my parents know that I spoke with you. If anything changes with her condition, I'll call you."

Just as Rel hung up, the doctor came out.

"Good news, we delivered the baby girl she weighs four pounds and five ounces. We are taking good care of her. She is early, so we have to watch her carefully."

"What about India? How is she doing?"

"Not well. We need you and your parents to come with us to give some blood. We don't have enough supply here and a donor from family is most effective in a situation like this." Rel looked at the doctor, then his parents.

"We won't be a match because my parents aren't her biological parents." The doctor looked puzzled.

"Your sister blood type is rare and she has lost a lot of blood. Does she have any family here?"

"I know someone who may be a match."

"We need that person to get here as soon as possible!"

Rel got on his phone and made the call to the one person that could save India's life.

"Is everything okay, Rel?" was what the female said on the other end of the phone.

"I need you! Can you be here as soon as possible? I'll explain everything once you get here."

"I'm on my way," Rel heard as he disconnected the call.

Rel buried his face in his hands. He couldn't believe that was how his night would end. He couldn't believe he had to kiss his baby girl goodbye forever. He didn't want to think that he would also have to kiss his sister goodbye as well. He had to believe that she would pull through.

Rel's parents walked up beside him.

"She's on her way," Rel said as they hugged.

To be continued...